a mind for trade

TOR BOOKS BY ANDRE NORTON

The Crystal Gryphon
Dare to Go A-Hunting
Flight in Yiktor
Forerunner
Forerunner: The Second Venture
Here Abide Monsters
Moon Called
Moon Mirror
The Prince Commands
Ralestone Luck
Stand and Deliver
Wheel of Stars
Wizards' Worlds
Wraiths of Time
Grandmasters' Choice (EDITOR)
The Jekyll Legacy (WITH ROBERT
  BLOCH)
Gryphon's Eyrie (WITH A. C.
  CRISPIN)
Songsmith (WITH A. C. CRISPIN)
Caroline (WITH ENID CUSHING)
Firehand (WITH P. M. GRIFFIN)
Redline the Stars (WITH P. M.
  GRIFFIN)
Sneeze on Sunday (WITH GRACE
  ALLEN HOGARTH)
*The Elvenbane: Book One of the
  Halfblood Chronicles* (WITH
  MERCEDES LACKEY)

*Elvenblood: Book Two of the
  Halfblood Chronicles* (WITH
  MERCEDES LACKEY)
House of Shadows (WITH PHYLLIS
  MILLER)
Empire of the Eagle (WITH SUSAN
  SHWARTZ)
Imperial Lady (WITH SUSAN
  SHWARTZ)

THE WITCH WORLD (EDITOR)
Four from the Witch World
Tales from the Witch World 1
Tales from the Witch World 2
Tales from the Witch World 3

WITCH WORLD: THE TURNING
I Storms of Victory (WITH P. M.
  GRIFFIN)
II Flight of Vengeance (WITH P. M.
  GRIFFIN & MARY SCHAUB)
III On Wings of Magic (WITH
  PATRICIA MATHEWS & SASHA
  MILLER)

MAGIC IN ITHKAR (EDITOR, WITH
  ROBERT ADAMS)
Magic in Ithkar 1
Magic in Ithkar 2
Magic in Ithkar 3
Magic in Ithkar 4

TOR BOOKS BY SHERWOOD SMITH
(WITH DAVE TROWBRIDGE)

The Phoenix in Flight
Ruler of Naught
A Prison Unsought
The Rifter's Covenant
The Thrones of Kronos

a mind for trade

A Great New *Solar Queen* Adventure

Andre Norton &
Sherwood Smith

A Tom Doherty Associates Book / New York

A MIND FOR TRADE

This book is printed on acid-free paper.

Edited by James Frenkel

A Tor Book
Published by Tom Doherty Associates, Inc.
175 Fifth Avenue
New York, NY 10010

Tor Books on the World Wide Web:
http://www.tor.com

Tor® is a registered trademark of Tom Doherty Associates, Inc.

Library of Congress Cataloging-in-Publication Data

Norton, Andre.
        A mind for trade   /   Andre Norton and Sherwood Smith.
            p.   cm.
        "A Tom Doherty Associates book."
        ISBN 0-312-85920-1
        I. Smith, Sherwood.   II. Title.
    PS3527.O632M55   1997
    813'.52—dc21   97-15364
                                                           CIP

First Edition: October 1997

Printed in the United States of America

0 9 8 7 6 5 4 3 2 1

With heartfelt thanks to Dave Trowbridge, tech wizard extraordinaire, for unstinting help.

—S.S.

1

"They're going to fire!"

The shout seemed to come from everywhere.

Dane Thorson tried to run, but his legs churned without propelling him forward. Terrified, he looked behind, saw sinister black shapes, like bombs, floating through the air. There were thousands of them. In the garish light around him ghosts drifted. Some of the faces were familiar. Childhood faces, half-remembered. From the Pool? No . . .

"Eeeeeee—yaaagh!"

The scream ripped through Dane's head, pulling him violently into consciousness.

He sat up in his bunk, blinking against the soft, steady bulkhead night-light as shreds and tatters of the dream drifted across his vision, and vanished. He was not running from impending attack, he was safely in his bunk aboard the *North Star,* where he was the cargo master.

He took a deep breath, and made more connections: the dream, the memories, were not his.

"Ali," he said. They were Ali Kamil's dreams, and memories—again.

He pulled on his clothes and hit the door control.

Out in the corridor he saw Ali leaning against the wall, motionless. Ali was also barefoot, his customarily suave, controlled face almost unrecognizable. Dane glanced at the engineer's tense forehead, where beads of sweat gleamed in his tangled dark hair, and wondered how much worse the dream had been for him.

There was no time for words; a moment later two small black-and-white blurs rocketed through the passageway, followed by Dane's new apprentice, Tooe, a Rigelian hybrid they'd found on the vast habitat called the Garden of Harmonious Exchange. Barely child-size, her bluish skin shining with exertion, she moved with a peculiar flat-footed grace in the pseudo-gravity of hyper, now set to the .85 standard of their destination.

Dane looked down at Alpha and Omega, the ship's cats, and then into Tooe's huge yellow eyes, waiting for her to catch her breath. And, he admitted ruefully, avoiding Ali's accusatory gaze.

Tooe and the cats obviously had been playing some kind of game. The little hybrid seemed to deal well with the adaptive gee shifts; better than the rest of the crew with the microgravity adaptation shift mandated by Craig Tau after their experiences on Exchange. Tooe was well adapted to the variable gravity of that vast construct, which was a home to humans, the insectlike Kanddoyd, and the heavy-world Shver.

The rest of the crew wasn't—Terran-descent humans preferred planets, like Hesprid IV, now less than a day away. But they were far beyond the Terran sphere of influence now, and much of their trading would be on the cylindrical habitats of Kanddoyd space. Hence both ships observed a complex cycle of gravity—actually the pseudo-gravity of hyper—to accustom the rest of the crew to a range of weight-mass ratios.

"Hear screech, me," Tooe said.

"Sorry." Ali smiled wryly. "I'll have to ask Rip what he's been slipping into our rations—"

"I resent that! No one seems to think my cookery is all that great, but no one has been poisoned yet." Rip Shannon and Jasper Weeks appeared side by side, a tall, handsome, dark figure and a short, pale one, both dressed for duty in their brown Free Trader uniforms. Despite Rip's joking tone his expression was concerned, as was Jasper's.

Ali said, "You couldn't have heard me yelling in my sleep all the way from the control deck."

Rip shook his head.

"Heard you here." Jasper tapped his forehead.

"Tooe hear you, in hydrolab." Tooe's crest flattened out as she pointed round the corner. She touched her ear. "Bad dream, Ali Kamil?"

"Bad dream, Tooe," Ali said with a faint smile.

"Second one," Tooe replied, her pupils slitting suddenly. "You yell two shifts ago. Tooe hears. Dr. Tau says, 'Tooe, do work.' You think dream is from bad food?"

"No." The voice came from the other end of the corridor: Dr. Craig Tau, senior member of the newly formed crew.

"I'm sorry," Ali said, his handsome face tight with strain. Dane could almost feel how much his crewmate hated the situation. Ali was not one to share emotions, much less data about his personal life. "I seem to have acquired the knack of making childhood nightmares into some kind of dream vid," Ali went on. Dane could feel his crewmate's effort to keep his tone light. "I wonder if I can collect an entertainment fee for general broadcast?"

Tau smiled slightly, then said, "I invite you four to meet me in the mess in . . . ten minutes? It's time, I believe, for a talk I probably should have had with you long ago. Tooe, why don't you hold down the control deck for now? We can brief you afterward."

The little Rigelian hybrid nodded, grinning.

"What's funny?" Dane asked.

Tooe gave a little hop, her blue, faintly scaled skin glossy with good health. "Hold down deck? Control deck holds me down!" Her crest flicked up in the shape that indicated a joke. "Space-leak holds me down." She hissed laughter through her teeth—Dane's explanation of how Ali could tune the engines to let hyperspace "leak through" to create varying amounts of pseudo-gravity had not been very successful.

Her crest snapped to a flatter angle as she added, "Snapout soon! Then real free fall before go into gravity well."

In, Dane thought. She still said "In," not "Down." He was afraid she still didn't have the concept of planetary gravity; intellectually she understood it well, but not physically, despite her fantastic adaptability. Dane didn't say anything. Time would tell, and he wasn't sure how much to say, and how much to leave to experience.

Tooe watched him for a moment, and then her crest flicked up, and she bounced away down the corridor and disappeared. The two cats followed.

Tau didn't wait for an answer. He returned to his cabin and Dane heard the door hiss closed.

The others exchanged looks and shrugs, then Dane said, "Whatever it's about, it can wait on a shower and something hot to drink."

Ali nodded and disappeared into his cabin.

Jasper watched him go, then said, "I'd better close down my work." He moved off in the direction of the engine compartments.

Free fall soon. Dane retreated to his cabin, wondering if it was Tooe's influence that had them all using the handholds, walls, and decking to propel themselves around in free fall, rather than walking with their boots magnetized as had been their habit for years aboard the *Solar Queen.*

He pushed his old uniform into the cleaning slot and glanced at the time. Still half a rest period left. He suspected he would not get back to sleep before Rip and Jasper went offshift and he and Ali were back on duty, but he wasn't worried. Except for Ali's weird dreams, so far the maiden voyage of the *North Star* had been uneventful enough. A lot of hard work, but they'd anticipated that. Rip had one more day in charge of the galley, then the rotation would put Dane there. At least there he could nap if he needed to.

He took a quick hot shower, got into his clean uniform, and left his cabin to go to the galley-mess.

The other three appeared at about the same time. Ali's dark hair was wet and slicked back, the color high in his handsome face. He dropped into one of the bolted chairs, smiling derisively. "If this is going to be a let's-talk-about-our-past bull session, Craig, I'd rather finish racking up my overdue sack time."

The medic, who had served aboard the *Solar Queen* longer than Dane had been a Free Trader, looked unperturbed. A plain, neat man who hardly seemed to have aged in the time Dane had known him, Craig Tau spoke in a low, even voice, and his manner was unemotional and straightforward. All the *Solar Queen*'s former apprentices respected him; he was honest, dedicated, and thorough.

Dane stayed silent. Despite Ali's banter, Dane knew his shipmate was tense and uneasy.

"I had hoped," Tau said, lacing his fingers together, "that this conversation could wait for a time. We all have too much to think about already: a new ship, new positions of responsibility for each of the four of you, a contract that may or may not break us out of this cycle of hard luck that has been riding our jets since we left Canuche. Add to that both ships being undercrewed and all the extra work that entails, I thought you had enough to think about."

"All right," Ali said. "I get the image here: it's sufficiently bad. How about giving it to us straight."

Tau looked up enquiringly. Rip nodded, his intelligent dark eyes concerned, and Dane felt himself nodding as well. Only Jasper Weeks—unfailingly polite and noncommittal, as were all Venusian colonists, Dane had learned—waited patiently for Tau to get to his subject any way he chose.

"Think back," Tau said. "To our adventures on the planet Sargol."

"Hard days to forget," Ali commented wryly. "Dane here smelling like a pleasure house feather-dancer every time he had to go trading with the Salariki—"

"—That Inter-Solar gang trying their damnedest to make us look like a plague ship," Rip added.

"—After the four of us did our best to turn ourselves inside out," Dane finished, wincing. "I don't think I've ever been that sick in my life. Well, I know I haven't."

Jasper looked up quickly, and Tau smiled at him. "No, Jasper, it's not a coincidence. You'll remember that the four of you who drank the Salariki warrior's cup were vilely sick, it's true—but when that pest the I-S gang sneaked aboard the *Queen* laid the rest of us out, it was you four whose immune systems were able to fight off the toxins."

"And so . . . ?" Ali prompted, his smile tight. "This relates to my nightmares?"

Tau said, "Just so—but have patience. The next item to recall is our mail run previous to the Canuche contract."

"Xecho—"

"—and Trewsworld," Dane said. He did not like to remember that one; in his own nightmares he still saw that dead man lying in his bunk, with Dane's own face.

"Remember what was slipped aboard the *Queen* that time?"

Jasper drew a deep breath. "Esperite."

Tau nodded.

Ali snorted. "Craig, my old friend, I value and esteem you, but if you're going to hop out with the news that we're going to turn into a bunch of psi-powered spacehounds, well, you've been studying that voodoo craziness too long."

Dane grinned, waiting for the medic to deny it. Rip was also smiling, but Jasper just sat, his pale, thin face unreadable as always, his gaze wide and unblinking.

Tau said after a long pause, "I'm very much afraid that's exactly what I am telling you."

✳   ✳   ✳

Tau watched Ali Kamil bury his face in his hands. The young engineer moaned with theatrical fervor, which made his three peers grin. Tau knew them all well, and despite Ali's flippant attitude, it was obvious that the news had hit him the hardest. In fact, Tau thought as he watched Kamil shake his head back and forth, the longer Ali joked, the more deeply he was upset.

Now Ali put his fingers in his ears and shook them, then looked up at Dane. "What's that, Viking? Can't hear you—think louder."

The tall, rawboned cargo master smiled a little, but his demeanor was one of slight embarrassment and vague discomfort. Again, this was no surprise to Tau. He had predicted fairly accurately their probable reactions; what he could not guess was what they would do with the knowledge.

"Any questions?" he asked.

Kamil looked up, his eyes narrowed. "Yes. How do we get rid of it?"

"Get rid of what?" Tau countered. "The syndrome itself? The changes in your nervous system that make it possible?"

"I suspect," Rip said with his calm smile, "that getting rid of it isn't exactly like excising a wart."

"I'm afraid not." Tau waited for them to absorb this.

Ali sighed. "You've obviously got more cheery news. Might as well have it all."

Tau sipped the rest of his jakek. The empty tube crushed automatically, and he sent it spinning to the recycler. "Let's go back before we go forward. I first began noticing something a few months ago: if one of you had had a bad night, invariably one of the others had one also. I began keeping a record of where you all slept while on various duties. If you were in your cabins, which were in relatively close proximity to each other, one's strong dreams tended to affect the others. If you were on duty elsewhere, there seemed to be no reaction."

"Then distance lessens it," Jasper said.

Tau nodded. "There is another item—and I have to say first that both were so subtle I forbore telling you in case you began to expect them—"

"Does the chief know about all this?" Ali cut in.

"Captain Jellico knows. Of course. As does Dr. Cofort."

Ali sighed.

"In fact, on my latest report I told them I would probably be speaking to you four soon."

Dane looked interested. "Did the Old Man have anything to say to that?"

Tau smiled. "Only that I had his sympathy."

"You?" Ali's dark eyes opened wide. "*You* have his sympathy? What about us?"

Dane laughed, and Jasper smiled.

Rip was silent, his gaze distant. Then he looked up at Tau. "That second thing you mentioned," he said. "Is it . . . sometimes . . . knowing where each other is?"

A zing of excitement sent Tau's heart racing, but he did his best not to show it. "Yes, that was the other item. I noticed it in particular when we were stranded on Exchange for so long. If one of you needed one of the others, you seemed to know without conscious thought where he was aboard the *Queen*— or that he was not aboard. Again, distance negated the syndrome."

Dane ran his big hands through his yellow hair, making it stand up in spikes. "I think—" He shook his head.

"You did notice it," Tau prompted. "I saw you react once."

Dane grinned, looking embarrassed. "But couldn't it just be that we know where the others are likely to be? We've been working together so long, we almost know the others' duties as well as we know our own."

"This is true," Tau agreed. "Which is another reason why I held off as long as possible telling you about this. I wanted to see if any of you would reach the same conclusions on your own."

"So that's the recent past." Ali lounged back on his chair. "What about the future? If Viking forgets to duck through a hatchway, am I going to get a bruise on my handsome brow? Or if Jasper misses his lunch during his duty-shift, am I going to wake up on alter-shift thinking about Venusian Fungus Soup?" Ali's tone was light and pleasant, and there was nothing but interest in the smooth face and heavy-lidded dark eyes, but Tau sensed that the young man was angry. To Ali, new strides in medical science and the development of human potential meant little besides the prospect of something—anything—crossing the boundaries of his privacy. This meant that perhaps you could not just go into your cabin and shut the door to close out your crewmates when you needed to be alone, and all four knew it.

"I can't tell you for certain," Tau said. "When it became apparent our credit problems were solved on Exchange, the captain authorized my purchase of the latest medical data. I've been in my cabin sorting through it ever since we left Mykosian space. I haven't found anything that directly relates to your case, which is not surprising, but I have come across some interesting data that leads me to speculate on the elasticity of human biological adaptations."

"Which means?" Ali prompted.

"Which means there are three alternatives, each leading in two directions. One, you do nothing, and nothing further happens. Possibly the syndrome even disappears. Or else the potential . . . increases."

"Choice two, we fight it?" Ali said, his smile twisted.

"That is one of the alternatives," Tau agreed. "We can experiment with attempts to damp the effect, and again either it works . . . or else your own bodies fight you." He paused to let the implications sink in.

Nothing showed in the three young faces before him, but he knew by the silence that they were considering this prospect as seriously as he.

"And third, we attempt to work with it. Again, it still might lead to nothing more than the four of you catching images from the others' strong dreams, and knowing where the others are at any given moment. Or . . ." He opened his hands.

"Or we end up in high-tech bars at the spaceports, playing cards for high stakes," Ali said with a bitter laugh. "Well, it's an easy way to make a fortune—seeing your opponents' hands through their own minds."

"Easy way to get yourself killed," Jasper said quietly.

"And who's to say we'll ever be able to read anything except from each other?" Rip put in. "I'm all for the third choice. Remember, if we learn how to work with it, maybe we can figure out how to shut it down when we don't want it."

Ali looked up, his lips parted. "Craig?"

Tau hesitated, then shook his head. "I'd like to be able to guarantee it, but I can't. There's too much here that we humans know little about."

Rip sighed, and glanced at the time.

Tau said, "Don't make any decisions now. Think. Talk it over among yourselves. If you want, next time we snap out to exchange reports, talk to the captain, or to Dr. Cofort. We can discuss what to do at a later date. We've all got plenty else to think about."

"The control deck is enough for me," Rip said. "Next snapout we emerge in Hesprid space. I hope we won't be finding any of Flindyk's leftover pirates waiting around for us."

They looked at one another, reminded of the circumstances under which they'd gained the ship they were in. The planet they were headed toward had been purchased with a contract by another Trader crew, for which that crew had been killed. Though the high-ranking Trade administrator who had secretly operated the piracy ring was now jailed and his ring broken, who was to say that the authorities had gotten them all?

"All the more reason," Ali drawled, "to resume my interrupted beauty sleep. If any of you spacehounds do manage to invade my slumbers, I'll expect you to add something amusing or at least stylish."

2

"One minute to snapout," Rip Shannon said into the general com.

He watched the displays showing the engines spinning up to the power level needed to thrust them back into normal space. He almost heard them; he certainly felt the vibration thrumming through the ship, and up through the deckplates to his chair. While his senses were busy gauging the familiar sound, his eyes scanned the ranks of lights on his console. At the communications controls sat Dane Thorson, his big hands rubbing absently against the safety webbing that held him in his seat as he watched his as-yet-blank screen.

Rip's control lights all gleamed a peaceful green; the countdown reached zero.

"Snapout."

Rip worked the ship controls.

"Roger snapout!"

As the corroborating report echoed over the general com

from Jasper in Engineering, the screens cleared of the weird lights of hyperspace, and the familiar fleeting nausea of snapout seized Rip. With an automatic reaction Rip magnetized his boots as his body pulled against his safety webbing. The pseudo-gravity of acceleration was gone; they were in free fall now, speeding at tremendous velocity through space.

Rip's gaze stayed on his console readouts as the sensors of the *North Star* slowly painted a picture of their course. "Let me get it first, let me get it first," he muttered to himself as he glanced up at the readout that showed a bright blip tracking them at a nearly matching velocity: the *Solar Queen.*

But just before Rip could assemble a coherent picture from his navputer, Dane said, "Incoming message—ID is the *Queen.*" He tabbed a key to put the message on the general com, and Steen Wilcox's voice came from the speaker, calm and matter-of-fact: "*Queen* to *Star.* I place us in the Hesprid system, approximately twenty light-minutes from the sun, about eighteen degrees above the ecliptic."

Rip grimaced as, within moments, his calculations produced the same information. "Confirm reading," he said, working to keep his voice as steady and calm as the *Solar Queen*'s experienced astrogator's.

"*Star* to *Queen*: confirmed," Dane said into the com.

"We've got an audience," Wilcox said a moment later. "Two. Two hundred seventy degrees mark four; two hundred ninety degrees mark four. Get 'em?"

Rip's fingers worked at his keyboard as he scanned back and forth across his sensors. "I—I—"

"Winked out." Wilcox's cheerful voice sounded heartless over the com.

Rip looked up at Dane, who just looked back in perplexity. This was not his job. He knew how to work the communications controls—they all did—but the standard contingency operations of a comtech were not something he'd memorized and could quote in his sleep.

"Standard communications call?" Rip murmured, feeling a wave of intense frustration. He'd wanted his piloting to be perfect, to match the *Queen*'s smooth, quick operations pace, but he simply did not have enough crewmembers.

Dane obediently said into the com, "Standard communications call?"

"Already done," came Wilcox's voice. "No response. Captain says for us to keep an ear open."

Keep an ear open. This was a casual way of stating it. Rip felt a mixture of pride and worry as he studied his familiar bank of instruments, trying to decide which would be best to assign the task of automatic scan-sweeps, and at what intervals. That Jellico and Wilcox didn't give him detailed, formal orders implied they felt he was on their own level of competence. It was a relief, and at the same time a worry. He suspected that part of Jellico's motivation was to encourage Rip.

Rubbing his sweaty fingers against his pants, Rip forced his problems out of his mind just as Wilcox's voice came: "Coordinates for rendezvous and planetary approach incoming."

Rip dashed his sleeve over his sweat-beaded upper lip and fought the urge to sigh with relief. This part was relatively easy. He fed the coordinates into his navputer, bouncing in his seat as the ship's jets stuttered and pulsed, adjusting the *North Star*'s orbit to the one transmitted by Wilcox, that would bring them to rendezvous in nine hours. Finally the orbital plot display coalesced into a single curve, and, after confirmation, Wilcox signed off.

With a distinct air of relief Dane unfastened his webbing and launched himself through the hatchway. Rip double-checked that the proper information was encoded on his quantumtape and then fed the tape in. For a short time he watched the autopilot take over the controls; when everything was running it was time to check with his own crew.

"Jasper?"

"Jets cooling and stable," came the prompt reply. "All green and good to go."

"Ali?"

"Engines off-line and stable, o my pilgrim," came the insouciant voice.

Pilgrim. Rip closed his eyes, thought of Dane, and—

Nothing.

He opened his eyes, looked over the controls, then sat back to take a moment's break. He'd earned it. Once again he called up an image of Dane. He saw the tall, strong-boned figure, the tousled yellow hair—

And knew that the "location" in his mind was just his imagination. He sighed. Every time he tried to locate Dane, Jasper, or Ali by this mysterious psi link that Craig Tau had told them about, it was his imagination that acted first. It seemed the only time it really worked was when he was unaware of the process.

"What good is that?" he muttered as he watched his readouts reflect the new course. A talent that only worked when he wasn't aware of it was about as useful as engines which only worked when the ship had planeted and everyone was on leave.

His hand hovered over the com-key, then pulled back. Talent. That was his opinion, but he knew that at least two of the others thought of it as a curse.

The four of them had decided not to work together on experiments with their putative abilities. Actually, Ali had decided, so vehemently the other three had gone along with him. But that didn't mean Rip couldn't experiment on his own. Now he wanted to talk to Dane or Jasper about what he'd observed, but wouldn't that make it seem he was breaking the agreement?

He sighed, scanning the screens a third time. He tabbed the final control to the autopilot, keying it to sound a general alarm if any anomaly showed up, and walked back to the galley to get something hot to drink.

He found Tooe there, seated on the ceiling. Only she wouldn't see it as the ceiling. Having lived in the microgravity at the Spin Axis of Exchange, she viewed the notions of "up" and "down" as merely a convenience to be decided on entering a space.

The *North Star* had been built to accommodate large humanoids—taller even than Dane—which meant many of the galley conveniences were stored high. So of course Tooe would simply see the ceiling as the floor, and reorient the conveniences to where she could reach them.

Rip had gotten used to living in free fall during their adventures on Exchange. Still, he was enough a Terra-born human that his stomach lurched at the sight of someone seated upside down on the ceiling. *Impossible!* his hindbrain seemed to gibber. He shut his eyes and forced his brain to reorient. When he opened his eyes, he was the one standing on the ceiling. He demagged his boots, pushed off gently, and flipped, landing next to Tooe, who was holding a drink bulb in both hands.

"Tired?" he asked, watching in fascination as her thin webbed fingers teased out a wobbling bubble of jakek. The pupils in her huge yellow eyes slitted as she watched its gyrations, then her blue tongue darted out and expertly slurped in the liquid sphere.

It was peculiar, how the little Rigelian hybrid liked to play with her food in microgee. Rip had at first been concerned; raised on Terra, he'd been taught to respect the dangers of liquids in free fall before he ever actually experienced weightlessness. But he knew that Tooe had lived most of her life in free fall, and watching her juggle liquid blobs or send them spinning and gyrating had proved to them all that she knew what she was doing. However much she played she had yet to make any mess, and they'd left her to it, thinking she'd get bored with her games. But as yet she hadn't.

"Not tired, me," Tooe said, extruding another rippling spheroid of liquid. "Short sleep, short work, short sleep, short work, natural to my biorhythms. Long work, long sleep harder."

She flipped over suddenly, her crest flicking out as she solemnly observed her bubble from another angle. Small and light and agile, she reminded Rip of a child, except she was legally adult age—and had signed on as a full crew member.

"She's smart," Dane had said when they left Exchange,

the Terran-Kanddoyd-Shveran Habitat on which Tooe had spent most of her life. "She learns at least as fast as we do— probably faster, and she knows more about cargo handling in free fall than any of us."

She'd rapidly assimilated Terran; she now read it as well as any of them, or nearly, and could write reasonably well. But her spoken language was still based on the quick patois, comprised of several languages, that she had used with her nestmates on Exchange.

Now she slurped up her bubble and grinned, showing a row of sharp white teeth. "Dane and Tooe finish mining-bots. Cargo holds ready. Much work." She brushed her hands together.

Rip nodded as he drew a bulb of fresh, hot jakek; he'd helped Dane a couple of times when Tooe was on her rest break. Dane's first job as cargo master had been to evaluate all the data on cielanite that they'd been able to purchase on Exchange, modify the *North Star*'s cargo holds to best accommodate the partially refined ore; and last, to design and build two general-purpose mining-bots to be modified for more specific functions once they knew just what they were facing. These would have to be transferred to the *Solar Queen*, which was the ship Jellico had decided would make the descent to Hesprid IV.

Again there had been almost too much work to be done for too few crewmembers to handle; Dane had not thought the journey in hyper long enough to get it all done, and consequently until recently had worked more than his share of shifts.

They all had.

"Need more people," Tooe said.

Rip looked up, saw the Rigelian's head canted as she studied him, her crest up in query mode. Her thoughts had been progressing parallel to his. It was oddly unsteadying. "We certainly do," he said, sipping his hot drink.

The problem, Rip thought as he watched Tooe play with

another bubble, was finding good, trustworthy crew. The original twelve aboard the *Solar Queen* had worked together so long they knew one another well; knew limits, strengths, and each would trust his life to the others. Previously they'd gotten new crew only on Terra, relying on the highly technical Profile Correlations computer that Traders everywhere nicknamed Psycho, to match them up with crewmates. But events had conspired to keep them away from Terra—and meanwhile they'd acquired two new people: Doctor Rael Cofort, recently married to the captain, and Tooe. Working with them, adjusting to them, seemed to be harder for the former crewmates of the *Queen* than for the new people.

Rip smiled to himself as he headed out the hatchway. So far they'd been lucky; he was just as glad that finding new people was Captain Jellico's worry. Rip wanted to pilot his own ship, but there were some responsibilities he'd be just as happy to leave to the Old Man.

Tooe watched Rip push through the door and disappear. Why did the kindly Rip Shannon frown so? At least they had talked a little. Too often recently he or Dane or Jasper would come into the galley, see Tooe, and then leave very soon. Three times she had seen those three, or two of the three, in serious talk— but when Tooe came near, their tone and subject would shift to the work at hand.

Tooe wondered aggrievedly if she were at fault, and cast her mind over her recent work. Dane had been pleased, had trusted her with many chores. She performed her shifts, was careful to clean up after herself, and did not touch anyone else's tools or belongings, all as Nunku had advised her. So she knew she had not caused any problems. Yet the Terran did not stay to talk.

To a certain extent Tooe had expected such behavior. "You do not leave one klinti and instantly make another," Nunku had warned her when she left Exchange to join this crew. Except it seemed that they frowned more, and talked secretly, the more since Craig Tau called the four of them together for that conference.

Tooe almost whistled her feelings, and stopped herself. She knew what to do about these times.

She launched herself across the galley to punch in the commands for a bowl of steamed rice. Then she zipped down to the hydroponics garden, where she ran her fingers through the foliage of her own private garden of roots. There were three ripe tiz-roots, blue-green, plump, and crunchy. She put them through the hydro-rinse and zapped back to the galley just as the timer for her rice sounded.

With quick motions she chopped up her roots and combined them into the rice. Capping the container, she shot through the hatch and bounced her way down to her cabin.

Inside, she set aside the food and tabbed her personal console to life. For a moment she sat and looked at the console, mute evidence that she was a real crewmember, someone of value. Until she had come aboard the *North Star,* she'd had very little in the way of belongings, and no space of her own. Now she had a cabin that was hers, no one else's. The others did not come in; if they wanted her, they made a noise outside and waited for her to come out, or else they summoned her over the com.

On Exchange, Tooe had lived secretly in an abandoned storage space in the Spin Axis of the habitat with a group of other young beings, all homeless and lost as she had been. They'd bonded into a klinti, which Tooe had tried once to translate into Terran for Rip. The nearest meanings she could find were clan, or family, though her klinti wasn't either. It had been hard to leave them, but she wanted more than anything to travel among the stars. And their leader Nunku, though only a little older than Tooe, but gifted with the ability to see into the minds of others as the ship-sensors saw into space, had helped her achieve this goal.

Nunku had also presented Tooe with a surprise just before

she left Exchange: a chip on which each of the members of the klinti had recorded messages to her.

Tooe called up that chip now, dividing her screen so that each face was there before her. Every time she felt cold inside, and her mind turned back to her life with the klinti instead of ahead to what she might learn next, she withdrew to her cabin and watched more of each message. Just a bit more. She hadn't reached the end yet; she hoped that emptiness in her middle would go away before she saw the last of the messages.

Now she uncovered her food container and took a bite. Most Terran foods were inedible, except for rice and carrots. Those were real delicacies; she didn't think she could ever get tired of rice.

Spooning a bite into her mouth, she scanned her screen. There was Nunku, long and thin, her gentle, wise gaze looking out at Tooe. Nunku sat behind the huge computer console that she had built herself from scavenged parts. She had taught everyone in the klinti how to make computers help them when other living beings could or would not.

Next to Nunku was Momo, small and round, with crimson skin. She touched Momo's image on the screen. Momo was the closest to a blood-sibling that Tooe had ever had. It was Momo's messages she'd listened to the most of; there was only forty-seven minutes, Terran measure, left of his portion. She would have to save his for days when the coldness in her insides felt like the vastness between the stars.

So she touched the control over Kithin's image. Kithin unfroze, her dark fur fluffing out. This was the third time Tooe had listened to Kithin; what had she spoken of before? Oh yes. Stars, and ships. Kithin was another who wanted very badly to travel.

". . . promise to send a message," Kithin said, her growly voice hesitant among the sibilants of Rigelian. Kithin had a gift for languages; she spoke more different tongues than anyone in the klinti. "I had vowed to myself I will go down to the heavy zone, just as you did, and exercise so that I might be able to dwell upon a planet and endure its gravity. Only you must tell me in your message what this is like, and how I can prepare for it . . ."

Tooe whistled sadly. She liked Kithin—one of her oldest friends—but she did not want to listen to messages about leaving the klinti. She wanted to pretend she was there with them, so she halted Kithin and activated Naddaklak's. The only Kanddoyd in the klinti, Naddaklak was always in trouble with the authorities, audacious, seldom truthful, but always entertaining. Naddaklak's message was funny, long silly stories about encounters with Kanddoyd and Shver authorities. In all of them the authorities came off badly and Naddaklak won. Tooe knew they were all false, but not lies so much as stories, just like the Terrans had in their story-vids. The Terrans had a real taste for things that had never happened; Tooe did not understand it, but she and the klinti had viewed them just the same, trying to learn something of the Terran mind.

Gradually, as her stomach filled with rice, the emptiness just above it filled with laughter, and Tooe was able to turn her mind back to her work, and to the prospect of landing on a planet for the very first time.

She stopped Naddaklak's message but did not close down her console. Instead she glanced at the time. Tau would be asleep, and Ali Kamil, the one who never talked to her. Dane was supposed to have started his sleep period, but she knew he'd be working; he seemed not to like sleeping at the same time as Ali.

Thinking back to that mysterious conference in the galley, and the somber conversations she'd seen since, she decided it was time to do some excavating in the computer.

3

"Standby for gees, one-eighth standard, twenty seconds, zero by ninety." Rip's voice was steady over the com. "On my mark, five . . . four . . ."

Dane and Tooe finished checking their vac-suits and braced themselves with the handholds just outside the cargo bay lock.

"Mark." The jets pulsed and the deck pushed against their feet. Twenty seconds later, Rip announced, "We're in cable range of the *Queen*. Relative velocity within parameters."

Dane stowed his duffel inside one of the general-purpose mining-bots. Tooe copied his movements, and waited silently. The design of the lock, more than any other part of the ship, announced its non-Terran origin. Built for microgravity operations, the *North Star*'s main cargo lock was on the ship's underside; they were standing on the opposite wall, their heads pointed toward the lock.

A moment later Rip announced: "Stotz reports johblocks launched."

Dane glanced down at Tooe, who looked completely lost in Rael Cofort's vac-suit. He had to make an effort not to laugh, noting to himself that one of the first things on the to-get list if this run was successful would be a fitted suit for Tooe.

If she stayed on as crew, of course.

"Ready?" he said.

"Ready." Her fluting voice came out of the suit's com unit.

A few moments later Dane heard the dull clank of the joh-blocks impacting the outer hull of the *North Star* on either side of the cargo bay. He envisioned the cables' atomically smooth gripping surfaces literally melding with the *Star*'s hull. The deck vibrated softly as Rip stuttered the jets gently, and Dane felt the soles of his boots push up against his feet again as the two ships, now firmly linked, began orbiting a common center of gravity, like a double star. Now the main lock was definitely overhead, even though their acceleration was barely perceptible as weight.

Dane tabbed the lock control, and they waited in silence as the pressure dropped incrementally and their two shadows slowly took on the peculiar razor-edged quality of an airless environment. "Check for leaks," he said, slapping the control on the front of his suit.

Tooe twinned his movement. Inside Dane's helmet the light showed a reassuring green, and he turned his attention to the lock console. When the blowout light glowed green, he keyed the outer lock, which slid silently open onto the jewel-pierced blackness of space overhead, framing the graceful needle shape of the *Queen*. He knew if he waited a moment he'd see the slow rotation of the ships sweep the edge of the *North Star*'s bay across a star, but there was no time for that.

"All right, Tooe, let's get those Geepees hooked up."

Dane saw Tooe's helmet light wink on and she clipped a light cable onto the nearest general-purpose mining-bot—called Geepees—and then swam up the ladder. He tabbed his light and did the same, followed her with less alacrity. At the edge of the lock they both hooked onto their respective cables. Then they turned to pull their Geepees into position.

Dane bent his legs, straightened his back, and began to draw the massive bot up out of the lock. At first it hardly moved, but he knew the secret was in a steady pull, not necessarily a strong one. Still, it was with mild satisfaction that he saw his bot come off the deck long before Tooe's, and he had clipped his bot to the main cable before hers even cleared the edge of the hatch. Crouching down, Dane pushed up against the bot, accelerating its slow motion toward the *Queen*, and floated away from the *North Star*.

He glided along the cable for a moment, making sure his bot moved smoothly. The cable-constrained orbit of the two ships made this part of the trip "uphill," so additional thrust would be needed. No problems presented themselves, so he braced himself under the Geepee and keyed his suit thrusters on. They flared briefly, propelling him and his cargo up along the cable. Turnover was barely perceptible, but now Dane found himself perched on top of the bot as it fell down the cable toward the *Queen;* mild vertigo seized him for a moment.

He triggered the temporary thrusters Ali had rigged on the front of the Geepee. The counter-blast of power pushed him into the bot as it decelerated, and two spots of light winked into existence on the *Queen*'s hull. Dane worked the controls in stuttering pulses, watching the two spots of laser light converge; projected from the thruster pack, the two beams would meet when the bot was within human depth perception, which was notoriously unreliable in the glare of space.

The spots merged and winked out; now Dane, concentrating fiercely, watched the highlights on the hull ahead of him. Dealing with mass as opposed to weight was still unfamiliar to him. Out of the corner of his vision he saw Tooe slowly overtaking him, her jets silent.

His was still slowing when he glanced over, and watched with a spurt of humor as Tooe triggered her jets just once, a long, low-intensity burn that brought her neatly to a halt within suit-cable distance of the *Queen*'s lock well ahead of Dane.

Now it was just a matter of unclipping from the main cable and guiding the Geepees as they fell slowly but inexorably into the *Queen*'s main lock. Stotz had rigged spring platforms to receive them. The Geepees could not be decelerated as they had been lifted—the prime rule of microgee was never to put yourself between two massive free objects.

Once the Geepees stopped jouncing Dane tabbed the lock shut. As Stotz and Kosti appeared in their suits, followed by the *Solar Queen*'s cargo master Jan Van Ryke, Dane realized just how unsuited the *Solar Queen* was to this type of operation, for the cable-orbit's acceleration made the back wall of the *Queen*—oriented as she was for vertical landings—into the floor.

Ali arrived a moment later, and for a time all were too busy for anything but brief communications. When the Geepees had been stowed safely for descent to a planet, Van Ryke sealed the cargo bay and they unsuited. Dane could feel the gees increase as he stowed his suit in the locker; the linked ships were spinning up to a quarter gee for comfort. Then Dane picked up his duffel and walked the short distance to his old cabin.

The *Queen* felt oddly unfamiliar. He walked along the wall of the corridor, threading his way past various outcroppings of ship systems and stepping over occasional hatches, outlined in lumenstrips of bright yellow-green. That reminder of distant Sol's imprint on humanity, tuning human eyes for the colors from the yellow-white sun of a chlorophyll planet, momentarily unsettled him as his mind tried to wrench the corridor into the microgravity layout of the *North Star*.

North Star—for just a moment, he was aware of Jasper and Rip on the *North Star*, orbiting opposite the *Queen*. A brief but intense wave of vertigo seized Dane, and his mind shook free of the image.

Dane looked around the cabin, his home for so long, trying to sort his emotions. How close and cramped it seemed, especially skewed ninety degrees! The cabin furnishings had been reoriented, locking into the clamps evident on every bulkhead, but he noted bright scratches on what was now the floor, evidence of how long the *Queen*'s vertical orientation had ruled their lives in Terran space. How dependent they had been on gravity! Were they growing away from the rest of humanity, out here, or merely adapting?

A strong hand whanged the decking outside Dane's open door, interrupting his musings. "Captain wants us." That growl belonged to Karl Kosti, the big man whose field of expertise was the machinery comprising the jets.

Dane followed the others up to the mess cabin. He smiled to himself as he noted that now, in partial gee, it was the human crewmembers who moved with a flat-footed shuffle, while Tooe moved freely, bouncing from bulkhead to bulkhead with a fine disregard for the mild acceleration of the two ships.

More evidence of ingrained habits faced him when they all crowded into the mess cabin. The *North Star* had a perfectly good cabin that had probably served as the former captain's ready room, but the new crew still held all their meetings, formal and informal, in the mess cabin on that ship as well.

After a moment's disorientation, Dane identified his usual place. He glanced at Tooe as she squeezed in next to him, then looked up to see Ali's gaze on him. Was Ali feeling the same disorientation? A sensation almost like looking down the corridor formed by two opposed mirrors made his head swim briefly, and he thought he saw a flicker of unease in the handsome tech's eyes.

He couldn't ask Ali, so he busied himself with looking around at the others, who exchanged brief comments as they crowded in.

Captain Jellico waited until everyone was quiet. He looked much the same as ever, Dane thought: tall, lean, blaster scar down one weathered cheek, keen eyes. The entire crew believed Jellico to be the best Free Trade captain in the starlanes, and nothing Dane had seen since he hired on had changed his mind about that.

"Slight alteration in plans," Jellico said without any preamble. "Wilcox reports at least two unidentified craft in-system." He nodded over at the lanky, thin navigation officer. "And Ya has tried to raise them, without success." Now he indicated the Martian-born communications officer. Ya shrugged his broad shoulders slightly.

"At this point we are still assuming that the planet is uninhabited," Jellico went on. "Unfortunately there's no way to be sure, especially given the violent weather and EM emissions from the cielanite deposits."

"EM?" asked Van Ryke, his white eyebrows quirking. "That wasn't in the survey. More of Flindyk's trickery?"

"Maybe," said Van Ryke, "but just as likely the general laxness of the Kanddoyds when it comes to gathering data on planets, which they have no use for. We're still in their sphere of influence."

"The magma pipes that cielanite is found in are strongly piezoelectric," said Johan Stotz. "Usually it's earthquakes that reveal cielanite deposits, and the signals can be detected light-years away. Here, it seems that the impact of violent storm waves on the volcanic islands causes huge electromagnetic pulses—radio waves that have very complex waveforms."

"The tides from the three moons make it even worse," said Tau.

"And look," said Tang Ya. He tabbed a control and the galley viewscreen lit up with a telescopic view of Hesprid IV. More than three-quarters of the globe was in darkness, strangely spotted with what looked like chains of Vereldian glowflies. Dane heard someone gasp as the realization hit them all simultaneously.

"Lightning," the communications tech confirmed. "When storms hit the islands, the EM pulses help create huge lightning storms."

"Which means almost nothing can get through," Jellico commented.

Tang Ya nodded once and tabbed off the display. "But I've heard nothing even in the calm periods," he added. "Not that we'll have many of those. The Hesprid sun is approaching its peak sunspot activity, so the weather, and the EM, are going to get much worse."

"It's a wonder the place hasn't burned to cinders," Ali Kamil drawled, "with all that energy."

"Looks pretty wet to me," Tau commented.

"In any case, we're going to have to assume that these others are possibly hostile," Jellico interjected, bringing the discussion back on topic. "And given the Patrol analysis of the weapon-scar on the *North Star* when we found her, we can't afford a confrontation. Even Patrol armor isn't much good against a colloid blaster."

The crew was silent. At the captain's mention of colloid blasters, Dane saw subtle reactions from some of the others— an angry narrowing of Ali's eyes, and a jutting of Kosti's jaw. Dane himself had never seen colloid blasters in action, but he knew what they were. Illegal except for use by armed Patrol craft, they used ship fuel to generate intense beams of particles and plasma. He even knew generally how it worked: cartridge feed, meaning burnout of the projector module each time. For those putting together the lethal beams an illegal catalyst whose major constituent was cielanite was the key element.

Hesprid IV produced cielanite. It didn't take any great leap of reasoning to figure that pirates who preyed on Traders mining cielanite could have used the cargo for their own purposes.

Dane shook his head slightly to chase away the dark thoughts. No use inventing fears before he had to face them.

Then he realized the captain was talking.

". . . so I am keeping six of us up here on the *North Star*," Jellico said. "Three will be on duty and three off, monitoring a constant signals watch."

"You still want us to take the *Solar Queen* down?" Dane asked.

Jellico's gray eyes rose briefly, and he nodded. "Rip's

landed the *Queen* in some pretty bad weather. As yet we don't
know how the *Star* handles in atmosphere, even a calm one.
And though we could land both, leaving us somewhat low on
fuel, that would give them—whatever their motives—high
end of the gee well. So it's best that one of us is in orbit monitoring things. Any questions?"

"Synchronous orbit?" Rip asked.

"No," Van Ryke interjected, his head slightly to one side,
his manner that of a man considering a possible move on a
chessboard. "High polar, I would suggest. Survey orbit. There
may be other resources here that would increase our payoff."

Tang Ya shook his head. "I don't much care for that. It will
be hard enough to maintain radio contact." He glanced at
Jellico. "And the redundancy our signals will need to punch
through will make them somewhat insecure—especially since
we don't know what kind of spy code might have been left in
the *North Star*'s systems."

Always assume someone's listening. Dane could almost
hear the com instructor's raspy voice at the Training Pool as
she impressed on them the primary rule of communications.

Captain Jellico sat still for just a moment, then nodded to
Van Ryke. "We never prospered by overlooking an opportunity," the bulky cargo master added.

No one spoke. Jellico gave a short nod, then said, "Polar
it is. Jan, you'll stay with me. Karl, you as well."

Jan Van Ryke, Dane's former master, gave a great sigh, his
bushy white brows arched in a slightly theatrical pained expression.

Jellico smiled just a little. "It was your idea. And if we do
find ourselves in communication with whoever is here, it's
your well-oiled tongue I'll be relying on to talk us out of any
trouble they might want to cause."

Karl Kosti looked slightly disappointed. Dane knew the
big man hated free fall—he'd probably been looking forward
to planetary gravity again. But he said nothing.

"How will we communicate, then?" asked Rip. "It'll take
a tight beam to punch through from the planet, but still . . ."

"We'll have to take that chance, despite the risk of inter- ception," said Jellico. "Try not to, and if you must, keep it terse, and don't rely on our codes." He smiled. "A lot easier for us to find you, and less chance of unfriendly ears. If we make contact with the ships and find them friendly, then stan- dard ciphers will do. If not, we'll pulse a code to you; as much as we can ram through the EM."

"What about a message torpedo?" asked Rip.

"The gods of space only know where it would land in that weather," said Ali Kamil, with a lazy shrug in the direction of the screen.

Rip nodded, his face faintly troubled. Jellico looked across at his wife, the beautiful Rael Cofort. Some kind of subtle sig- nal passed between them, and Dane wondered what they'd agreed on—or if they'd agreed.

Jellico said, "Then let's go!"

Dane watched the captain and some of the others go out, thinking, *The Old Man and Dr. Cofort haven't any psi con- nection that Tau's mentioned—but it sure looks like they have the next best thing.*

The captain and the doctor faded from his mind when he looked down into Tooe's huge yellow eyes. Her crest was raised at an alert angle he'd only seen once before, and she said, "Pirates, these others?"

"Maybe," Dane said reluctantly—as if his answer would make the threat real. "Hope not. Cielanite is rare enough to attract thieves—within the law, like Flindyk and his gang on Exchange, and without." He thought again about how cielan- ite was the main constituent of the illegal catalyst that ener- gized colloid blasters, and winced slightly.

"They chase us onto planet?"

Dane grinned. "Not likely. Remember gravity, Tooe. It's not just a small area you visit and leave when you get tired of feeling its pull. It costs a lot in fuel to land on a planet, and it'll cost more to leave when we're loaded up."

"I understand fuel, me," she said. "So this why we don't take two ships down?"

"Correct. We'd be too short on fuel unless Stotz was able to both process the raw ore and rig us a fuel catalyst for the two heavy elements in the cielanite. And we may not have the resources for both. Anyway, if someone's going to attack us, they won't do it dirtside, where it's much harder. They'll try to zap us out here, probably when we're climbing into or out of the gravity well."

She nodded. "Ship vulnerable then."

"Right."

"If it's pirates, they can't be too big an operation," Van Ryke said from behind. "Or they'd be down there mining now."

"Either that or attacking us," came Wilcox's quiet voice, as he finished a bulb of jakek.

"They're most likely a Survey team—or else independent scouters," Van Ryke went on, his manner reassuring as he watched Tooe. "It makes sense to be cautious. After all, they don't know who we are—for all they know, we could be pirates, out looking for ships to jack."

Tooe's crest tipped on one side into query mode, and her eyes seemed less intense as she thought that over.

Van Ryke touched her thin shoulder. "I suspect the biggest challenge for you will be getting used to weight."

"What weight?" Kosti joked, looming over the little Rigelian. "She'll get down there and she'll still float."

"Right," Ali drawled from the hatchway. "She'll still be sitting on the ceiling munching her crunchies."

"And the rest of us will brain ourselves, thinking we're still in free fall," Wilcox said, with a smile at Tooe.

Tooe listened to them making jokes. She knew they were jokes, even if the words did not seem funny. She liked it when they made jokes, because she felt reassured when they smiled and laughed. Going into a gravity well could not be so terrible if they joked—and they would know, for they had done it many times.

"I will not float, me," she said to Karl Kosti, as they started out. "I have mass!" She smacked her chest. "I will therefore have weight!"

"But not much, little cargo-wrangler," the big man said, laughing as he handed himself downdeck. "Not much!"

"What mass you do have needs strapping in," Jan said. "I believe the adventure is beginning." He looked up at Dane, his white brows making a shape that Tooe knew signalled an emotional change, but as yet she could not read it. "Good journey, my boy. You as well, Tooe."

He and the others transferring to the *North Star* suited up, and were soon jetting along the link to the other ship. Tooe watched them on the cargo-bay screen. When they were safely aboard and Rip Shannon conveyed the order to disengage the ships, Dane let Tooe work the controls.

Then it was time to get into the acceleration couch. Tooe hated that; she desperately wanted to stay at the console, where she could see everything.

Dane shook his head. "Tooe, this won't be like working in the heavy-gee gym on Exchange. You have to get into the couch. I wouldn't want to be caught outside mine, and I'm from Terra."

Tooe tried to hide her disappointment as she worked the webbing over her in the way they'd practiced. When she was ready, she looked across at the cargo master's console, wishing she could link up to Rip's piloting console so she could watch the landing.

"Here, Tooe," said Dane suddenly, his fingers playing briefly across the control tabs in his seat, and moments later her console screen lit. With delight she realized her wish had been granted.

She sent a quick glance at Dane, reminded of the psi link. Had he somehow read her thoughts? Except she had felt nothing, and he didn't act like a being who sensed thoughts. She thought back to the psi-sensitives in the klinti, and shook her head. He didn't read her thoughts; he sensed what she would like. This meant he was starting to know Tooe.

Pleased, she settled into her couch to watch her console. For a time she forgot all else, absorbed in the bright graphics of the display, happily tapping her way through various readouts and views, ignoring the brief bursts of acceleration that bounced her smoothly one way and then another, just like playing with the rubberdubber game that Momo had rigged from stretchy cargo straps they'd found in a long-forgotten locker in the heart of the Spin Axis of her former home on Exchange.

Then she saw Rip Shannon tense. Her body unconsciously tensed as she waited for something to happen. Nothing did, in the immediate sense. But as Hesprid IV loomed larger in the main viewscreen, the momentary accelerations became more frequent, and harsher. Now there was constant acceleration underlying all the bouncing, tugging at her guts. This wasn't like the smooth change between adaptation shifts on board the *North Star.* Tooe felt like she'd eaten too many Daddatik sweetnuts, and they were trying to burrow deeper into her stomach. Now it wasn't fun anymore.

It was then that the planet flipped abruptly, turning from a big ball out there into something vast and dangerous far below, something sucking her *down,* and Tooe experienced vertigo for the first time. And still she got heavier and heavier.

Now she could hear a sound like an overloaded ventilator, shrill and harsh. She tapped at her keys slowly, her fingers feeling like bloated Poapi-fruits, but all ship systems that she could see were green, except that the hull was heating up.

"Air's getting thick," a voice spoke over the comlink. Jasper, that was who. His voice sounded different, but Tooe's head hurt too much for her to figure out why.

"Huge high-pressure area," Rip replied abstractedly. "Ran into the bulge. More to come."

Despite her own misery, Tooe could hear the tension in the familiar mellow voice, which matched the set of Rip's shoulders and the swift stabbing of his fingers on his console. But then she puzzled out the sense of his words. Wind! She was hearing the sound of the *Solar Queen*'s sleek hull ripping through the air of Hesprid IV. Now her instincts warred with understanding, as a part of her insisted: rupture!

Fighting panic, she scanned the schematic of the ship on her screen, but all the hull sensors indicated the ship was still intact. She fought hard against the danger sense, swallowing constantly. That hurt, too.

Time began to pass in fragments for Tooe as she struggled against the sickening sensations. What made it worse was the realization that she'd have to go through this again to get away from the planet.

The viewscreen was now gray with clouds streaking past as the *Queen* tore through the atmosphere. Faint flickers of greenish blue and very occasional glimpses of a gray sea far below were all Tooe could see, but on the radar a peak loomed ahead.

"That's it," Rip exclaimed. "Biggest island in the chain, most cielanite, too. And practically the only place we can land."

"If this is calm," came Ali's voice as the ship shuddered briefly through a wind shear, "I don't want to know what counts as a storm."

"We're just at the leading edge of a terminator storm, racing ahead of sunrise," replied Rip, speaking slowly as he concentrated on his piloting. "Jones's teeth! Look at that lightning! We'll be down and cabled before it hits if we move smartly."

This was actually the easiest part of the descent, Dane had told Tooe, when the ship was actually flying. The landing would be much trickier.

But for Tooe, the actual landing was a blurred misery of jerky accelerations that grew ever stronger, and a weight that dragged at every part of her, growing ever greater in the same direction no matter what the ship did. Her eyes teared so violently that she couldn't see the screen, and she lost track of time.

Then, one final bump, and as acceleration went steady,

the final horror hit Tooe. You couldn't turn planetary gravity on and off like pseudo. It wasn't going to stop, not until they went through that all over again. With that thought, the little Rigelian hybrid let go her grasp on the world around her and slipped into unconsciousness.

4

At the last moment, a sudden flaw in the wind snatched at the *Solar Queen,* and Rip grounded her more heavily than he'd intended.

"Full sensor scan," he ordered on the general channel, and a bloom of windows on his console displayed Craig Tau's response from his console in the lab. Rip didn't remove his hands from the pilot console—the *Queen*'s normal thrusters were still powered up, the autopilot now balancing the tall, needle-shaped vessel against the growing gusts of wind. "Floodlights on."

Millions of candlepower flared from the belt of lights circling the *Queen*'s sharp nose, revealing the violent reality behind the passionless readouts and displays all around them. Behind him he heard a sudden exclamation from Dane.

"Tooe!"

Rip stole a glance at the linkup to the cargo bay—the autopilot felt stable—and saw Dane scramble up from his console and over to Tooe, who lay almost invisible in the oversize

embrace of her acceleration couch. The big man slapped the
red medic button at the head of the couch, then stopped, his
hands hovering in indecision. What little Rip could see of
Tooe, before his concern over the *Queen*'s exposure to the
wind pulled his gaze back to the main screen, was almost the
same gray as the utilitarian leather of the couch.
The com crackled to life as Craig Tau responded to the
emergency signal. "She's grav-sick," said Tau, looking directly
at him from the screen. "I need to stabilize her right away;
she's very shocky, if I'm reading her right. You can move her
safely."
Rip swore he could feel Dane's and Ali's gazes on him.
Was that just the knowledge of his responsibility as captain
here, or was it a psi-borne emotion from Dane? "Rip? I want
to get her down to the lab right away."
Rip swiveled around in his now upright seat as Craig's
face winked out. "Dane, go ahead and take her. Ali, grab an
echo from his console and monitor."
The cargo-bay linkup blanked, and Rip turned his attention to the main screen once more. He studied what the floodlights revealed, which wasn't much. He saw the shapes of tall
trees that reminded him of Terran redwoods; the frequent
lightning flashes indicated some kind of foliage, though he
couldn't see details. This storm was only a few hours deep at
the speed it was moving, not much more than a squall line for
this planet, but the variap radar had indicated some savage
wind shears in it, as well as the telltale hooks of incipient tornadoes.
But their landing spot was clear enough, if Stotz was right.
"Ali, deploy the guy-bots," he ordered; moments later the
muffled report of the guy cannons in the nose of the *Queen*
rumbled through the bridge. At the edge of the light he could
see the squat form of one of the eight-legged bots splash into
the mud. It stumped forward a few meters and then squatted
down, the cable linking it to the ship glistening like a spiderweb in the light from the *Queen*. A brief burst of light under
the bot's belly hurled steam and spray in every direction as it

explosively augered an anchor into the ground. The explosions under the three bots, equilaterally deployed around the ship, tapped mildly at the soles of his boots, reminding him to demag them. Then the *Queen* creaked and her slight swaying diminished rapidly as the winches tightened the guys.

"No wonder Stotz made such a fuss over them, back on Canuche," said Ali. "Always seemed like a luxury, until now—kind of thing Macgregory would have on his yacht."

"I'm sure he does," replied Rip, smiling as he turned away from the console and stretched in relief. "But Johan isn't one to be taken in by glitter."

A moment later the hatch opened, revealing Dane and Craig Tau.

"She's still out, but stable," said Tau as they entered. "It may have been more the psychological shock than the physical, since her vital signs tightened up right away." He shook his head, his expression rueful. "She seemed to be adapting so well—with those hollow bones and their hybrid calcium system she was building up good bone mass. I don't know what happened."

Rip nodded. He cast a glance at Thorson, saw mostly the top of the cargo master's yellow head. His gaze was on the decking, a sure sign of a somber mood.

Then he realized that the others were looking at him in silence, waiting for orders.

Tau spoke first. "We're cabled down and sealed up. What do the sensors say?"

"Humanoid infrared and carbon dixoide traces, mass at high end of human scale," Ali replied as Tau leaned over to look at the display.

"Humanoid?" Dane looked up in surprise. "Pirates? They landed?"

Ali gave an elaborate shrug. "Can't be native life; Tau says that's confined to the oceans, and though there's apparently plenty of it, none of the varieties match the standards for sentience." He sent a look at Rip. "So . . . ?"

"So no one goes out until we have light," Rip said slowly.

"Meantime, standard procedure: we'll break out the sleep-rods and set up watches. Ali, send out query signals, in case whoever is out there is legit. We've got low tide right now, so the EM shouldn't be a problem for a little while."

Ali shook his head. "Still a lot of interference, but I'll keep trying. Captain Jellico is still in range, for another two hours," Ali said, glancing at his chrono. "Want me to report?"

Again Rip looked at the others, saw Stotz shake his head slightly.

"No," Rip said, now sure his first instinct was right. "Just bounce the safe-down signal off the moon and let it scatter. Ya will pick it up. Beyond that we have to assume that whatever we say will be overheard. We'll only contact the *Queen* if there's an emergency."

Ali's brows rose faintly. "Aye," he said, tapping at keys.

Tau and the others left to return to their stations.

Rip stayed in the command chair, watching the blank com screen. Ali sent the query, to no response. Time passed slowly; for something to do, Rip called up the infrared sensor reading from Tau's instruments, and saw blurry shapes indicating beings whose body temps ranged well within humanoid limits. They were in clusters, some of them relatively near the ship. Assault dugouts—or shelters?

But an hour passed, and then another, and nothing happened. No communication, no movement of anything besides slowly subsiding wind and heavy rain outside the ship.

Rip thought of something, and reached to tab the intercom. "Tau?"

"Here." The medic's voice came from his lab.

"How far is the range on your temperature sensors?"

"Just our immediate surroundings. But unless they can baffle my readings, our neighbors haven't moved."

"Thanks." Rip tabbed off, feeling the unaccustomed pressure in his hand joints. He absently flexed his fingers.

After a time the intercom blinked, and Rip keyed it.

Tau's voice said, "I have fine-tuned my readings as much as I can, and I don't find any evidence of a ship."

From the engine room came Stotz's voice, "You wouldn't, if their ship's gone totally cold."

"How often do we ever go totally cold? Even when we're planeted for a lengthy stay, we're at low power in order to run life support, the computers, and hydro." Tau sounded calm and matter-of-fact.

"True," Stotz returned somewhat drily. "But it's good to note all possibilities."

Rip realized the others were not so much reporting as reminding him of the many aspects of the situation that he might overlook, but no one wanted to come right out and say so. He felt a weird mixture of gratitude and irritation; the latter mostly at himself for not projecting the kind of competent front that was second nature to Jellico. *He probably had his crew convinced he was in perfect control the very first time he took command,* Rip thought. He sighed, feeling the unaccustomed grip of gravity as tension in the back of his neck and across his brow. Rubbing his fingers around his eye sockets, he considered the medic's words. His thoughts were distracted by the sense that he was being watched by someone familiar. He turned—and Dane Thorson appeared in the hatchway, looking tired and slightly apologetic.

"One thing we never found out," Dane said, "was whether the *Ariadne* had its full crew complement on board when she was hijacked by Flindyk's gang. If they split their crew and left half here, the *Ariadne* could go back to Exchange with a full cargo, return with supplies, and find a cargo waiting to be loaded right away."

Ali whistled. "Never thought of that—but you might very well be right, Viking."

"It makes sense," Rip said slowly. "We've been running that same ship with a half-crew, so we know it can be done."

"If it's so," Ali said, tapping idly at his console, "then we're the pirates. At least, so we'd appear to them. They have to have a 'scope—if we'd split crew like that, a good telescope would be as important as a comlink."

"So . . . if they saw the *Ariadne* in orbit overhead, then

they know we have their ship," Dane said. He winced and gave his head a shake. "Bad way to find out their crewmates joined Sanford Jones and his ghost ship."

Rip laid his palms on his knees. "I know what I have to do." He keyed the com screen to life. "Ali, let's broadcast on a spread-spectrum signal on the Trade band."

Ali stretched out his hands over his console, but paused and looked up, his mouth wry. "You know, our neighbors outside could very well be pirates."

Rip took a deep breath, then shook his head. "We'll have to take that chance."

Ali gave a slight shrug and went to work.

The red light above the com screen changed to green, which meant that Rip and the others on the command deck were being broadcast. Rip gave a twitch to his Free Trader uniform, and said, "I am Rip Shannon, piloting the *Solar Queen*. In orbit is the ship once named the *Ariadne,* now named the *North Star.* We found her in orbit in the Mykos system; our snapout intersected with her orbit . . ." Slowly, calmly, he told the story.

At the end, he had Ali broadcast two tapes from the log: their first contact with the *Ariadne,* showing plainly the scoring down her side, and "Starvenger," the false name provided by the pirates, painted on her hull.

Then he had Flindyk's arrest and arraignment broadcast as well.

It was a risk, to reveal themselves without knowing who might be watching, and to what end. Rip hated talking to a one-way vidscreen. But he felt it was the least they owed the *Ariadne*'s crew—if the unknowns *were* the *Ariadne*'s crew— and he noted that neither of the others protested further.

When he was done, he said slowly, watching the com light over the receiving screen, "And so that's why we're here. We have the Charter, issued by the Trade Commission, and we're here to mine cielanite. I'm sorry to have to be the bearer of this news." He felt the end was lame, and winced as he reached to tab the comlink off.

For a protracted moment all three waited, and when there was no response, Rip looked around at the others. "Meanwhile, since there isn't much else we can do, why don't we eat, and those not on watch can get some rest? If we've got a rough night ahead, let's be ready for it."

Dane went out first, Ali staying behind on watch. Rip noted slowness and awkward angles in the cargo master's movements. Rip stood up, felt his head twinge, and his stomach muscles gripped warningly. He winced, and took some time to work his muscles before descending the ladder. Landing the *Queen* had left him with a body full of knots.

He'd expected that the long journey through hyper, with its pseudo gravity, would readapt them to full acceleration, but it seemed not. That worried him. Was the psi just part of something else that was happening to them? Or was the rest of the crew adapting to the new conditions in Kanddoyd space, where variable gee was the norm?

As he ran through a set of muscle-loosening movements, he reflected on the fact that he hadn't skimped in working out on the weight machines. Tau had made certain that they all did their time in the workouts, to keep up the level of calcium in their bones despite the microgravity shifts. It wasn't that Rip's muscles ached, but that everything still felt a little out of place.

Finally he moved out with care and descended the ladder. Standing on the deckplates next to the ladder to the next level was Dane Thorson. The cargo master made a face as he rubbed his temples.

"Fall?" Rip asked.

Dane grinned sheepishly. "Nope. Moved too fast, I guess. Almost took a dive through that hatch—hit my forehead." He jerked his thumb behind him.

"Tooe all right?" Rip asked.

"That's where I'm headed. Craig asked me to check on her," Dane said.

Rip shook his head. He knew the little Rigelian had spent time on Exchange in the Terran-gravity areas, but that always had been for short periods. Remembering what he felt like when he visited the heavy-grav Shver area on Exchange, he could understand why she'd collapsed. "Let me come with you."

They found Tooe lying on her bunk. Sinbad, the *Queen*'s cat, sat near her head, grooming himself. To all appearances he was completely unconcerned about the sudden return to gravity.

As soon as Tooe saw Rip and Dane she made a valiant effort to get up. "Tooe work now," she said, but her eyes were half-closed, her pupils huge with her effort.

Rip looked in dismay at the webbed crest that stretched over her skull from brow to nape. It was limp and grayish blue. Her fingers were stiff with the effort it took her to remain upright, and the coloring of her scaled skin had dulled from her normal, healthy blue-green to a kind of greenish gray that really did look like the use-scarred synth-leather of the *Queen*'s acceleration couches.

"I'm getting Tau," he said.

Dane motioned to Tooe. "Get back in that bunk."

"I work, me," Tooe said. Even her voice seemed flattened.

"No you aren't," Dane said. "Any more than I'd be up and working if I had just landed on the Shver planet. Your body has to adjust, and it takes time."

Jasper appeared just behind Rip, his naturally pale face looking strained.

Rip slid out of Tooe's cabin, leaving Dane there to reassure his apprentice.

"Is she all right?" Jasper asked.

"I'm about to send Tau in," Rip said. "Though she's insisting she can get up and take her shift, so she can't be dying. Problem?"

Jasper grimaced. "Nothing that a dose of free fall couldn't cure. Wonder why she never had problems during the geeshifts in hyper?"

"Tau's working on that. Go get some sleep," Rip said.

"We don't know what's going to happen—or how long it'll take when it does happen. Someone needs to be fresh."

Jasper gave a nod of agreement, and, working his neck, disappeared. Rip followed more slowly, his mind a jumble of different thoughts all needing immediate focus. Remembering what Jellico had told him once, he made himself stop in the galley. Mura had coffee waiting—a silent testament to the stresses of the landing.

Rip picked up a mug, making sure it didn't tip. For a moment he watched the liquid behaving like liquids were supposed to—only it looked strange. *Half of command is knowing how to get your emergencies into priority order,* the captain had said. Rip sipped half of the coffee, trying to get his thoughts sorted. Then he set the mug down and left.

When he reached the cargo deck, he met Craig Tau coming out of Tooe's cabin.

"I thought she was coming out of shock," the medic said, shaking his head ruefully. "But her hybrid metabolism went right through homeostasis into overdrive, trying to force calcium into her bones in response to the gee stress. The sudden calcium depletion hit her synapses hard and made her nervous system unstable." He rubbed his temples. "It seems the adaptation shifts weren't long enough to really switch her over to a high-gee metabolism, so it hit her all at once."

"Prognosis?" Dane asked.

"She'll live," Tau said. "I've got her on a heavy calcium replacement drip, and we'll transition her to liquids and then solid food." He frowned wryly. "I should have seen it sooner. Her body was trying a little too hard too fast."

"That's Tooe," said Rip.

The medic turned to him. "Speaking of too much, your advice to Weeks was good—and I think you should follow it. I don't think anything is going to happen for the remainder of the night, but if it does, you'll be the first to know."

Rip opened his mouth to argue, but his brain wouldn't supply the words. He realized it would be foolish to force himself to stay awake, like some kind of trash-vid hero. *If I do, my commands will make as much sense as theirs do,* he thought with an inward laugh. "I'm off, then. Thanks." A few minutes later he stretched out gratefully on his bunk, and fell asleep.

It seemed about five minutes later the buzz of his alarm speared into his dreams. He fought for consciousness. It was like swimming up from the bottom of a well, with an anchor dragging at his body. No, with a spaceship sitting on his chest, holding him under water.

With difficulty he forced his eyes open.

The spaceship on his chest was gravity. He stayed flat, doing relaxing breathing. Slowly a semblance of energy returned, and he sat up with care, then got to his feet. A needle-hard hot shower helped more, and he dressed as quickly as he could, resolving to drink something stimulating before he did anything else.

He found Dane and Frank Mura in the galley, both looking tired. The steward nodded at a fresh pot of jakek, with mugs stacked beside it. No more drink-bulbs. Rip poured some liquid into the mug, hefting its weight. Some things felt comfortingly natural, and mugs of hot liquid rated high on the list.

"Storm's abated," Dane said.

"Heavy fog moving in." The new voice was Johan Stotz's. "But that force-five wind has died out, at least."

"Good," Rip said, swallowing another hot mouthful of the jakek. "Let's take a look around."

"Cap'n would want you covered," Stotz said.

Rip nodded. "Two of you in the main hatch, sleeprods. We'll take 'em as well." He finished the drink, then glanced at Dane, who plainly was waiting. "Let's get it over with."

Shortly after that he and Thorson stood in the main lock, and Rip tabbed the outer hatch. They watched as the ramp lowered, and a wave of cold, wet air blew in and bathed Rip's face. He smelled salt and greenery and an odd trace of scent that reminded him strongly of damp wool, and he sneezed.

Next to him, Dane sneezed as well. They'd been used to the sterile ship's air so long, Rip had forgotten the rich scents of a planet—not that he'd smell them for long. Already his nose was clogging up, and he made a mental note to visit Tau first thing, assuming they returned safely, and get sprayjected for allergies.

The ramp boomed softly to the muddy ground. Behind them the ship was silent; she'd had plenty of hours to cool down from the descent. The ramp lights glared in the weak light of the thick fog. Rip made out a tangle of huge trees, so tall their tops were lost in the fog. He shivered in his tunic; he was also unused to weather.

He and Dane started down, then Rip was startled to hear a quick hiss of static from the comlink in the hatch behind them. He paused, and Ali said, "Shannon! Thorson! I think you'd better hear this."

Rip and Dane looked at each other, and Rip retreated up the ramp. In silence Dane followed.

In the lock, Stotz hit the com-key with his fist, and said, "They're here."

Instead of Ali's voice, there was a squawk of static, as if someone was having to find their frequency manually, and then a heavily accented voice said in Trade speech, "Do not walk forth! Bide in your transport until the sun is gone!"

Rip looked at the others.

Stotz frowned. "Tau ran tests on the air, and the scanner has cleared all known toxins to humans."

As if in answer again there came a burst of static, under which they heard the rapid chatter of voices. Rip gripped his sleeprod unconsciously, staring out at the foggy landscape.

"Danger," came the accented voice. "Monsters!"

5

"Creatures—monsters," came the voice. "Sunlight danger only. They move in the fog. Vacuum suits ward them not."

Dane Thorson peered out into the fog, but saw nothing. He turned back to Rip, who leaned against the bulkhead right next to the com, as if the proximity to the electronic device brought him closer to the unknown speaker. "So you want us to wait for darkness before emerging, is that right?" Rip asked.

"Wait for dark. Wait for dark."

Then the com went dead.

Craig Tau appeared in the hatchway.

"What do you think?" Rip Shannon asked him.

"Pending discussion, let's seal up."

Dane was relieved when Rip closed and sealed the outer hatch. Suddenly that thick fog outside seemed sinister. Not, he told himself, that he believed in monsters—but maybe these mystery people lurked out there with weapons.

Johan Stotz said quietly, "Our unknown friends might have a reason to keep us in here for a while."

"Such as moving in to set up an ambush?" Rip asked.

"Just what I was thinking," Tau admitted.

Rip nodded. "Then let's reactivate all our sensors and scan the perimeter as thoroughly as possible. If they notice, and comment, we're testing."

"If they notice, and comment, they are almost certainly preparing for a fight." Ali's drawling voice was heard a moment before he appeared in the inner hatchway. He leaned lazily against a bulkhead and gave them one of his ironic smiles. "Remember, there is no evidence of another ship. Jasper's got the com right now," he added. "In case our mystery friends feel the urge to send more entertaining communications."

"If what you say is true, then these people must be aware that their only way off might be the *Queen*—with us or without us," Tau said.

And again the others looked at Rip, their expressions varying. It was up to him to make the orders, but Dane wondered if Rip did not know what to say. What would Jellico say?

Almost as if from memory, he heard the clipped tones of the captain: *Break out the sleeprods, and set up watches.*

The others were obviously thinking along the same lines, for Rip repeated the same words out loud, and Dane had the satisfaction of seeing Stotz nod slightly, and Tau's face relax. This order was pretty much what they expected, then. What else?

Rip turned to Ali. "I know you've been up for much longer than your shift, but can you stay it a little longer? You're good at talking—see what you can learn from them. Even if it's all lies, at least we'll be able to pinpoint where they are. Maybe their numbers as well."

Ali lifted one shoulder in a slightly theatrical shrug. Dane recalled the time when Ali's vid-actor gestures had annoyed him. Now he felt oddly reassured.

Stotz said, "I wish the Old Man was in range—"

Ali stretched, glanced at the time, and said, "Another six hours and seventeen minutes. Except we need to remember that any message we send up will doubtless be listened to. We simply tell the captain that we've discovered others here, and wait for his instructions."

"No doubt carefully worded." Rip grinned. "All right. In six hours we can dump all this into the Old Man's lap. Until then, let's get as much data as we can."

Ali laced his fingers together, turned them inside out until the knuckles cracked, then he wrung his hands. "Even keying hurts. We were in free fall too long. I feel like I mass as much as a Dirjwartian thundersaur."

Rip laughed, or started to. Suddenly his laugh turned into a fierce, jaw-cracking yawn—one that Dane caught. He yawned himself, his eyes tearing.

Tau smiled at them. "I prescribe some rack time, you two. You know, if anyone makes contact, it'll be you—and that would go better if you're rested."

Dane nodded, feeling that he'd never obeyed an order with more pleasure.

Several hours of heavy sleep later, he woke suddenly, sat up— and nearly fell out of bed. For a moment his body seemed one big cramp, and his lungs labored for air, but he lay back down, slowing his breathing, and then got up more slowly.

A hot shower woke him some more, enough so that his mind filled with questions. But before he went in search of answers, he checked on Tooe, who responded weakly to his knock. She lay in her bunk, her color more gray than her normal healthy greenish blue. Her crest lay limp, and her eyes seemed dull.

Dane frowned, noting the full glass of liquid next to her. "Have you eaten?" he asked. "Drunk?"

"No," she said. Even her voice seemed flattened. "My insides like it not." She wound her fingers together. "It strangles me." The little alien scratched at a bandage in the crook of her elbow. "Hate needles, tied up."

"That stuff in the glass," Dane persisted. "Looks like one of Tau's medicinal concoctions. Why don't you get it down—it might help."

"No," she said, sounding wistful. "Food—liquid. Strangle my throat."

Dane bit back the impulse to stand over her and make her try to drink. He nodded, then said, "I'll check on you later," hoping that would be enough to get her to take whatever Tau had given her. Then he withdrew.

He found all the others except Johan Stotz gathered in the tight quarters of the mess cabin. They all had food and drink before them; Frank Mura tipped his head toward the galley, and half a minute later Dane had a plate of fresh, hot food in one hand and a mug of good, strong coffee in the other. As he sat down, he saw Sinbad bound in, a plump orange streak.

"What's the news?" Dane asked, picking up his fork.

Jasper Weeks said, "They contacted me just a while ago. They are indeed from the *Ariadne*."

Dane whistled softly. "That's bad."

"Besides the obvious, there's another problem." Rip set his mug down and leaned back in his chair. "They no longer hold the Charter—"

"Of course," Ali said, bending down to stroke Sinbad, who wound round his legs and purred happily.

"—which means," Rip continued, unperturbed, "whatever they've mined since the date of the transfer is ours. How to establish that is going to take some ticklish negotiating."

Dane Thorson looked up, his expression pained. "And Van Ryke is on the other ship."

Tau smiled a little. "Which means it's your problem."

Dane swallowed some coffee, then said, "I need to know what kind of people I'm dealing with before I can think out an approach."

Rip said, "How about this. At sunset you and I will go out and see if they'll come to us within the light perimeter of our ship. The plan is the same as this morning: the rest of you can be armed and ready just behind the hatches. If we establish any kind of reasonable communication, then we'll take it from there."

Mura nodded. "May's well get started on the negotiating now. We can't start mining until we've gotten this straightened out with those people out there."

Ali said, "Jasper received the initial contact, but I've been trying to chat with them. As far as I can tell they weren't shareholders, just crew, so they probably had no legal claim on the ship."

"We can't know that," Dane said. "It was presumed that the entire crew had died when Flindyk's pirates took the ship and changed the name. Who exactly were considered heirs?"

"We have that on record," Mura said reassuringly. "We just checked. The heirs were listed as kin to the captain—as long as these out here don't have a nearer kin claim to the captain, then we can safely assume they were just paid crew."

"I don't know the ins and out of Trade Law," Jasper said quietly, "but I've never heard that paid crew have claims. Instead, I've heard of people being stranded on planets when their ships have run into various kinds of legal trouble."

"So have I, come to think of it," Ali put in, giving them a slanting smile. "I'm sure we're protected legally by anyone's system. Whether these gentle people outside will agree—and abide by Trade's decisions—is what Dane and Rip need to ascertain. I don't envy them the task, either," he added with his usual smiling drawl.

"Go get some sleep," Tau said, jerking his thumb behind him. "You can find out the next exciting installment when you wake up."

Ali sauntered out.

Rip sighed. "Let me see if Stotz has heard anything, and then we may as well get it over with, Thorson, after you eat. The sun has just set."

Dane nodded, and Rip went out—moving with care, Dane noted.

Frank Mura retreated to the galley, and soon sounds emanated from there. Dane turned to the medic, who was just finishing his coffee. "Tooe won't eat," he said.

Tau frowned. "Did you tell her she will not recover her strength unless she does?"

"She knows. She said the food will choke her. Even liquids choke her."

Tau's brow cleared suddenly, and he almost laughed. "Weight."

Dane stared, puzzled. "What?" Suddenly he got it. "I never did see her eat during the Hesprid adaptation shift. Of course. Her throat's used to the mass, but not the weight. I never asked, but I'll bet my next year's pay that Tooe only worked out in heavy-grav, and never ate there. *I* sure never ate anything down in Shver territory on Exchange—couldn't get used to foods weighing sixty percent more than usual. She's going from virtually zero to point-eight-five, eighty-five percent of Terran gravity!"

"I know what to do," said Tau. "We'll get her used to it slowly. I can talk to Frank, and we'll aerate her liquids for now. That'll get her swallowing—and, probably, playing with her food again. Unless I'm mistaken, she'll enjoy seeing how water behaves in grav. And when she gets hungry enough, she'll stop spritzing her mouth and start experimenting with small bites."

Relieved, Dane glanced at the time, and the medic said, "You and Rip had better get ready for your encounter. Leave this to me."

Dane was glad to comply. The truth was, even though he'd just woken up, he still wanted to go right back to his bunk and spend a good stretch of hours just lying there. The inexorable pull of gravity made his joints ache, but what really hurt was his head. Was it his imagination, that weird sense that Rip's tension was pulling energy right out of him? He'd never felt that before—which made him suspicious. Ever since Tau had told them about that possible psi link, Dane's dreams had been playing tricks on him, such as pulling up memories of stupid tri-D stories about psis and mysterious brainpowers. He knew Rip was tense. They all saw it. They all felt tense as well.

When he met Rip out in the narrow accessway, the astrogator-pilot silently handed Dane a sleeprod.

"These going to be enough?" Dane asked.

"Hope we don't have to find out," Rip said. And he indicated the outer lock. "Let's get this over."

Once again they lowered the ramp. Dane sniffed appreciatively at the air outside, cold as it was.

Then he forgot the cold, the smells, and everything else, when he saw the four figures standing close together in a line just at the edge of the pool of light. Dane was used to towering over most humans he met, but these four made him feel short.

He heard a slight intake of breath from Rip, and looked over; there was no expression to be seen beyond friendliness in Shannon's dark, pleasant face. He stopped a few feet from the bottom of the ramp, and Dane stopped with him.

"I am Rip Shannon, astrogator-pilot of the Free Trader ship *Solar Queen*," Rip said. "My cargo master here is Dane Thorson."

They waited. What sounded like whispered growls came from the figures; the sound was partly obscured as a great gust of wind soughed through the mighty trees. In the distance, just faintly, came the rise and fall of voices in a minor-key melodic line that made the hairs on the back of Dane's neck prickle.

Then one of the four stepped forward. In the deep voice that could only come from a massive chest, he said, "I be Lossin, locutor of the Free Trader vessel *Ariadne*-that-was."

"I be Tazcin," said another.

"Vrothin."

"Kamsin."

Dane could tell nothing from those deep, low voices. Were they angry, afraid, indifferent? He scanned them again, fighting the urge to touch his sleeprod. He didn't trust the way they stood in a row like that, shoulder to shoulder, their arms touching. It seemed aggressive, except they had no weapons, and made no overt move of threat.

Dane, calculating how long it must have been since the *Ariadne* had left, wondered if this crew was low on supplies.

Rip hesitated, then said in his mildest voice, "Our first concern is these monsters you mentioned at daybreak. Can you tell us more about them?"

In the background the voices rose again, sustaining a high, eerie note. Dane wondered if it was mourning music.

"We have made a recording from our archives. Trade, for your data of *Ariadne*-that-was."

The other three made some kind of hand-sign, and two of them growled something in low voices. It sounded to Dane like a ritual phrase, though he could not guess at its meaning.

Rip approached Lossin with slow, easy steps, and held his hand out. Lossin dropped something onto his palm, then said, "Floaters—we call these *ghestin* Floaters—come only in sun time, and fog. We do nothing in sun time. Rains come soon." He pointed upward.

A sudden gust of chill wind swept over the rocks, sending bits of mud stinging Dane's face. Lossin and his companions did not move. Only their thick fur ruffling marked the effect of the weather; the gust brought to Dane a whiff of a distinctive odor that propelled him for a brief moment back to childhood. He could not identify it, though.

"Thank you," Rip said. "We will view it now. May we contact you with any questions?"

Lossin said, "You are here. Trade has given Charter to you. Our camp is now your camp. Our ore is now your ore. Our ship—"

One of the four made a sudden move, then paused. Then as Dane and Rip watched, the person abruptly ducked back a few steps and withdrew rapidly into the inky darkness under the huge trees.

There wasn't anything to say—at least, Dane couldn't think of anything, and apparently Rip couldn't either.

"Thank you for the tape," the navigator-pilot said in an uncharacteristically subdued voice, and in silence Dane and Rip retreated back into the *Solar Queen*.

6

★

The chip that Lossin gave them was designed for the old external input system on the *North Star*, of course. But before the ships had left Exchange, Tang Ya had built conversion hardware and software so that the systems of the *North Star* and the *Solar Queen*—which was designed to use quantum-tapes—were now compatible.

Dane saw Stotz close the outer hatch, and in silence the engineer fell in behind Rip. Though no one had said anything as yet, they found Ali waiting on the control deck. Dane glanced at Kamil's tight expression, the challenging glitter in his dark eyes, and wondered what had angered him.

But there was no time to consider the engineer's moods. Rip activated the big screen, and after a moment keyed the chip to general broadcast, so that the others elsewhere in the *Queen* could bring it up on their screens if they wanted.

A flash of unfamiliar script appeared and disappeared, and then they found themselves watching an automated vid-scan of the same clearing that Dane and Rip had just walked in, only seen from a different angle. For a few seconds they listened to an unseen speaker talk in a language unfamiliar to Dane—the tone made it clear she was reporting. After a moment Rip tabbed the mute, and they continued to watch the scan, now in silence. Dane calculated that the *Ariadne* had landed about a hundred meters southwest of the *Queen*'s present position. He recognized two of the gigantic trees they'd just left, the great branches undulating in the continuous strong wind.

The scene changed abruptly; now figures moved about. Dane recognized the actions, if not the tools. Crewmembers were taking samples of soil and plant life, and measuring air currents. As thin wisps of fog obscured the higher tree branches, two crewmembers, humanoids wearing the brown of Free Traders, walked cautiously downhill between the trees, marking a pathway and stopping to scan and report as they went. Behind them walked an unseen person carrying the vid recorder.

They emerged from the shelter of the trees into a clearing and stepped into a fairly thick fog bank. The recorder was perhaps twenty meters behind; the operator had paused to take close views of some of the plants.

Suddenly the vid jerked and swerved. The two in the clearing had stopped, and stared up at something in the fog.

Rip tapped the audio key again, and Dane heard the rapid exchange of voices, higher in tone, sharp. He felt his own adrenaline spike; he leaned forward, as if the movement would bring the scene into clearer view.

The vid operator tabbed the zoom, and vid now focused on the fog. The vague outline of a turnip-shaped thing, light gray in color, hovered above the two on the pathway. Another one was just barely in view, perhaps ten meters above the first. Dane squinted, and thought he could see the vague outline of others even higher up. His neck muscles tightened.

"Balloons," Stotz murmured. "Look like balloons."

As they watched, the two in the clearing exchanged rapid words, one of them reporting into a comlink. Then the creature above them compressed slightly, and what looked like ribbon rolled down, dangling in the wind. The ribbons brushed one crewmember's head, with horrific results. Dane felt his throat go dry as the man stiffened, his body vibrating as if undergoing electric shock. He screamed, a terrible sound.

"Damp that," Ali snapped.

Rip had already extended his hand; he tapped the mute, and the wrenching sound stopped abruptly. But on the screen the terror had not ended. Blood erupted from the man's nose and ears, and he fell to the pathway in a boneless way that indicated he was dead before he reached the ground.

The woman with him had frozen still for a moment; she suddenly turned and started to run, but her initial pause condemned her. She had scarcely gone two steps before another of the things lowered its ribbons, which touched her. Now they could see more clearly, for she was closer to the vid operator, and facing them square on. She flung her arms over her head, but the ribbons contacted her wrist, and adhered to her flesh where they touched. Dane and the others were forced to watch her undergo the same violent death as her crewmate. Hers, in fact, seemed to last longer. Several times Dane wanted to tell Rip to stop it, or to get up and go away himself, but he forced himself to view it all. This was important; he would be facing the same danger.

While the woman was dying, the vid operator kept the vid going, but it jerked and jiggled. Dane figured she (if the operator was the same voice they'd heard reporting the initial vid-scan) was either yelling orders or begging for help. Probably both.

Then one of the gray things started lowering within a frighteningly close distance to the vid operator, and the screen abruptly went dead.

"I hope she got away," Rip said into the shocked silence.

After another pause, Dane said, "We'd better get helmets."

"Except that second person was not touched on the head, but her wrist," Stotz pointed out.

"Biohaz suits, then?"

"The others said in their first warning that that wouldn't work." Rip gave his head a shake, as if to dispell bad images. "It seemed to me that those people died of a jolt of electricity."

"Or some kind of poison that instantly traumatizes the neurological system," Ali murmured. "Either way, you won't catch me out during daylight hours, suit or no suit."

"Agreed." Rip sighed. "We'll send this up to Captain Jellico, but I know what he'll say. This means it's going to be considerably tougher to get at that cielanite, for we don't have the energy budget for night mining. Not in this climate."

"Our friends out there must have equipment designed for this planet, though," Stotz said. "If they've managed to maintain it despite being marooned." He turned to Dane. "Think you can work a trade?"

Dane was thinking rapidly. "I'll try." He remembered the low growling voices, the ritual gestures. The one who ran off so suddenly. In a sudden surge of doubt, he said, "I wish Jan was here."

"We don't have Van Ryke," Rip said slowly. "And I don't think we're going to get him. Especially now—these people out there have no ship, no fuel. We are their only hope of lifting off. Bringing the *North Star* down would just double the chances of a jacking, if they're that desperate, or worse, actually allied with the pirates—if those are pirates above us."

"Even if they're honest, from the looks of these people on the vid, each will cost upwards of three hundred kilos of ore or refined cielanite at liftoff," Ali said.

"But the cost of that depends on how far refined it is," said Stotz. "If we can refine it further—assuming they've kept up their mining—" He fell silent, considering.

By the laws of Trade, they couldn't leave the Traders there—but what would it cost them to lift them off? How would this affect their profit? Would they be reduced to seeking another desperate gamble like staking everything on another Survey auction in order to recoup their losses, or would they lose the *North Star*?

Rip's voice broke into his thoughts. "There must be a way to approach them. I consider their sharing this data an act of good faith. They know who we are—they know we have their ship. They could as easily have sat tight in their camp, wherever it is, and let those Floaters zap us one by one."

Stotz was now drumming his fingers on a console. "Cielanite is a possible fuel, although a touchy one. If we can refine it far enough to bring it into range of the catalysts we have . . . but that depends on how much mining equipment they have . . ."

"That could be the trade we need," said Dane, feeling a sense of relief at the possible solution to the problem. "The law gives us their ore, but not their equipment. If they lease it to us, that could save us enough of our energy budget to compensate for their liftoff mass."

"I'd better do some simulations," Stotz said. "Be ready for what they'll offer so we can come right back at them with a counteroffer if we need to." He fingered his jawline, got to his feet. "Epsilon converters, probably," he muttered, his gaze turning inward. He muttered a few more phrases in his incomprehensible engineer jargon, then stopped and sent a look at Rip.

Shannon nodded; orders asked for and received. Stotz disappeared.

Rip looked up at Dane. "We'll turn this data over to Tau, and see what he can extrapolate from it. But in the meantime we'd better get some fast answers to some questions before we proceed any farther."

Dane nodded reluctantly. "Comlink first, I hope."

Shannon gave a brief nod, and an even briefer smile. "But you know we're going to have to go out there eventually."

Ali Kamil stood under the shower and let the water beat against his eyelids. He had turned the pressure and the temperature up as high as he could bear it. The roar in his ears, the hot sting on his skin, all closed him in, smothered him in the comfort of narrow awareness—narrow focus.

He breathed deeply of the steam, and felt stress and anger leach out of him. When his skin felt tender but his mind had calmed, he shut off the water and watched the last of it gurgle down the drain on its way to the hydro-recycler. For a moment he let himself imagine the molecules of H_2O tumbling down through the pipes to the machines he himself tended . . . then his awareness expanded to the technological grid of the ship—not the outer hull, or skin, but the spine, connected by electronic cabling like nerves, all leading to the skull—the control deck—

And without warning he heard them both there, Rip and Dane. Rip was speaking—at least Ali "heard" his voice, as if muffled underwater. And then, before conscious thought could reject it, his mind, quick as a nerve-synapse, zapped out and located Jasper, found him down in Ali's own area, the engines.

Ali pressed his hands over his face and head, as if trying to hold his brains in. That was what this damned psi-thing felt like, as if his brains were leaking out. No, as if his skull had dissolved, and his brains were mixing in with the other three men's and Ali's identity was escaping, to be smeared through the heads of Rip and Jasper and Dane.

A sudden, ferocious anger seized him. Why him? The only thing—the *only* thing he had come to trust, to value, was his privacy. He'd lost everything else—family, friends, home—in the Crater War; since then he'd learned never to get too close to people because it was simply too easy for them to walk away, or get transferred, or sick. Or killed. Wealth came and went—the tides of fortune. None of that really mattered. He had adjusted to the meteroids of material gain and loss that crashed through one's personal hull, but all passed on.

This—this curse was not going away, and he could not go anywhere to get away from *it*. And—he gritted his teeth—there was no worse personal trespass. He knew, for during one

short but eventful period of life he'd challenged the fates by
participating in them all.

Why couldn't it be Thorson who kept seeing and hearing
the others so clearly? "Head as thick as a rock," Ali muttered
as he pulled on his clean uniform.

Except he knew that wasn't fair. The big Viking looked as
impassive as a rock, and he invariably reacted to events with
a stolid front that indicated a lack of emotions, but that was
a lie, and Kamil knew it was a lie.

What about Rip? Ali had been friends with Shannon ever
since Kamil had come on board the *Queen*, an angry, moody
apprentice engineer with a very bad record. Rip had accepted
him with the same calm friendliness with which he accepted
the entire universe. It was an intelligent, deliberate calm, the
kind that indicated a balanced inner gyroscope, Ali had sub-
sequently found out, for of course he had tried Rip's limits. He
did that to everyone he might have to come to trust. Rip's
calm was not the blind, passive calm of the follower; he was
a natural-born leader. It was he who wanted to experiment
with this curse—and it was he, ironically, who displayed the
least sign of being pestered by it.

Except for Jasper. It was hard to tell how much he felt, for
his demeanor never changed. Ali ran a comb through his hair,
considering Jasper. It was all too easy to forget about Jasper,
for he was small and unprepossessing and his manners were
the self-effacing politesse of the third-generation Venusian
colonist. Jasper rarely spoke except to the point in mess cabin
gatherings, and on leave time, he seldom if ever went out. He
seemed completely content to sit in his cabin listening to musical tapes from across a hundred worlds, and carving intricate
little statues out of the weird blue-green woods he ordered
from his home colonies. Ordered. He didn't go back to buy
them himself.

Ali had never been to any of the Venusian colonies. A
friend had once admiringly said that a person could drop his
wallet, containing his entire life savings in nonbonded chits, in

one of the biggest colony's busiest streets and come back a week later and find it there. Or if he didn't find it there, he'd go to the nearest lost-and-found operated by the street cleaners, and there it would be. Ali's friend had expressed appreciation, but to Ali it had given shivers. What kind of control created such a society? As Ali thought back, he realized Jasper had never said anything about his home at all—bad or good. But he'd also never gone back for a visit, even when they'd been permitted to enter Sol's system.

How intense was this psi connection for Jasper—and what kind of thoughts did Jasper have on the matter? Ali knew that it was enough for him that the others had agreed not to talk. This meant Jasper would say nothing, even if he was reading Ali's thoughts right at that moment.

With a grimace of self-disgust Ali decided he'd brooded in self-pity long enough. It was time to pay a visit to the medic and get some kind of drug . . . but he knew that Tau would try once again to impress on him the scientific importance of this idiocy, and Ali didn't want to face that now.

So the obvious choice was to go up to the control deck and find out what was going on. After all, the busier he kept himself, the less time he had to brood about this curse.

He found Dane and Rip sitting at the comlink. Both glanced up when he entered. Rip's dark eyes looked tired, and his tunic was partially unfastened, a rare slip in his habitual spruce appearance that served as mute evidence for how many sleep periods he'd scanted, or skipped entirely.

"What's the word?" Ali dropped down into the astrogator's empty seat.

"Nothing," Dane said somberly.

"You mean, they can't answer your questions, or they won't?"

"We don't know," Rip said, thumbing his eye sockets. "They won't answer. We tried every channel, we tried different questions. The quantum sensors indicate the messages were received, but they're not answering. Dane even found a few words of their language, and we tried that. Nothing."

"Mura thinks they might be preparing to take the *Queen*, since we have their ship," Dane said.

Ali whistled. "That would mean they planeted with weapons. How many Traders do that?"

Rip shrugged slightly; they'd considered that aspect. "Impasse."

Ali grinned at him. "So now it's time for you to follow your own advice to me."

Dane gave Rip a significant look.

Ali lounged back. "I take it I'm not the first to offer this friendly piece of advice?"

"Tau's been up here. Mura. Stotz. Next we'll have Jasper up here ranting and raving at you," Dane said in a wooden voice.

The idea of Jasper even raising his voice was so strange that they all laughed.

"All right," Rip said, getting up. He winced, and Ali felt a twinge of headache that he knew was not his own. This annoyed him. But he gave no sign, either in face or voice. "Let me know if anything changes."

Ali wondered if they'd run this problem past Jellico, but he glanced at the triple chrono he'd set up. Three time measures flashed: one, the *North Star*'s orbital pattern, displaying when the ship was in communication range and when it wasn't, and how long in and out of each cycle remained. The second display was Terran biological time, the twenty-four-hour cycle on which their bodies' internal clocks centered in permanent obedience to the rhythms of distant Earth. The third was Hesprid IV's time—the nineteen-hour day divided up into twenty-four "hours" of about forty-five Standard Minutes each.

The *North Star* chrono showed it would be less than an hour before Jellico was due back in range, which meant most of the time Ali had been asleep he'd been in communication silence.

Dane stood up, ducking his head under the hatchway. "I need something to eat," he said.

Ali followed him down to the mess cabin. There they

found Jasper, Johan, and Frank gathered. All three looked up. "Still no word?" Mura asked.

Dane gave a flick of his hand that indicated a negative, and went over to draw a mug of hot drink. "Craig racked up finally?" he asked over his shoulder.

"We said we were going to jump him and knock him out with one of his own drugs," Stotz said, with one of his rare smiles. "He'd just finished lecturing us on how this nineteen-hour cycle was going to wreak havoc on our Terran biorhythms, despite the hormone therapy and a change in diet—"

"We can expect to have one good day out of four," Frank cut in wryly.

"—but then I counted up, out loud, how many hours it had been since he'd been in his cabin, and he finally up and went."

"Thinks he needs to oversee Rip?" Ali asked, dropping into a chair.

"Rip thinks so," Dane commented.

"Making him twice as jittery," Ali finished. "Well, I'll stroll down and have a chat with the good doctor when he wakes up. Meantime, what do you think about this sudden silence out there?"

Stotz frowned. "I was just saying that it reminds me too much of Limbo. That so-called Dr. Rich who was after the Forerunner artifacts. Just after you joined the crew." He nodded toward Dane.

"I remember." Thorson made a slight grimace. "But he was bad news from the minute we took him on board. I don't want to go blasting into yon Trader camp with sleeprods charged, when for all we know they're off having some kind of funeral ritual."

"Nobody leaves a camp untended, especially the comlink," Ali cut in. "I don't care how religious they might be."

"They still might think we're pirates preparing for attack," Mura put in.

"Or, they're preparing an attack." That was Jasper's quiet voice.

"So do we go down there and attack first? And with what?"

Into the sudden silence came a low, rumbling thrum. Ali realized the ship was vibrating. He half rose, then felt the deckplates reverberate under his feet. "Something hit the ship," he said, moving in one quick stride to activate the port-screens.

The outside scanners showed blackness; then lightning strobed, too shortly to reveal more than a glimpse of their surroundings. Impatiently Ali tripped the perimeter lights, and then stood back as they stared out at a powerful deluge. The wind had kicked up so strongly that the heavy rain was nearly horizontal. At the edge of the light perimeter they saw tossing branches; some of the trees were swaying at angles Ali would have thought impossible without actually uprooting.

"Nobody is attacking in this weather, unless they have an armored groundcrawler," Frank said.

"How are we going to *mine* in that?" Thorson muttered.

"And Tau said that this is summer," Jasper added softly.

As they watched, the ship vibrated again, under another mighty buffeting from the gale-force winds. Ali fancied he could hear the winches humming as they compensated. The lightning seemed to be increasing, the bolts more frequent and longer in duration. Thunder drummed through the hull as the storm intensified.

"One thing's sure," Jasper said. "We won't be talking to the *North Star* until this dies down. The EMP is kicking up like I wouldn't have thought possible."

"One more reason to stay in the *Queen* during a storm," said Mura. "The EM readouts are at unhealthy levels—might even have neural and immune system effects on us." He nodded toward the screen. "I don't know what effect it's having on them."

"It's only going to get worse as the sunspot cycle peaks,"

Ali added. "And even inside the *Queen* we may see some effects. It's already hitting the computers—their error rate is up, and processing efficiency is down almost a percent."

"All of which puts a time limit on our being here—a much tighter one than the Charter time," Jasper said. "Tau can offset the health effects to a point; beyond that we'd require expensive medtech that will outcost any theoretical profit."

"Don't want to test that theory," Dane muttered.

"The trouble is," Ali said as he shut down the exterior lights and closed the screen down, "all this merely postpones the problem with our friends out there, it doesn't answer it."

But a new voice piped up from behind, causing them all to turn round sharply: "I know, me!"

It was Tooe. She stood rather limply in the hatchway, her crest half-raised at a hopeful angle.

Dane sprang up and guided his apprentice to one of the padded seats. "What do you know?" he asked.

"No more sleep for Tooe," she said, looking around at them with her great yellow eyes. Ali noted that she had some of her brightness back. "I call up comp, see tape. Kithin people!"

"What?" Mura looked perplexed.

Dane grinned suddenly. "Of course—that's what they reminded me of. Kithin, one of the people in Tooe's klinti back on Exchange. Go on, Tooe."

The apprentice looked back and forth at them, reminding Ali forcibly of a bird with new crumbs. "I know Kithin talk, I talk them."

"But you can't," Ali said. "They won't answer the comlink."

Tooe shook her head quickly. "You do not hear. No, you hear, but you do not understand. Lossin says, *Our camp is now your camp, our ore is now your ore.* Kithin people live in habitats like Exchange, but not rich. Things scarce . . . things important. Honor important. Charter is ours, ship is ours, camp is now ours, comlink ours."

"You mean, they've left their camp? Expecting us to take it over?" Dane asked.

Tooe gave her quick nod, then winced and rubbed at her neck with her thin, webbed fingers.

"By the Eleven Hells of Treloar!" Mura exclaimed, slamming his hands down on the table. "That's it! I've heard Van Ryke talk about them before. These Tath—that's what they call themselves—have been in habitats for generations, habitats made from welding old ships together. They apparently don't have much in the way of personal property, but what is theirs is guarded fiercely, yet shared when there's need. All kinds of questions of honor bound up there, way beyond the legalities of Trade."

"But we have to honor Trade Law," Jasper pointed out.

Dane added wryly, "Or the Patrol will be on our backs in a big way."

"Let me get this straight," Ali said. "They'll sit out there in that hurricane because of a sense of honor?"

Tooe gave a tiny nod this time, and whistled one of her trills. "They wait for us to tell them, come back to camp. Use camp, use things. Things ours now. Not theirs; we give things back, then they use. But owe us honor-obligation."

It was Jasper who now gave a sober nod. "Their culture probably depends a lot on trust," he murmured. "I expect they had little else when they began."

Ali stared at the pallid little man, feeling his viewpoint skew round. It made him almost dizzy, as if the ship had been picked up and spun by a giant hand. Was Jasper talking about more than these unknown Tath—like maybe Venusian colonists?

Ali clamped his mouth shut, wondering how much Jasper had picked up of his thoughts. He did not show his irritation, but he resolved to himself that when Tau woke up from his sleep-shift, the medic would find him in the lab, waiting.

"Hate to think of those people out in this weather without any protection," Dane said with a glance at the blank screen.

"They'd weather it better than we would," Frank said. "I don't know too much about the Tath, but I do know that that fur protects them from the foulest weather."

Dane grinned suddenly.

"Speak up," Ali said, feeling almost giddy from the combination of Dane's and Jasper's relief, and his own. "What's so funny? Seems to me we've had a dearth of jokes of late."

"When Rip and I met them. There was a . . . distinctive smell. I just realized what it reminded me of." His grin widened.

"And . . . ?" Frank prompted.

Dane laughed. "Wet dog," he said.

7

The storm lashed at the *Queen* for two days. At the height of the gale the thunder was almost a continuous rumble through the hull, but that wasn't why those who customarily slept on the upper decks bunked down in the tiny passenger cabins lower in the ship. Rip Shannon said trying to sleep up in his cabin on the control deck made him realize for the first time what seasickness meant.

A portion of those two days Dane spent in helping Stotz run his simulations and then, based on extrapolations of the most likely outcomes, begin matching the tools and basic parts that would likely be necessary for rebuilding the mining-bots into refining machinery.

"We'll likely still need the ultrasonic crushing equipment," said Stotz, "and certainly the catalytic separators, but the rest of these Geepees are probably going to be redundant."

Tooe came down to help. She didn't lift anything, but her quick fingers were deft at wiring.

"We not move ship?" she asked when the work began. "Very exposed place."

Stotz gave his head a shake. "We can't move the ship, but we can add extra guy cables. We'll shake and shimmy, but we'll be stable enough."

"When we do unload the Geepees, we'd better clear off the boulders upwind of us," Kamil drawled. He was also there to help. "There's a reason there aren't any hills here. I don't like to think of a two-ton rock smashing into the *Queen* just when I'm settling down to get my beauty sleep."

Tooe grinned at the term "beauty sleep" but she didn't speak. Seeing her smile made Dane smile too. He still hadn't quite figured out her sense of humor. Seemingly random things would suddenly send her into hoots and trills of laughter; and though she seemed quite happy to explain if she was asked, somehow it seemed inappropriate to continually ask someone to explain what she thought funny. He didn't want to imply there was something wrong with her humor.

Stotz just lifted an eyebrow slightly, but went right on with his work. He and Tau had contrived a daunting number of instruments to be placed out for measuring everything from temperature fluctuations to the water and mineral content of wind, rain, and whatever else the weather threw their way. On the first calm night, the scientific arm of the crew would be out planting these things all over, as well as adding the extra guy cables to stablize the ship. Dane knew that he and Rip were scheduled to attempt contact once again with Lossin and the others.

Two days passed. Though there was no change in the weather, Dane was glad to find that each day made a tremendous difference in how he felt. Unless he clambered up three flight decks at once, he didn't notice gravity much of the time anymore. The biggest problem was altering habits he'd slowly developed in microgravity.

Not that he had the problems that poor Tooe had. Tau had contrived an aeration device for her, and that enabled her to get nourishment. But twice, as Dane watched, she absently parked her drink in the air, expecting it to stay there, as she reached for something else—and both times before he could open his mouth to warn her it dropped painfully on her foot.

The first time, she stopped and crouched down, intently watching the liquid spread out in a spill, her crest spiking up at an alert angle.

Dane heard a slight noise and looked up, to see Ali trying halfheartedly to repress a laugh.

"Like water better in spheres," Tooe said finally, looking up. She got the liquid scoop from its place in the tool rack and watched intently as it slurped up the mess and sent it to the recycler.

So everyone kept busy on various tasks.

The third day dawned with a pale, watery light filtering below a solid bank of white clouds. For the first time the visibility was relatively good, and he could see gray-blue ocean stretching out endlessly in all directions save the south. The giant trees seemed unharmed, their big, rubbery-looking green leaves shiny in the light. Dane suspected those leaves were tougher than plasweave.

During the course of the day Dane checked the portscreens a number of times, and saw fog banks hovering here and there. Were there Floaters in them? Probably. The cold thrill of evil so near made it impossible not to look for them. Yet there was nothing horrible in the sight. The fog even had a kind of alien, delicate beauty, the way it drifted in dreamy patches over the water, and round the great trees.

Night finally came, without another storm. The measuring instruments were ready, positioned for easy carrying in the outer hatchway lock. Everyone was now awake; they weren't even trying, as yet, to match their sleep cycles with the planetary diurnal rhythm. There was too much work to be done, and everyone seemed to feel like Dane did: mentally restless, but physically strained due to the long time spent away from gravity.

When night had fallen, Ali Kamil came out, carrying a box. "Here's my contribution," he said with one of his twisted smiles, and began handing out roundish objects to each person gathered in the mess cabin to discuss last-minute plans.

"Helmets," Rip said with obvious pleasure. "With lights attached."

Ali shrugged. "Got the idea from the Floaters, actually. These are probably useless against them, but the helmet idea itself seemed good. The lights will run for ten hours. There's an intensifier here"—he demonstrated a control—"but then the power packs will only run five hours max. However, you can carry extra power packs clipped to your belts; I didn't want to add more weight to the helmets."

"Good thinking," Mura said feelingly. "What's here, a comlink?"

"Easier than the pocket links we usually carry. Since we're always going to be working at night, and probably in rotten weather, I figured these would become part of daily wear." He handed Tooe hers, which he had altered to fit over her crest.

Tooe whistled happily, turning the helmet over and over in her fingers. "Is good, Ali Kamil. Is good."

"Not elegant," Ali said with his faint, slightly mocking smile. "I doubt they'll start any fashions when we get back to civilization. But they are tough; I used high-density plass to absorb most of the impact of the occasional flying rock or falling branch."

Dane took his, and fitted it on his head. Ali had used his engineer's mind to devise a comfortable and easily operated item. Dane was just as glad that now he wouldn't have to wear the awkward helmet light he'd hastily contrived in his cabin during his rare free time.

Rip fitted his on, gave a nod to Ali, then looked around. "Ready?"

Four of them were going out for the first extended expedition. Tooe had wanted badly to accompany Rip and Dane—and Dane would have felt better with her along for this initial contact with the stranded crew of the *Ariadne*—but Tau had decreed that Tooe must stay near the ship for a little while longer because he didn't trust her not to overtax her strength.

Dane had spent most of his time studying the data files on the Tath. As he walked down the ramp with Rip Shannon, he felt he was as prepared as he could be—but long experience had taught him never to be overconfident even about very detailed files. Too often there was some crucial fact either left out or misrepresented. Though Tooe only knew one Tath, and that one had been left behind on Exchange at a young age, he was sure that her ability with the Tathi language would give them extra insight in understanding these people.

They started downhill between the trees. Dane could see his breath in the chill air. The lights that Ali had built into their helmets were powerful, showing that the rudiments of a pathway had been worn on the ground and then had grown over; spiky grasses were noticeably shorter in a winding trail leading south.

Very soon they entered a clearing. Dane felt a kind of sick coldness inside when he recognized it as the site of the Floater attack. He and Rip both hurried their steps, and Rip cast Dane an ironic smile at the instinctive reaction they'd both shared.

Across the clearing, and through the trees again. Both walked slowly and deliberately. The ground was muddy, but too rocky to make sinking a danger. The path they proceeded down seemed to be a kind of spine along the hillside; the ground fell away on both sides. Dane saw the boles of mighty trees growing from ground he couldn't see. The trees reached at least a hundred meters upward.

They kept moving steadily downhill. Dane thought grimly of the climb back up—then decided *not* to think of it. He'd face that reality when he came to it.

He was beginning to wonder if they'd passed the campsite and were lost when Rip stopped, and sniffed the air. Dane cautiously sniffed as well, not liking the freezing burn along his sinuses. There was a faint whiff of smoke.

"This way," Rip said, pointing to the west.

They picked their way down through the boulder-strewn cliffside, fetching up against the huge trees for frequent rests. Going downhill was not appreciably easier than going up, not at such a slope; Dane felt his calves and thighs cramping and wondered how long he would last.

But after they'd caught their breath against a gigantic tree that had to have a diameter of six meters at least, they picked their way around it, clambering over the knee-high roots, and saw faint lights glimmering in the undergrowth just a little ways further downhill.

Neither made an attempt to keep their footfalls silent. It was bad enough to be invading the camp without an invitation; they did not want to seem like they were sneaking.

When they reached the campsite, they found nine shadows waiting for them. Dane caught a glimpse of small tents arranged round a central cooking place, and though this camp was located among an especially thick grove of trees, he winced in sympathy, wondering how pleasant this could have been during the storm. Those trees must not have afforded much shelter from the icy deluge.

No one spoke as they neared the waiting Traders. Their helmet lights shone in unblinking eyes. Dane saw that there were four Tath, and five beings from other worlds. All of these latter five were humanoid, but there the resemblance ended. All nine wore Free Trader brown tunics.

There was no time to study them more closely.

Rip halted, and Dane as well. A quick glance from Rip, and Dane cleared his throat, dry from breathing harshly on the long walk.

"We restore to you your camp," he said. "Everything you took from *Ariadne*," he said firmly. "Our people do not want any tools or possessions from the ship of the dead. *Ariadne* has a new name, new people, new tools and possessions. She is now *North Star.*"

That much he had planned, with Tooe's help. He said it in Trade, and then he said it in Tathi, hoping the four who were not Tath would understand—or at least not be offended.

It got an effect—though he couldn't tell if the reaction was bad or good, as the growly voices murmured. Dane was distracted as one of the smaller beings swayed, and was braced by another. They silently withdrew toward one of the tents.

The others closed ranks, and regarded Dane and Rip impassively.

Dane looked over at Rip for clues, to meet a blank look. Of course. This was his job. Dane turned his gaze back to the Traders. The Tath still stood quite close, shoulder to shoulder, and Dane felt a flash of irritation. Were they hoping to intimidate him into some kind of concession by crowding him like that?

Clearly something else was needed.

Dane thought rapidly, part of his brain distracted by the bone-chilling cold. If this was summer, how were they going to work successfully during winter nights?

Suddenly Rip cleared his throat. Dane could feel Rip's impulse of compassion—or was that his own emotion? For a moment he felt vertigo, as if he had double vision. He closed his eyes.

Rip spoke. "When we are ready to go, we will take you to the nearest port so you can get on with your lives."

Silence.

One Tath murmured. Lossin turned his head—translating.

All along the row the Traders stood still. Then two or three murmured, long antiphonal phrases with the rise and fall of ritual chants.

Dane felt an unsettling sensation inside. Somehow he and Rip had done wrong. Or was he misreading them?

Then Lossin said, "Our lives are yours."

Again the murmurs.

Then Lossin said, in the same growling voice, flat-toned, "We bring ore to you."

Dane opened his mouth, trying to come up with an appropriate answer, but the Traders did not wait. One by one, in total silence, they turned away and began the walk to their camp.

"Wait," Dane said.

They all stopped at once, exchanging looks. A couple of them talked, and the tallest Tath said something in a quick voice, silencing them.

Once again they ranged themselves in a tight line, facing Dane and Rip.

"That crewmember." Dane pointed down toward their camp at the lit tent, in whose walls shadows could be seen moving about. "You have someone sick? Can we help?"

"Parkku end life in freedom," Lossin pronounced, still in that flat voice.

Then, just as before, the Traders withdrew, this time dispersing in perfect silence to their tents.

Dane and Rip watched until they had all disappeared. Then Rip looked a question at Dane. "Do you sense any kind of invitation to join them?"

Dane shrugged, feeling defeated, though he didn't know why. Frustration, tiredness, anger warred in him. "About as much as I'd welcome a Norsundrian vampire-wasp in my cabin at night."

Rip grimaced. "To tell the truth, I feel like we've been dismissed."

"Not dismissed," Dane said heavily. "Closed out."

There was nothing to do but start the long trek back to the *Queen*.

8

⭐

"No!" Tooe's voice was shrill. "No good!" And she talked on in rapid Rigelian, mixing in what sounded to Rip like a few words of the Tathi language.

Rip saw Dane frown in concentration. The cargo master's understanding of Rigelian, after weeks of talking with Tooe, was as good as hers of Terran—or nearly. But he seldom spoke in the difficult, hissing language. "Life-obligation?" he said at last, and shook his head.

Tooe whistled, a rapid series of notes that indicated distress. Then she turned to Rip. "Gift of life mean you own life. Bad, bad, bad—"

"—Unless we want slaves?" Dane interjected drily. "By the lords of space! When we mess up, we really mess up nova-size."

"Slaves?" Rip repeated in amazement. "What? This isn't more of the ghost superstition, is it?"

"No!" Tooe exclaimed, her voice going high again.

"Explain, please?" Rip asked, working his neck. Would

this day ever end? The hike back to the *Queen* had taken
even longer than the trip out, and at the end, when they were
already struggling just to stay upright, they had been pounded
by a sudden shower of rain. He was exhausted, longing for
his bed.

Most of the crew had already gone to their cabins; the
Hesprid-IV chrono lacked just a couple of hours until sunup.
Only Tau and Tooe had remained awake, waiting in the mess
cabin for their return.

Suddenly Rip felt a flicker of double awareness—Jasper
and Ali, both soundly asleep. Tiredness seemed to flood
through him, dragging at limbs and brain. As Tooe began to
talk, he forced himself to his feet, and drew a hot mug of
jakek.

"Gifts outside clan groups only in treaty," Tooe said.
"Small gift mean small obligation, but big gift, gift of lives,
mean obligation of lives. Tath Traders have camp, have equipment. You take ore, go away, they finish lives here. You offer
gift, take them to port, that means give life back. They owe life
to you if they take offer."

Rip groaned. "I wish I'd kept my mouth shut." He
couldn't help grimacing at Dane. "You weren't in any hurry to
stop me."

Dane sighed. "Because I felt the same sense of pity—
compassion—whatever. I thought it was a fine gesture."

Tooe's crest flickered. "You not read files?"

"Of course I read the files," Dane said, so tired he was unable to hide his exasperation. Not that Tooe seemed per-
turbed; she apparently knew as well as Rip did that the cargo
master wasn't angry with Tooe, but with himself. "I read
about the obligation business—of course—but I equated that
with treaty-making. It translated out in my mind to a kind of
Trade. Barter. Things for service. But my understanding was
that both sides agreed to the conditions first. I thought Rip's
offer would escape that because he set no conditions. He offered them passage freely."

Tooe shook her head, her crest flicking up. "But they know

lives are condition. Either life finish here, or life given back on ship. See now?"

"See now," Dane said gravely. "Tooe, you're overdue for rest. Go get some sleep. We'll talk again in the morning. I know I'm going to need your help when I go back to face them, and I want you fresh and ready for action."

Tooe looked from one to the other, her crest at a hopeful angle. Then she got up and walked out.

Rip opened his mouth, was surprised when Dane raised a hand to stop him from speaking. In silence they listened to the tuneless clangor of the ladder as Tooe went down to the lower deck. Then Dane said, "I want to make her our locutor, and go back to the camp tomorrow night and straighten things out."

"Locutor?" Rip repeated. "But from what you told me, that's an official spokesperson. She's so new to the crew, and barely nineteen years old—"

Dane shook his head impatiently. "I was just about her age when I first signed on aboard the *Queen,* raw from the Pool. Sure she has a lot to learn, but she knows that—she's been studying Trade data going years back. Just as I did in Pool. And I graduated knowing how little I knew. Yet Van trusted me enough to give me some real responsibilities within my first couple of journeys."

Rip felt the pressure of decision weighing on him. Had Jellico found it this hard? *Jellico put me in charge of the* Queen, he thought. *How did he feel handing off his own ship to someone who was still an apprentice only half a year ago?*

Age—experience—ability. Somehow a captain, if he or she wanted to be a good captain, had to be able to evaluate them all, and a host of lesser virtues and vices, and not judge a person on just a single quality. Rip realized he had some thinking to do.

He looked up and saw question in Tau's eyes. The medic and Dane were both waiting for an answer.

"Good idea," Rip said.

And Tau nodded, his approval obvious.

"You two finish planning," he said with a smile. "I'm for the rack."

Then Rip realized that, as he'd been evaluating Tooe, he himself had been taking a kind of test without knowing it. And he'd passed.

Daylight was well advanced when Rip woke up. He checked the viewport, saw the diffuse white light of fog.

When he got down to the mess cabin, he found Dane already there, watching a white screen. Rip walked up, realized he was looking at the exterior view. The fog was so thick that the ground was difficult to make out.

"I see them," Dane murmured. "Floaters. I'm sure of it."

Rip squinted at the screen. Dane damped the glare with a quick touch to the keypad.

Rip shook his head, his gaze still on the screen. "I don't see anything."

"Watch."

They stood side by side. Soon Rip was able to discern subtle patterns in the thick mist. Rip felt almost mesmerized by the swirling vapors. A couple of times he thought he saw the gleam of pearly gray drifting in the fog, never too close, but then it would fade, and he figured he was just seeing the landscape through the less dense vapors.

"Floater-patrol?" came a new voice.

Rip glanced over his shoulder. Ali sauntered in, his eyes slightly puffy. Rip knew the engineer was taking some kind of drug which he'd gotten from Tau. He wondered, looking at those eyes, if Ali was doubling his dose.

Dane said without looking away from the screen, "I think they're out there."

"Hear 'em up here, eh, Viking?" Ali tapped his head.

Dane didn't see the gesture. His back was still to the mess. Nor did he answer.

Ali shrugged, casting an amused glance Rip's way, and he

sauntered over to get himself a substantial breakfast. Rip, watching him dig in, decided that whatever drug Kamil was taking did not interfere with his appetite any.

Tooe showed up a few moments later. Today, Rip noted with approval, there was a little of her characteristic bounce to her walk—though necessarily muted by the unrelenting gravity. She fixed a bowl of the chilled, chopped tubers she was so fond of, mixing them with rice, and plopped onto a chair, planting her webbed toes on the the edge of the seat, her knobby knees at her ears, her thin elbows tucked close next to her body. Her half-crouch half-squat looked highly uncomfortable to Rip, but she seemed content as she attacked her food.

Johann Stotz appeared then and cast an appraising glance around. "We need an inventory on the Traders' supplies and equipment as soon as you can get it," he said to Dane without preamble. "We don't have enough supplies of our own to be duplicating anything."

"We still need to straighten out last night's misunderstanding," Dane said.

"Do it." Johan paused to sip at his jakek, and he sighed. "Craig and I ran some numbers on the wind velocities and the tidal movements, and we're both afraid we won't get much done if the winters are as bad as we predict. And we were conservative. If we're to pay our way back on this venture, we need to get moving."

"We're going back tonight," Rip said. "That is, if the fog lifts. And another force-nine storm doesn't hit." To Tooe he said, "You are now appointed our locutor. You'll be going with us."

Tooe looked up, her crest flicking at its most alert angle. The little being radiated pride and enthusiasm. "I help!" she fluted. "I talk Tathi."

Everyone was grinning. Rip indicated Stotz as he said, "Keep Johan's requirements in mind. We'll plan this in more detail later."

Craig Tau walked in right then, and Rip said, "I forgot to tell you last night. One of them appears to be ill. We asked about her, but were given the brush-off."

" '—Parkku end life in freedom,' " Dane said. "The exact words, or close enough." He glanced over at Tooe. "I suppose this means more of the obligation business."

Tooe nodded vigorously.

"Anyway, if we get everything straightened out, we might be needing your medical services."

"What kind of biology are we talking about here?" Tau asked.

Dane said, "I didn't get a good look. Small person, humanoid—they're all humanoids. Dappled skin, browns of various shades. Looked like elephant hide. I only glimpsed the hands and face; the rest of her was in uniform." He indicated his own brown Free Trader tunic.

"Parkku," Tau said. "Sounds like a Berran. Small features? Broad back, reminds you almost of a turtle?"

Dane snapped his fingers. "Now that you mention it."

Tau nodded. "Berrans don't often leave their world. Rest of the universe is too hot for them." He smiled slightly. "This crew is better adapted to this planet than any of us. The Tath fur is waterproof and keeps them well insulated, and the Berrans are used to subzero temperatures and scouring winds."

"Sounds like Hesprid IV is a picnic spot for them," Ali drawled, lounging back in his chair. "Cheery thought."

"If we can clear away the misunderstandings and get them to team with us, at least for the duration, then that might work to our advantage," Mura said from the hatchway to the galley.

Tooe nodded. "We fix," she said, and whistled a quick flight of notes. Then she smacked her scrawny chest. "I know about Tath, me. They live for Trade!"

A few hours later, Rip recalled those words as he watched the Tath slowly emerge from their camp.

He and Dane and Tooe had gotten into winter gear. All three had on their helmets, which lit the way as they fought a rising wind. This trip to the camp seemed to take much longer than the first; whether it was the wind, or anticipation, Rip wasn't sure. He just wished they had some kind of transport. Clambering over rocks in a howling gale did not add to anyone's peace of mind.

He saw Dane hovering just behind Tooe, who struggled against the wind and the uneven terrain. She was wearing— for what Rip suspected was the first time in her life—the shoes that Dane has insisted they get for her when she first signed on as crew. She had insisted that they were comfortable, but she walked as if someone had slipped eggs into them. Rip suspected that the effort it took to balance on the rough, steeply inclined hillside added strain to her muscles. She never complained though, just tweeted rather limp-sounding thanks when Dane caught her just as she was about to trip or fall. This happened more often than Rip liked—especially toward the end of their trek.

But they reached the camp without further incident, and as soon as the Traders appeared, Tooe gathered energy from somewhere inside her and launched into a flood of Tathi words. She probably spoke too quickly; Rip heard what he rather thought were phrases of Rigelian here and there, and some Terran, but the Traders listened without interrupting.

When she finished, they started talking rapidly with one another, showing more animation than he and Dane had ever seen from them. Not just the Tath, but the others; Rip realized one of the Tath was translating to the others when he heard Trade patois mixed with another language.

He also realized as he watched the interplay that Lossin, the locutor, was not the leader. Like Tooe, he seemed to have been chosen for his ability with Terran. It was to a tall female whose fur was sprinkled with silver streaking that the others kept turning. She was the quietest of the four Tath, listening to everyone.

Finally she spoke, rapidly and softly, in a low, mellow

voice that reminded Rip of some kind of wind instrument. Lossin then approached Tooe. "Tazcin speaks. We Trade." The grayish-furred leader loomed over Tooe, and held out her hand, palm out, fingers pointing up. Tooe flicked her thin blue hand up, palm out as well, and the hands met.

Then Tooe's crest flicked upright. She turned to Dane and Rip, her attitude triumphant. "They hear us now! We trade for ore, we trade for passage, we trade for camp things, we trade for medicine—"

Dane laughed. "Damp down, Tooe. One thing at a time!"

Tooe whirled about. "What first, Lossin?"

Rip felt the urge to laugh, and squelched it. It was amply obvious that Tooe was thoroughly enjoying herself. He did not want to risk making the wrong move, though, so he stood silent and passive-seeming—just as their leader did.

"Camp," Lossin said, pointing back up the mountain. "We show you."

"We see. Then trade," Tooe said with a nod.

This, apparently, seemed eminently reasonable to everyone. The *Ariadne* Traders—except the sick one—formed into a single-file line and started walking. Dane and Tooe fell in behind. As he followed, Rip wondered why he hadn't thought of "see, then trade" before. Or more importantly, why hadn't Dane?

Because I told him how I wanted the talk to go, Rip thought, his mood sobering. *And then I made the supposedly compassionate gesture that made things worse. And Dane was apparently unsure enough of himself—being as new to cargo master as I am to captain—that he followed.*

Rip did not like to think what would have happened if they had not taken Tooe on as a new crewmember.

And it would have happened under his captaincy.

9

Dane keyed his helmet comlink on and reported quietly: "We're in."

And a second later he sensed a flash of triumph from Jasper and Ali. The direction was distinct: he knew they were on the *Queen*'s control deck. A moment later the peculiar mental flash altered—Ali was irritated.

It was all so swift, and so vivid, that Dane wondered if he'd imagined it. He certainly would have assumed so before Tau's memorable psi discussion, he realized. After all, he would expect them to be waiting for word, and even the emotional reactions were predictable.

But he knew it had been real. He couldn't predict when he'd make those connections, and he certainly couldn't control them, but he knew they were real.

As they climbed a steep trail, he glanced back at Rip. Shannon's pleasant, dark face wore a closed expression; he was either concentrating on thoughts of his own, or else on the difficulty of the trail. There was no sign from him of his having experienced a similar psi flash.

"Cave ahead," Lossin said, pointing toward an outcropping of volcanic rock.

They all glanced up; Tooe slipped on a stone, and chirped her distress. Dane shot his hand out and caught her arm before she could fall back on the trail. He resolved as he uprighted her again that he was going to have to teach her how to fall when she lost her balance; when tired she tended to react as if she were in null grav, reaching for the nearest object to bounce herself off of. In this case she would have smashed into a mossy boulder.

She tweeted her thanks, and turned back to the climb, her crest flattened out in concentration-and-effort mode. Noting it, Dane enjoyed a private grin. There was no psi connection with his little Rigelian apprentice, but he didn't need one. That flexible webbed crest, and her expressive whistles and chirps, made her emotions clear enough. As they rounded the last of the outcropping of rock and walked across a wide, flattened area, he wondered if she was even capable of hiding her reactions.

The cave was a dark fissure in the side of the mountain. The *Queen*'s Traders followed the others inside.

"Flitters there," Lossin said, pointing farther inside the cave, the floor of which had been blasted smooth. One of the other Tath tabbed a control on his belt, activating a remote, and lights flooded on. Deep inside the cave they saw four flitters parked: awkward, joint-winged craft, resembling an unlikely cross between a bat and the more familiar fan-ducted Terran vehicles. Dane stole a glance at Rip and saw an expression that echoed his own feelings: such craft would deserve the term flitter far more than the almost stolid Terran machines they were used to. The Tath, it seemed, had a very different esthetic of engineering.

But despite the strangeness of the craft, and the fact that they obviously couldn't lift much more than their human cargo, Dane felt his heart accelerate. If they could get the use of those! . . .

He glanced back, met a slight nod from Rip. The navigator's lips were moving: he was already reporting to those waiting at the *Queen.* Good.

"One water transport, established five kilometers that way," Lossin added, waving.

Dane nodded. It would be stored nearest their launch point for the current mining site, of course. That made good sense.

"Now last climb—behold, here is camp," Lossin said. But he didn't move forward, instead pointing to a truncated pyramid of some earthlike substance, vague in the gloom. "Your cielanite."

Dane and Rip approached the cache, which resolved into a neat stack of what looked like rocks. But their shape was almost organic, short chains of spheres melted into each other, almost like some kind of bacterium.

Dane picked one up. It was light, rough, porous; his helmet lamp struck glints of light from the water in the pores as he hefted it. What kind of mining device would refine the ore into such an odd form?

"Looks like some sort of scoria or pumice," said Rip. He slipped a small sample of the sphere-chains into his beltpack. "Stotz will need to analyze it to build his refiner."

Rip said to Lossin, "Your mining machinery, is it automatic?"

After a brief exchange with his fellow Tath, Lossin replied, "The *ethianhuru* are autonomous, yes."

"Autonomous," Tooe said. "Goes by self—like a creature?"

"Correct," the Tath replied.

Tooe gave a quick nod and chirped a note or two. "Kanddoyd tech," she said to Dane. "*Ethianhuru*—mining slugs, it means. Some of Kandder tech come from Tathi Trade."

Dane nodded back, thinking that Stotz needed to know

how much cielanite might be awaiting them on the island when the latest series of storms abated. But what was a "mining slug"?

Without further comment the Tath turned away and led them up a very steep trail into a cluster of fantastically giant trees. The darkness was so intense here that the *Queen*'s Traders all flicked on their high-intensity lamps—even Tooe.

Dense, rubbery shrubs grew close to the mighty trees, half-obscuring roots that were several meters thick. Dane glanced up, awed at the gigantic scale of the trees. The trunk of the nearest tree started maybe ten meters over his head. Below that, all around, was the root system. He wondered as the others picked their way carefully over the smooth, stonelike roots just how far down those roots reached into the island.

He thought about the planetary report that Craig had given them. The trees had a linked root system that reached all the way downhill to a salt fog zone created by the crashing of the storm waves on the rocks below at high tide. Some even grew in the tidal zone, and the rhythmic wash of salt water did not harm their growth; Tau had pointed out salt deposits below the trees. The report speculated that the trees used the salts to create the high conductivity that made them relatively immune to lightning damage, instead grounding it harmlessly.

He glanced at the others of his party, and saw them all looking up at the great trees. Tooe whistled, and, seeing Dane's glance, she said, "One tree—big as all Exchange, it looks!"

"Does seem that way," Rip said, turning to the Tath. "I hope we don't have to climb?"

"Here is lift," Lossin said, indicating for them to follow around to the lee side of the nearest tree.

Dane scanned the narrow elevator that was built right onto the mighty bole, knowing that Jasper and Ali would both pester him with questions about its unique construction. It was a simple wooden box, but its construction had a sparse elegance to his eyes. The gloom hid the cable where it attached to the top, but the rest of the cable glistened wetly in his helmet light as his eyes followed it up into darkness. There was a track of some lighter wood along the elevator's path. Wear from friction? He couldn't see what held the box against the trunk when it rose—surely they didn't let it dangle free?

Faint washes of light from unseen sources brought tree branches and leaves into silhouette as Dane's eyes adjusted. A sudden gust of frigid wind brought icy, stinging needles of frozen rain, and Dane was glad to crowd into the narrow elevator. Lossin squeezed in with them; the other Traders remained behind.

Lossin pressed a button and they rose slowly, buffeted by occasional blasts of wind. The little box had a queasy, bouncy feel to it, as though the mechanism that lifted it was wearing out. It also seemed to pull in against the tree trunk, then back out again in a regular rhythm. Dane thought he heard a peculiar ripping noise in the same rhythm, like the catch-tabs on clothing, but before he could look for the source, he became aware of a small hand clutching the back of his coat. He glanced over his shoulder and saw to his dismay that Tooe's face had gone a peculiar greenish gray.

Her eyes lifted to his, huge and dilated. "Up and down," she murmured, her voice barely audible over the howling of the rising wind. Dane had to lean close to hear her. "Not used to up and down, not with a very bad down." She closed her eyes and swallowed. "Tooe has control," she added firmly. "I learn. Up and down, not in and out."

Dane nodded, trying to be encouraging.

The lift jerked to a stop. Tooe tightened her grip on Dane's coat.

Dane followed the others out of the lift, and then everything went out of his head as he stared around in amazement.

It was as though he stood at the center of a vast spiderweb, gossamer spun between the huge trees, here thickening to support rounded structures like giant bird nests, there thinning to invisibility. As he turned his head to look around, a faint shimmer caught his eye, one of many, he realized. He bent over and looked closer. His heart jumped as he saw a rip in the fabric of the web—the arrow of stress from it pointed at his feet. His boots were overstressing the fabric, which was apparently designed with the furred feet of the Tath in mind.

Dane started to back away, but a tug on his coat kept him in place. Still clutching the fabric, Tooe squatted in front of the tear and gently poked at it. Her curiosity had at least partially overcome her acrophobia.

Tooe's finger stopped just short of the shimmer. "It reweaves itself!" she exclaimed. "Grows like tree?" She looked up at Lossin.

Lossin gestured with his great, furry hands. "Sessile . . ." The Tath paused, said something Dane didn't understand.

"Stomach foot?" Tooe said doubtfully.

Dane straightened up and looked at Rip, who greatly surprised him by chuckling and pointing. "Gastropod. Barnacles. Tree barnacles."

It was a cluster of rough, misshapen cones sunk into the bark of the tree, each with a web of filaments emerging from its tip. Above it Dane noticed a balloonlike swelling that grew as he watched. There was a popping sound, and the balloon collapsed suddenly. A briny mist momentarily tickled their skins. "Vines bring salt water, nutrients up to keep them alive," said Lossin.

"You found these here?" asked Dane. "Part of the tree root system?"

Lossin's expression meant nothing to him as the Tath answered. "No. Tath build these."

Build? Dane felt his stomach lurch slightly—and felt an inner tickle accompanied by an image of Rip. A shared reaction? Since he couldn't ask, he ignored it, and turned his thoughts to the data at hand. The Tath were bioengineers, a discipline rigidly controlled in the Federation. He turned and looked more closely at the lift, and saw the mat of thin, fibrous tentacles sprouting from it where it touched the tree trunk. That explained the lighter track on the wood, and the ripping sound: it was a kind of living catch-tab!

Dane looked over at Rip and saw that he had pulled the

lump of cielanite ore from his pouch and was looking at it. The navigator met his glance and raised an eyebrow expressively as he put away the ore again.

"Stotz may have to do more reengineering than he thought" was Rip's only comment.

Dane mulled over the implications of that as Lossin turned and led them along a catwalk with an arching narrow roof overhead. To Dane's surprise, the structure was fairly rigid even far out from the trees—it swayed, but not the way a similar Terran-built structure would. It felt alive under his feet, and his toes curled reflexively. Tooe, of course, displayed no reaction other than interest, except when she happened to glance down—and her grip tightened on his coat. Bioengineering was nothing new to her; she'd seen it on Exchange, so for her it was natural and even desirable. Gravity was the menace for her.

Lossin led them to one of the thatchlike structures, but did not bid them enter. Fortunately, although technically they were still outside, and the temperature was still very cold, relatively little wind and rain penetrated the thick canopy of leaves overhead.

Meanwhile, the rest of the Traders arrived. Dane realized that they still had not taken back their own camp, and again he regretted the mistakes that he and Rip had so nearly made.

For a moment they all stood, then Tazcin, the leader, gestured to her crew, and after some glances at the Terrans, all but three of the Tath moved off in various directions, three plunging down one or another of the woven catwalks, walking with a peculiar rhythm that worked with the sway. Others went up ladders and kindled lights. Within moments a spicy, herbal scent drifted in the tamed wind.

"Tooe? Do you recognize that scent?" As he spoke Dane realized her grip on his coat had loosened. The aroma forgotten, he whirled around just in time to see her start to fall.

Rip, the closest, caught her just before she landed, and he laid her gently down. She clung tightly to his hand, her eyes tightly shut.

"I'm falling!" she keened on a plangent note that made Dane's jaw tighten. "Cannot stand up, me. I fall."

The three Traders still with them exchanged quick remarks. Lossin pointed to Tooe and said, "This Rigelian. Lives previous in varigrav?"

"Yes," Dane exclaimed.

Lossin nodded his shaggy head. "As did we. Give her some of our *glostuin?*"

Rip looked up. "Is it safe for her metabolism?"

Dane said, "I'll check." He keyed his comlink, and requested Jasper to relay the question to Tau.

Moments later he said in relief, "It should be fine."

Lossin turned and relayed the message in his own language.

A minute or so later a tall, thin feline being ran down one of the catwalks. Dane watched, mesmerized; the person, a male, was astoundingly graceful, his silver tail flicking back and forth to help him balance. He leaped with soundless step onto the platform and knelt beside Tooe, a sprayjector in one hand.

This he applied gently to her neck. A tiny screen flashed readouts that Dane couldn't interpret, but the medic seemed satisfied. He triggered the spray. Moments later Tooe's coloring slowly returned to normal, and she relaxed her death grip on the navigator's hands. Rip stood slowly, flexing his fingers.

The feline stood as well. His great slanted green eyes took them all in, and he said in a scratchy voice, "Dizzinessss. Inner ear takesss time to adjusssst. Hassss your medic a ssssupply of *glostuin?* Sssshe will need it for the heightsssss."

Again Dane contacted the *Queen,* and then returned a positive answer. By then Tooe had recovered enough to stand.

"Do you want to return to the ship?" Dane asked.

She gave her head a resolute shake. "Tooe well now. See everything."

Dane looked at Rip, who shrugged, spreading his hands. He would not decide for Tooe.

"Then let's finish the tour," Dane said.

Lossin made a sign of agreement, and they proceeded out onto one of the catwalks. This time the feline medic walked with Tooe, supporting her arm. Dane dropped back and left him to it. It was hard enough for him to balance for himself. He clung to the cables strung at either side, sliding his hands slowly between each step.

To keep his mind off the wiggling catwalk—and the unguessable drop below—Dane observed the feline medic, who walked just in front of him. At first Dane thought he might be the only member of the other Traders who was not humanoid. Was he an Arvas? But he was smaller, and his hands were human, with five fingers. Probably one of the genetically altered human strains, Dane realized. For what purpose? Climbing, obviously. He moved with the beauty of a cat—but he had a cat's unlovely voice.

He seemed to be a good medic. Tooe appeared much recovered, but the medic still kept right with her, watching carefully.

They finally reached the next platform, after what seemed to Dane a kilometer-long walk, and he sighed in relief. Now they were in a cluster of platforms—which were surprisingly neat despite their thatchy appearance—all connected by ladders as well as catwalks.

Lossin took them rapidly up and down them all, explaining as they went. As Craig had surmised, the trees were actually the safest place to be during lightning storms, for their conductive outer layers helped make the forest into a huge Faraday cage almost as effective as the *Queen*'s hull metal.

To Dane's surprise, only the medic had his own platform. All the Tath slept together in a quadruple hammock arrangement where they could touch one another if they wished. It seemed horribly crowded to Dane—even more crowded than the small compartments on the *Queen*. At least on the ship each had his or her own cabin.

Two more platforms were for sleeping, each with two occupants. Then there was a small platform, more sheltered than any of the others except the galley-and-mess area, which housed the sick. Here they found the dappled being that Dane had seen before.

This time the medic drew Tooe aside and talked to her in his yowly, hissing voice. Apparently he knew Rigelian, for it was in that language that he spoke.

While this was going on, Rip followed Lossin to the last platform, which seemed to house their computer and communication equipment. This platform was the most stable, tucked right against the bole of the mighty tree.

Dane watched them go upward. As he observed Rip's slender form in his bulky winter gear working his way up the ladder he got another one of those flashes—Rip's intense interest. No, it was stronger than that. Purpose. Rip wanted something.

Comp equipment—of course.

Dane gave in to impulse. "Lossin."

The Tath paused at the top of the ladder and peered down. Rip disappeared from view. Dane felt a flash of triumph and a kind of weird dismay: he had been right, then.

He called to Lossin, "Translate here? What's the Trade for medicine for Parkku?"

Tooe looked at Dane in surprise. Could the others read her reaction? Tooe knew he spoke Rigelian.

But the feline medic altered his posture in one of those fluid, balletic motions, and directed a quick stream of words at the silent Tath. Then Lossin faced Dane, and said, "Parkku immune system suffering from allergens in air. Dr. Siere needs fresh supply of medicine. In turn, share data we gathered on local fauna, not in Survey tapes."

Rip appeared behind Lossin, standing at ease—as if he'd been there all along.

Dane said, "Suggest to the doctor that he accompany us back to the ship to talk to our medic. That way you can get the medication right away."

Siere gave a quick nod, his ears flicking forward. "Do thisss," he said in Terran Trade. "I sssshall go with you."

Lossin turned away, and started talking to Rip on the upper platform. Siere led the way back to the lift platform. Tooe followed silently. Once or twice she cast odd looks at Dane, her crest cocked at the familiar question angle.

She did not speak again during the trip down the lift. She was quiet even when one of the silent Tath appeared in one of the flitters. A second one trailed them on the swift journey back to the *Queen*.

Dane was relieved not to have to walk. The wind had risen steadily, and hail and freezing rain clattered over the viewscreen of the flitter; the ride was as uncomfortable as Dane had surmised on first sight of the ungainly craft. Huge gusts of wind sent them sidling, as if smacked by a vast hand, but the Tath pilot appeared unfazed.

But they reached the *Queen* safely. The driver gave them a brief nod, set the vehicle down, then she slid out and ran to the other flitter. It, too, had settled to the rock-strewn ground, its running lights blinking in stationary mode.

Rip dropped into the control seat, his fingers moving almost without hesitation over the control console. "Jasper," Rip said into his com unit, "open the cargo hatch."

Dane studied the unfamiliar console. It was laid out very differently from the flitters he'd learned to operate, but the same sorts of controls seemed to obtain. It appeared that the wings served the function that on Terran machines was fulfilled by side ducts and deflectors. On the ship the cargo hatch slid open. At the same time the flitter rose on its belly fan, and under Rip's guidance it slid hesitantly into the cargo bay, and then settled to the decking between the two mining-bots that Dane and the others had brought over from the *North Star.*

The cargo hatch slid shut, and Rip opened the flitter door.

"This way," he said to Dr. Siere, who moved out of the flitter in a quick, flowing motion that reminded Dane strongly of Sinbad, the ship's cat.

Tau met them at the inner hatch. "Dr. Siere?"

"Thisss issss a pleasure," Siere said in his scratchy voice, making a polite gesture. "Dr. Tau."

The two medics disappeared.

Moments later Rip's beltcom beeped. He touched the hatch communicator.

"Better come up to the com room." Jasper's voice held an edge beyond his usual terseness.

Rip slapped the com off and walked through the hatch without a word; Tooe and Dane followed more slowly. The navigator-turned-captain seemed to be lost in thought. Tooe looked from one to the other without speaking.

They went up to the com room, where Jasper swiveled away from the display screen, where they could see Tau accompanying Siere to the waiting flitter. Dawn was just graying the eastern horizon; the medic hurried back into the ship, and the door shut.

"Siere's from Tarquain," said Jasper, slightly tipping his head back toward the screen. "Their hearing is extremely acute. I didn't want to risk being overheard."

Ali slipped in the door. "Something to report?"

For answer, Jasper reached over and tapped the console. A speaker came to life, but all that emerged was a kind of gasping noise, repeated three times.

"They bounced it off the second moon," Jasper continued, his naturally pale face taut with strain. "Right at the limit—almost lost in the noise. I can almost guarantee that the pirates didn't hear it."

"Three ships," said Rip. "Unfriendly."

They watched the flitter slip away, moving round the trees and disappearing from view. Then Rip closed down the external viewport.

"I feel better about Lossin, now," he said. "Not that I did anything wrong—just tried to check their communications setup." He shook his head. "Couldn't read it, of course, and didn't have a detector to read its frequency setting."

"You think they're listening to the *North Star*?" Dane asked.

Rip shrugged. "I don't know. But it's something to consider."

Tooe's crest flickered in a complicated reaction, then she said, "Dane. You ask for translation. You hear Rigelian, or not hear it?"

Dane hesitated. Tooe had never lied to him—but she had to know what lies were, having lived on Exchange, and among the Kanddoyds. They were probably the galaxy's masters of indirect discourse.

He looked up, to find Ali's eyes on him. But the engineer was uncharacteristically quiet.

It seemed a bad precedent to set with a new crewmember. On the other hand, he was reluctant to tell her that he'd asked Lossin to translate in order to distract him so that Rip could do whatever he'd needed to do on their computer platform. He didn't want to say why he'd done it, and he knew that Tooe was quite capable of questioning him until she'd gotten every scrap of data that she wanted. As yet none of the other crew members knew about the psi link.

Dane shrugged, choosing his words.

Then Rip rescued him. "I wanted Dane to distract Lossin," he said. "I wanted to check their com unit. Just to know. But I hoped to do it without them knowing I was checking. Seemed easier, after the mistakes we made before." He smiled.

Tooe nodded slowly, her crest still at inquiry mode.

Then Ali spoke. "So you think they know there are three pirate ships orbiting this planet, apparently waiting for us to lift?"

"One way or the other," Rip replied.

Dane felt his heart slam in his chest.

"And we can't ask," he said.

10

★

Jellico reflexively anchored himself more firmly in the micro-gravity of the freely orbiting *North Star* as Karl Kosti whirled around the engine room of the ship, touching various readouts and giving succinct—sometimes cryptic—explanations of the data on each. Unlike the *Solar Queen,* every millimeter of which Jellico knew well enough to maneuver in without light, this ship was still unfamiliar—something he and his crew of five had been working almost nonstop to rectify.

Kosti said, "There are some decidedly odd tweaks in these engines, just as Ali warned me. And some of them make sense if you're used to varigrav." He pulled himself into a low framework of pipes linking two of the engine cores.

"How's that?" asked Jellico, knowing that Kosti was this talkative to take his mind off free fall, which the big jet tech loathed. The *Queen* had only been orbiting a couple of Standard Days, but already it felt like a week.

"Excuse me," Kosti said as he abruptly twisted around in the maze of pipes enclosing him. Now his face was upside-down to Jellico, and the captain was struck by how meaningless, at least at first, an upside-down face was. Was Kosti seeing the same thing?

"These plasma guides, for example," Kosti mused as he applied a sonic impeller to a dull gray pipe. "This maze is part of the tuning, and it's also an efficient work cage for maintenance in micrograv." He braced himself against the pipes behind him and triggered the big, hypodermic-like tool.

A muffled bang hammered Jellico's ears; he let the impact wash past. "What you're saying is, the designers of this ship are better engineers than Terrans?"

Kosti grinned at him. "Yes. Out here. But you'll never see a design like this in central Terran space. Not really built for planetside."

Jellico knew his crew as well as he knew the *Queen*. He repressed the urge to smile, and permitted himself a small nod of agreement. He knew Karl had disagreed about sending the four apprentices down in the *Queen*, though Kosti hadn't said anything. Not after the decision was stated as an order. Apparently the grizzled jet tech now thought better of his disagreement. The hint was good enough for Jellico. He was pleased to be corroborated; no need to rub anyone's nose in a change of mind.

But Kosti, apparently, was not satisfied with an apology by implication. "I thought you were coddling Shannon by sending him and his bunch down in the *Queen*," he admitted, squinting at Jellico. "Did you run the calcs on how much more fuel the *Star* would gulp in landing planetside, or was that one of your lucky guesses?"

"It was one of my . . . guesses," Jellico admitted in his turn, letting the smile come. That was as far as he'd go in speaking of his own priorities for his decision; he knew that it was too easy to figure from a stated list of positive factors the negatives that might have been balanced against them, and he did not want anyone worrying unduly about Rip Shannon's fitness for this assignment.

That was his own worry, part of the responsibilities of command.

But apparently he was not, after all, as subtle as he thought; Kosti touched a readout connected to some unfamiliar tubing, grunted, then said, "You trained 'em. They'll pull it off."

"We trained 'em," Jellico said.

Kosti extricated himself from the work cage and magged his boots to stand in front of Jellico. His craggy face creased in an expression of humorous irony. "So if they fail, we fail as well."

Jellico was considering what to say when the com interrupted. Kosti braced himself against recoil and tapped the comlink with a huge fist.

"Captain." It was Rael Cofort, her soft voice brisk and businesslike, as it always was on duty. "When you have a moment, would you stop by the survey lab?"

Jan Van Ryke, the cargo master, added in his mellow voice, "You have to see this."

Kosti keyed the transmit, and Jellico said, "On my way."

He turned to Karl. "How much ore could we lift with this ship? If we didn't have to worry about evasive action."

Kosti shook his head. "Nominally, in excess of forty thousand metric tons. But converting cielanite is tricky business, and I don't know how stable the tuning parameters for these engines are. The *Queen* could—will—handle it. This ship . . ."

He rubbed his heavy jaw, his eyes now completely serious. "I'd throw away ten thousand tons for the sake of the engines, unless the cielanite ore is highly refined."

"That bad?"

Kosti shrugged his massive shoulders. "Not too much difference between a blown-out engine and a colloid blaster—except an engine only does it once."

Jellico's mood was somber as he bounce-pulled himself along in free fall toward the survey lab, which had been converted from a cargo hold.

He considered Kosti's words—and what had been unsaid. His crew were not only trustworthy, but adaptable. Two necessities if a ship captain wanted to live to a reasonable age in an indifferent universe.

Adaptability meant considering all possibilities. What Kosti had implied, and Jellico understood, was the fact that if the unknown ships turned out to be unfriendly, Jellico would have to sacrifice the cargo capacity of the *North Star* just to pull any profit out of this trip—out of the contract. There wouldn't be any way to refuel the ship; therefore, the *Star* would have enough fuel to either engage in evasive maneuvers to cover the takeoff of the *Queen*—or to flee to a rendezvous with the *Queen* later to refuel.

Not both.

As he handed himself past the last closed cargo bay to the new lab that the scientists in the crew had set up, he dismissed the problem for later consideration. Entering the lab, he let his gaze take in the impressive banks of instrumentation patched together from the piece-kits his crew had built over years of successful Trading, and come to rest at the last on the fair countenance of Dr. Rael Cofort, his wife.

She was immediately aware of his presence; she glanced across the lab, her dark blue eyes smiling. Even wearing the severe non-gender-specific gear of the lab technician, with her rich auburn hair severely pulled back and braided on the crown of her head, she was beautiful—a beauty enhanced by her intelligent, fast-assessing gaze, her sensitive, expressive mouth. In a long and lonely life he had never thought to find this kind of companionship—not just of the body, but of the heart, of the mind. Every time he saw her after an interval apart, he reexperienced a belief in the miraculous.

"Come look," Rael said, gesturing.

Jellico handed himself into the high-ceilinged room with its huge viewscreen. Van Ryke, his bushy white brows knit, was busy at an adjacent console, tapping commands as a stream of data filled the bottom of the big viewscreen.

Rael hovered directly in front of the screen, her slim body at a relaxed angle; more experienced with free fall than the

Queen's Traders had been, she had adapted quickly to microgravity.

"Look," she said, gesturing at the display with her free hand; a sticky-glove anchored her other to the viewscreen. An orbital plot spilled across the screen, six points of light in synchronous orbit around Hesprid IV. "Tang Ya found six comsats the Traders of the *Ariadne* put in orbit. He's more than tripled our data feed."

Jellico thrust himself away from the entry and came to rest across the hold from the bottom of the screen, well below Rael, which left her plenty of maneuvering room without blocking his view.

Her hand brushed across the vast planet below. Bright swirls of cloud glared sunlight up at them from the dayside half. Beyond the terminator, the lands of night shone dimly, illumined by the reflection from the three moons.

As Jellico watched, the lab lights flicked off, leaving Rael a harlequin figure of light and shadow against the glow of Hesprid IV. And in the darkness of the planetary surface below her outspread fingers, as though cast by magic, faint pulses of light ringed outward, like ripples from pebbles cast in a pond.

"False color," Van Ryke spoke from behind him.

The screen flickered, and now the pulses had complex internal structures, delicate webs of color, fractal in complexity.

"Up into the infrared, even some ultraviolet from high atmospheric layers," the cargo master went on.

"Resonances from the cielanite EM pulses dayside," said Rael.

"More cielanite?" Jellico asked.

"No," said Van Ryke. He brought the lights back up.

Jellico could hear the faint rhythmic sound of her gloves pulling loose as Rael hand-over-handed down the screen to join them.

"But almost everything else at the high end of the periodic table. All the major superheavies. A rich prize."

"One worth killing for, to some," said Jellico, connections

flashing in his mind like puzzle pieces snapping into place. "Now Flindyk's plot makes real sense," he said.

"Exactly," Van Ryke said, smiling benignly. A tall, broadly built man, his unlined face and shock of white hair as well as his calm, melodious voice gave no hint to the subtle intellect and impressive memory that made him one of the best Traders Jellico had ever met. "Once the Patrol, acting in accordance with the Terran-Kanddoyd-Shver Treaty, hear of this planet's riches, they'll put a base here, because it can be largely self-sustaining."

"And mining will be a concession, carefully controlled by the three-way government at Exchange," Rael said.

"At immense profit," Jellico murmured, scanning the viewscreen again as he imagined how many rare elements were to be found down below, and in what quantities—and no indigenous sentients.

"Profit," Van Ryke repeated. "The prospect of which seems to generate a corresponding greed."

Rael frowned. "That's why they killed the *Ariadne*'s crew, then," she said. "Not just to keep the planet for themselves, but to keep the Patrol from hearing about the planet's resources; that would have been the first thing Trade Admin would have reported, once the *Ariadne* docked at Exchange."

"Right," Jellico said. "So if our mysterious company out here has anything to do with Flindyk's organization, they're going to see to it that none of us live long enough to talk."

Rael Cofort reached for another bulb of jakek as she studied Míceál Jellico's face. Lean, blaster-scarred, hard-boned, her beloved looked exactly like what he was: a tough Free Trader captain who never compromised his convictions. One glance at his narrow gray eyes, the steady gaze of one who always told the truth as he saw it, and even the most undiscerning would know him for an honest man. He was her safe harbor; after a life of dangers and sudden changes, she'd found a mate to match her. Wherever Míceál Jellico went was home to Rael.

She smiled at him as she sipped at her jakek.

Jellico paused in collecting their dishes and glanced up inquiringly.

Obligingly she said, "I was just trying to picture you fast-talking some wild-eyed pirate."

"Not likely. Leave that to Jan." He grinned, then leaned forward, bracing himself against a bulkhead, and hit the cage containing the blue hoobat Queex.

The cage rocked; the weird creature that looked like a parrot crossed with a toad clung with all six claws to a branch inside the cage and squawked happily. The specially sprung cage would rock and shake for hours now, keeping Queex content.

"Time for the shift change," Jellico said, lifting his chin in the direction of the control cabin.

The captain, Rael, and the other four crewmembers had set themselves eight-hour shifts; the idea was to be rested, but all of them had spent rest time doing "just one more chore."

Jellico had had to force Steen Wilcox to his cabin, after he'd stayed awake twenty-four hours after the long shift that had brought them out of hyper, saw the two ships cabled together, and the *Queen* launched on its mission.

Tang Ya was now on the control deck, but he, too, had gone too long without rest. The ship was on auto, but the com—until they knew who else was out there—required constant attention.

Jellico's thoughts were paralleling hers—again. He said, "You've been at it for two shifts. Are you going to get some rest?"

"Same two shifts you've been working," Rael said, smiling at him. "I'm fine. And I have plenty to do, correlating the fresh data. We'll be in range of the *Queen* in, what, six hours? Anyway, I'd like to squirt down some data for Tau, which means it needs to be prepared. I'll take the next shift as a rest period."

Which meant they could be together. Jellico gave her a brief grin, then he picked up the dishes and swung himself out of the cabin.

Rael followed, intending to find out if Ya had culled any news from the com before she retreated to the survey lab and buried herself in the mountains of statistics the instruments had been gathering.

With the jakek bulb still in one hand, she used the other to propel herself after the captain, who moved with the speed and efficiency of the born athlete.

Ya looked up in obvious relief when they arrived, though he said nothing. They'd all gone too long without rest, but it had seemed more important to master this unfamiliar ship as quickly as possible. No one had disagreed with the captain when he split the crew unevenly, eight to go planetside and only six to maintain the *Star;* they would need all eight if they were to mine enough ore to make the trip worthwhile.

"Any news?" Rael asked Ya. "Nothing," the Martian-born comtech said, stretching before he released himself from his seat. "So I've put in another shift playing with this computer."

"And?" Jellico prompted.

Ya shrugged his broad shoulders. "I guess I know it about as well as I'm going to." He levered himself up, reaching with one long arm to swing himself out of the com couch. "I'm for something to eat, and rack time, in that order."

"Good. I'll take over." Jellico moved above him, ready to drop onto the couch and strap himself in. His blue eyes were already scanning the readouts. Rael watched him at it, enjoying the speed with which he assessed the situation—then saw him frown.

Feeling a spurt of alarm, Rael shifted her gaze to the com console.

"What's this?" Ya jerked himself back into the couch, and one hand fastened him in as the other tapped keys.

Data flashed across the screen, too quick for Rael to comprehend, but Ya followed it without difficulty. "Unknowns—signal via moonbounce."

Jellico gave a short nod. "So we don't know where they are—"

"But they have an idea of where we are."

Jellico exchanged a glance with Rael, then said, "Put them on."

Ya worked his console, and the com screen displayed the head and shoulders of a woman. She looked about Jellico's age, her features somewhat blocky, her skin deeply lined. Rael stared in silence. The screen began to jitter.

"Damp that static," Jellico murmured.

"Not static," Ya replied, his hands busy at his keypads. Other screens lit, some blooming into multiple windows. Scans, Rael realized, watching for the other ship.

As they watched, the woman's face seemed to break up, then crystallize; Rael realized the instability in the picture was because of the weakness of the signal. At the same time, she saw in Ya's and the captain's faces that they realized it as well.

"Umik Lim, communications officer for Trade ship *Golden Sails* out of Ovaelo III. Our sister ship, *Wind Runner,* is Ovaeli."

The woman spoke Trade lingo with a heavy accent. Rael frowned at the screen, wondering what it was that bothered her. Ovaelo system? she thought—and Jellico typed the words into the computer, which threw a prompt overlay on the screen.

Rael scanned it swiftly as Ya identified himself and the *North Star.* Ovaelo III appeared to be an ocean world like Hesprid, but with far better weather. Also, the planet had .85 gee.

". . . you did not respond to our initial com query?" Ya was saying.

The woman's eyes shifted from Ya to Jellico and back, then she glanced down—probably at a readout corresponding to the ones running below and around the screen on the *Star*—and said, "We feared you might be brigands, and so we maintained silence."

What made you change your mind? Rael thought, glad she was out of view of the vid transmitter—and then she realized what bothered her. She knew what the transmit on the *Star* projected: the comtech, of course, and the captain as well, and if the others moved their couches into forward position, you could see at least part of a shoulder, or arm, plus a portion of the instrumentation. Behind the woman there was only a flat surface, impossible to judge; she could be sitting in a bare cabin, or else there might be a sheet of something directly behind her head. Nothing else was visible, no crewmates, no equipment.

"We are having trouble," Umik Lim went on. "Trying to contact our landing party. Overdue to rejoin us. EM is too strong for our communications equipment."

Ya's hand barely moved; Jellico glanced at the screen, but Rael saw no corroborative data on the overlay. Only the one ship was evident. Where was the other?

"When you enter system, we see two ships," Umik Lim went on. "Your second one?"

"The *Solar Queen,* our second ship, is planetside exploring mineral deposits," Ya said. "We are duly authorized to exploit this planet; the contract is registered at the Garden of Harmonious Exchange, according to the treaty, and with the Free Trade Administration."

"When we come here, no one here. No one claims. Free planet to survey," Umik Lim said.

"It's a big planet," Jellico said, speaking for the first time. "Once you collect your landing party, you are free to take whatever you mined, as long as you leave the system."

Umik Lim said, "We are here before your contract signed, maybe?"

"If you were, then why did you not register the find at Exchange?"

"Ovaeli law states, finder of planet is new owner," Umik Lim said.

"But we are not in Ovaeli space," Jellico said evenly.

Umik Lim glanced quickly aside, then jerked her chin down in a semblance of a nod. "This we know. Law here is different—I explain Ovaeli laws. We think we can claim planet, until now. We meet, my captain says, make treaty between us? Then we depart."

As Jellico hesitated, the image of the woman abruptly cleared. Ya tapped at his keys, and script overlaid the woman's face: SWITCHING TO DIRECT.

A subscreen suddenly windowed up, displaying orbital

plots around Hesprid, a ship creeping up over the limb of the planet.

Rael realized the tactical situation: the others had revealed themselves in a safe orbit, leaving both parties poised to escape, yet on very slowly closing courses. So far, so good.

They're behaving as though they are what they say they are, she thought.

Another screen showed the limb of Hesprid in real time. Rael saw a dim spark above the curve, shimmering with the instability of an enhanced image.

NO SIGN OF THE OTHER SHIP, Tang Ya tapped onto the screen overlay.

"We can make a treaty by comlink," Jellico said. "You did not know that this planet, Hesprid IV, was claimed. We'll squirt over the legal data." He nodded at Ya, who tapped at his keys.

Rael saw the data-transfer light flicker. Umik Lim paused, as though reading—or listening—then said, "Our custom is for treaty to be made in meeting. No false coms when two captains meet, touch palms. We record meeting, then our treaty is legal on Ovaelo. Comlink treaty not legal."

Ya glanced over at Jellico, who hesitated, scanning the data running across the screen. Rael did as well: so far, at least, the woman's words and the signals corresponded.

"Very well," Jellico began.

Just then the intership com bleeped, and Ya quickly transferred the sound to his headset. A moment later he worked at his console, and on the screen a new line of data appeared—this from Van Ryke, down in the survey lab.

PUTTING THIS EXPENSIVE SURVEY GEAR TO GOOD USE. THE GEE-ANOMALY SENSORS SAY THAT SHIP IS UNDER 1.6 GRAVITIES INTERNALLY.

One-point-six? Rael glanced back at the information on Ovaelo, and there it was, just as she remembered: GRAVITY .85.

One-point-six gravs . . . she remembered a moment later. This was the preferred gravitic pull of the Shver, the huge, elephantine beings who shared Exchange with the Kanddoyds and humans.

And a moment later, Ya typed on the screen: SHVER?

Jellico glanced at it, then continued. "Very well. Name a rendezvous point, please." Rael's heart was thumping in her chest; even so, she felt the urge to laugh. Jellico had asked them to name a rendezvous point, but he hadn't promised to meet them at it. Even in danger, he had difficulty lying.

No one spoke further as Umik Lim—or whoever she really was—relayed coordinates for a meet point. Ya acknowledged them; there was a brief exchange of niceties, and then the com winked out.

"Shver," Jellico said grimly.

Rael recalled what she had learned about these beings. Their homeworld was overcrowded, and their society favored strength, aggression, and ability. In their own sphere of influence, they were busy conquering worlds most favorable to Shver adaptation—whether those planets were inhabited or not.

"They have to appear to abide by the Exchange Treaty, or else they'll get the Patrol after them—and the Kanddoyds, who are much more technologically advanced," Rael said. "But it makes sense that they would only pay lip service to the treaty way out in these frontier areas."

Ya smiled sourly. "They certainly made it plain enough on Exchange that they looked down—"

"In more ways than one," Van Ryke chortled, appearing in the hatchway.

Rael bit back a laugh at the image of the tall, massively built Shver towering over everyone else. No one got in their way on Exchange—and they never stepped aside for anyone.

"—that they looked down on everyone else," Ya finished, shooting a look of tolerant scorn at the cargo master.

"I suspect what's closer is that the Shver feel challenged by the Kanddoyd relationship with the Patrol," Jellico mused. "Within their own lights they are relatively law-abiding. More so than the silver-tongued Kanddoyds, who will praise you to your face while helping themselves to your pockets, if they think they can get away with it."

Van Ryke nodded, his white brows quirked. "I suspect the Shver, concerned with their own overcrowding problems, are also sensitive to the prospect of a growing human presence. We are one of the most adaptable races—and one of the fastest growing, under ideal circumstances."

"But human colonization was ruled out, except in specifically agreed-on systems," Ya said. "I remember going over that treaty word by word."

Van Ryke shrugged. "Treaties get broken. And the Kanddoyds would be the ones to do it—apologetic, flattering, obsequious . . ."

"I can just hear them," Rael murmured, smiling as she recalled some dealings with the strange beetlelike beings.

The cargo master smiled benignly. "Exactly. Anyway, the Shver's manueverings with the Kanddoyd would be hampered by a Patrol base on Hesprid IV, bringing with it too much traffic, too many eyes, too much commerce."

"But it's unlikely they're official Shver units," Jellico said. "Not with a heavy-world human aboard."

Rael interjected, "That's one of the things that was bothering me about that vid the entire time I watched. The most obvious discrepancy was how the rest of her cabin was blocked from the vid transmit. More subtly, I realize now that the structure of her features, the deep lining, all would be characteristic of humanoids bred for heavy grav."

Jellico tapped with his fingers on the arm of his couch. "Except standard Shver tactics call for five ships, or seven, or three ships. No even numbers: there is always a flagship, even of the smallest fleet."

"If there is a third ship out here," Van Ryke said, "we can be sure they're planning a surprise when we reach the rendezvous."

"And so?" Ya asked, loosening himself once more from the com couch.

"We won't," Jellico said.

He reached forward, working his console. A display came to life, showing a swirling storm system on the planet below, with the land masses outlined in glowing white lines. "Our present orbit takes us across the *Queen*'s position, after this storm passes. Instead, we'll retro in, pick up velocity, and skip off the atmosphere at the height of the storm. We'll use the EM pulses to cover our course change."

"And then Dead Dog," Van Ryke said, in a tone of delight.

Jellico nodded.

Rael repeated, " 'Dead dog'?"

Jellico gave her a tight smile. "One of those tactical achievements you come up with when you're an unarmed ship facing two or possibly more ships that are, more than likely, armed—and with illegal arms at that."

Van Ryke's expressive brows soared. "What it translates out to is: no power except some shielded DC fans to keep the air circulating."

No power. Engines shut down, cold. No jets. Rael contemplated the consequences in dismay, though she gave no outer sign of it. Engines could not be turned on and off like a water tap. The *Star* would be helpless if discovered. In fact, they wouldn't even know they'd been caught until a colloid blaster breached their hull—they'd be flying blind for hours after the bounce, until they were far enough away to make a quick peek safe.

"With the three moons in their present configuration, we've got the makings of a great billiards game," Jellico said, his narrowed gaze gleaming with challenge. Rael suddenly realized just how great a challenge they faced, for Jellico had never piloted the *North Star* through an ablative orbit. Its blockier construction would make it handle very differently from the sleek *Solar Queen*.

"What do we tell the *Queen*?" Rael asked to take her mind off the danger.

Jellico looked at Tang Ya, who shook his head. "Can't punch much of anything through an EM mess like that, not securely. Have to wait for the storm to pass and the wave action to die down. We'll be doggo by then."

"They'll reveal themselves when we make our break. We'll pulse the number off a moon, then," said Jellico. "Minimal information for the Shver, and enough for Rip and the others."

"What about a call to the Patrol?" Rael asked.

"They'll know it," Ya said, twisting about to look at her. "Simple enough to put a spider-eye between Hesprid and the relay."

Rael had a brief, vivid image of the gossamer web of conductive monofilament, hundreds of kilometers across, spun out of a ship between them and the Patrol relay far out in space. Light pressure from the Hesprid system's sun would eventually blow it past the relay out into interstellar space, but until then, it would faithfully record any signal coming from the planet's vicinity. The pirates couldn't destroy the relay, for loss of its polling signal would equally well alert the Patrol. She nodded in agreement; so did Jellico.

"The relay's fifteen light-days out," said Teng Ya. "That gives us at least thirty days until they know we've squawked."

"At that point they'll have to set themselves up to intercept the *Queen*," said Jellico. "They'll know they've lost the planet, and they'll just want what they can get away with."

"And they won't care how they get it," said Kosti. "If we alert the Patrol, I suggest we send a message they can't ignore—a Nova Class Alert."

Rael said automatically, "Which is for war, or threatening X-Tee contact, or planetary disaster—if they determine a call is frivolous, we'd be in serious trouble."

"We're in that now." Jellico said, "We're close enough on the last two. Let's risk it." He nodded and began setting up a course. "We'll make our break at 19:20; that'll give us maximum cover from the EM."

Rael glanced at the time, realized what the cut in power would mean to the many projects she had running, and ducked out to make her own preparations.

At 19:20, they were all strapped into their couches.

"On my mark," Jellico said, his voice tight, his focus laser-narrow. Next to him, Steen Wilcox, his longtime navigational officer, sat, working his console. "Three, two, one. Mark."

The swift relay of orders given and acknowledged were steady and familiar. Then Rael felt the ship hum with power through her couch. Moments later came the pressure of acceleration, like one of the Shver sitting on her chest. *Two Shver*, she thought hazily; they were up to 3.5 gees, and the acceleration was still climbing.

To keep her mind off the discomfort, she watched the orbital plot on the screen before her. Abruptly another blip appeared over the limb of the planet ahead—but too high for an intercept, now. Or was it? The Shver could take more acceleration than they could. The blip brightened as the computer detected its jets firing. They would try.

The next thirty minutes were a haze of growing discomfort as they dropped into the planet's upper atmosphere. The hull began to ping from stress, and Rael thought she could hear a high, faint shriek underlying the rumble of the jets.

And just as the orbital plot fuzzed out from EM overload and went static, a third blip lifted over the planet, a classic three-point intercept.

Three ships. Forming a trap.

Her vision grayed as the gees suddenly surged, tearing at her guts as Jellico triggered the jets and literally bounced the *North Star* off the near vacuum of high atmosphere.

Then, abruptly, they were in free fall, falling away from the planet at high velocity without power. Invisible. Undetectable.

All but one of the displays went dark. The emergency lights came on, dim and reddish orange. The remaining screen flickered as the computer projected their course, and lines sprang from the four dots on it: three red course lines converging from the Shver ships on a point behind the fleeing green dot that represented the *North Star.*

Rael closed her eyes, her breath hissing out in relief. They had sprung the trap and escaped.

At least for now.

11

![star decoration]

The *Queen's* crew were all gathered in the mess cabin.

"The first question is, are these Traders in league with the pirates?"

That was Rip Shannon. Tooe watched the navigator. He was nervous. Tooe thought he was a good leader, but she strongly suspected that he did not like being a leader when he had to make a decision that had two or more consequences, and which would affect everyone else. Tooe knew the signs. It had been the same with Nunku, the leader of her klinti on Exchange. They would both be happier taking all the risks, and the consequences, themselves, if they could.

"Anything is possible," Tau said. "But I don't think these Traders are in league with anyone. The situation with Parkku, and the medication, would indicate a stranded party who is low on supplies."

"Unless it's a ruse," the cook-steward, Frank Mura, said.

"Seems a very elaborate ruse," Dane said. He seemed preoccupied. He'd been this way ever since they had returned from the campsite. "If they'd wanted us to believe—"

"Siere's data is very good," Tau said. "Some of his discoveries will probably save our lives; there are some virulent microbes in these winds, some of them brought from distant islands, so they didn't show up on the preliminary tests."

"I'll be adding the immune mods to the food," Mura put in. "But you have to consider that this could be a way to get us to trust them. After all, we could have figured out the same data, given time—"

"If—if—if!" Ali cut in. His voice was not slow now, it was quick and impatient. "We can spin out 'ifs' all day, and never get any answers. Either we trust them, or we don't. If we don't, give me a definite reason, not another load of 'ifs.' Makes more sense to trust them until we see some sign—something definite—that we shouldn't."

Johan Stotz said, "I'm with Ali. We have to get that cielanite, and then we've got to figure out some way to get this ship into orbit without being either hijacked or blasted out of the sky. The sooner we get started, and the more hands we have helping, the better our chances."

"The Traders will be with us when we leave this planet," Rip reminded them.

"They could always have a plan to take over the ship—" Dane said.

"We can counter that easily enough," Rip said, with a quick glance at Ali. "Steen has programmed plenty of trapdoors and the like in the computer systems—no one's going to get control of the *Queen* that way."

Ali chopped the air with his hands. "Enough with the far future. Almost as bad as the 'what-ifs.' Let's get Lossin and his gang on the comlink and plan tonight's work," he said. "Assuming, of course, the fog disappears—taking with it whatever might be riding along."

Everyone looked at the external viewport, which showed thick, swirling vapor obscuring the scenery. There was some wind, but it only made the cottony moisture weave and curl in hypnotic patterns. Tooe did not like looking out at that fog. Ali, Jasper, Dane, and Rip looked at the viewports often. Tooe watched them doing it, wondering if they sensed the Floaters by their psi-link. She also knew that they only half believed in the psi-link, or at least that was what they had told Craig Tau. She'd delved into the data files and found his reports on the subject.

She also knew that she wasn't supposed to be mining the data files without permission. She felt a little bad, but not bad enough to regret it. What she'd found helped her to understand these Terrans a little better.

For instance, she thought she understood why Dane had been preoccupied just now. She had talked to him more than any of the others, and she knew when he was not telling her everything he knew. Mostly that was memories. He didn't like to talk about his past. She accepted that. But he'd betrayed the same little signs of regret—hesitant voice, not meeting her eyes—when she had asked him about his pretending not to understand Rigelian. She'd also seen how Rip was suddenly alert, and very still, when Dane talked.

Tooe wondered if there had been some kind of contact with Rip caused by the psi link, and the two didn't want to talk about it. It seemed probable—the result of Ali's angry denial of the subject.

Tooe knew about that, and about the drugs he was taking in order to mute the possible development of the link. She suspected the drugs would not help. They might even cause a problem—something Tau had discussed as a possibility. Terrans knew very little about psi links.

Tooe knew more, but only by accident. There were two among her klinti on Harmonious Exchange who had psi talents. For some people that was a fact of life. It had, like anything else, its good and its bad aspects.

But Terrans were funny about it. She knew now why Dane got that tone of deepest regret when he mentioned his adventures on Trewsworld, especially if he referred to the brachs who had become sentient through prolonged exposure to esperite. He felt bad about these little beings, so alone now; their brains had changed, forever. They were no longer brachs, nor were they human. Tooe suspected he saw himself, and the other three, in the same way. Dane was afraid that developing the psi link would make him less of a human.

What is *human?* she thought. And the answer: *I don't know.*

So she kept her thoughts to herself.

". . . open communication, then, with Jellico," Rip was saying.

"Bearing in mind that the pirates are probably listening as well," Stotz said.

Rip nodded. "They know the *Queen* is here, so they're probably deployed in orbits that preclude communication silence. At any given time at least one of them will be in com range."

"Steen will know all that," Ali said, still impatient. "Leave it to him. And the Old Man. They've dealt with pirates before. We need to get at this job if we're ever going to lift off this summer paradise."

Mura laughed. "Summer paradise indeed." He disappeared in the direction of the hydro-lab deck.

The others agreed quickly on going ahead with the mining. Tooe listened carefully, relieved that no one questioned the deals she had made. Whether they thought she had done well or not, they had accepted her palm-touch with Lossin as a formal contract. The first trade had already been completed, when Siere, the medic, brought the data chip and then departed with the medicine he needed for Parkku.

The second item was the flitter in the cargo bay. That was for the use of the *Queen*'s crew.

After everyone had spoken Rip Shannon got up to contact Lossin, and through him Tazcin—thus initiating all the other trades that they had discussed.

Tooe felt proud, and relieved, and frightened, at having everyone acting on her word. Had she done well? The Tath had understood her, but that was not surprising. She had pretended she was talking to her old friend Kithin. It had worked fine. But being a good Trader, when she wasn't always sure about the exact worth of the items they discussed, that part bothered her.

She waited until Dane was alone.

"Come on, cargo-apprentice," he said with a smile. "Let's get all our data entered into the log."

"Is good?" she asked, rising from her chair and following him out the hatchway. As always, she felt the hard deckplates pressing up on her feet. This time, at least, she didn't feel the cold, because she still had on the shoes. They were good for that, she decided. But they confined so!

"The items you promised from our stores are fine. The work ratio—the medicine—the items that intersect with others' departments, we'll find out about. I don't think anyone is outraged. They know you had to think fast. I'll submit a report to Jan Van Ryke when we can, but I suspect he's going to be more pleased than not."

Tooe's relief was so strong it felt, just for a moment, that the gravs had lifted.

"Thunk!"

Dane was barely aware of the noise. It worked its way into his dream. A strange dream. The horizon was oddly short. People were so polite, so soft-spoken they reminded Dane of robots. Not in a bad sense. Different from Terra.

"*Klank!*"

A bad flitter? Dane realized he was with Jasper. No, he *was* Jasper. He was Jasper, and he was worried about the flitter. Was the engine disabled?

"*Plink! Clatter-clatter . . .*"

Dane opened his eyes, gazing uncomprehendingly at the close confines of the cabin he had slept in for years. Recognition returned suddenly, inner and outer. He was Dane Thorson, not Jasper Weeks, and he was in his cabin aboard the *Queen,* and not in Mzinga City, Venus Colony Five . . .

"Pok!"

He recognized the sound then, and laughed. He didn't have to go into the empty cargo bay to identify it. He could just picture Tooe in there, tossing cogs and bolts and whatever detritus she could lay her hands on, watching trajectory and ricochet as if they were magic. And to someone who was used to the straight lines of micrograv, they *were* magic.

Would she ever get tired of it?

He shook his head, still grinning, as he grabbed his clothes out of the cleaner and headed for the san-unit for a fast shower.

When he started up the ladder to the galley, he felt the unmistakable thrum and joggle of the ship around him that meant they were under the full battery of another storm.

He found Stotz and Weeks already there. Jasper ate steadily, his gaze on his plate. Did he know about Dane's dream? Probably. Dane winced inwardly, half-sorry and half-glad that they weren't to talk about it. Even though he could hardly be blamed—and he knew Jasper would not blame him—he still felt as if he'd made a personal trespass against the very private jet tech.

"Storm's lessening," Johan said, waving his fork toward the vidscreen. "Sunset in half an hour. We might make it yet."

Dane felt a surge of anticipation. Action, that was what he needed; what they all needed. The need to fight the elements in order to get the cielanite would help get their minds off this psi stuff, even if only because they were too tired to think.

Rip appeared in the mess cabin just before the exterior viewport showed the sun setting.

"Been talking with Tazcin," Rip said. "Hammering out details of our Trading."

"We still on for the tour of the mining site?"

Rip nodded. "You and Johan—tonight, 00:30 local time. There's a lot of atmospheric instability, and we could get squalls or worse, but it looks like a good time for it. Lossin and Siere will go with you. They have a rule that a medic needs to be on hand for the trips."

"That dangerous?" Johan looked up, his straight brows slightly furrowed. Nothing ever seemed to upset the engineer.

"Parkku better?" Tooe appeared in the hatchway.

Rip gave her a nod. "Fast recovery, now that she's on meds again," he said to Tooe, then he turned back to Stotz. "That's what they say. Craig volunteered to take his turns going out."

"Good." That was Ali.

Rip gave him a brief smile. "You and Jasper aren't going to the mining site—at least, not until you get what they've already pulled out refined and stashed aboard here."

"How much might that be?"

"Not nearly as much as we'd hoped, for a number of reasons, mostly tidal scouring, since the mining-slugs need a littoral environment for most efficient ore extraction."

Ali stroked his jaw. "Speaking just from the esthetic view—thinking of their cable-weaving treesnails and so on—what does their mysterious miningtech look like?"

The crew looked at Stotz, who smiled and shook his head. "That will be my surprise," he said. "But they can't be worse than the haggis—which was the inspiration for the ore-bots machines I put together."

Rip gave a sudden laugh. "Dane's duel! I'd forgotten that."

"Not me," Dane said, sensing everyone's relief—however momentary—at the ridiculous memory of his so-called duel with the mighty Shver. "My ribs still ache from my attempt to play Wilcox's bagpipe in one-point-six gees."

"Johan surprise?" Tooe put in, her crest flicking through a series of reactions. "I think, Johan smell something bad, in Trader camp."

Ali snorted a laugh. "She's right, Stotz," he drawled. "After talking to Taczin, you looked like you'd found a phlegm-spider in your salad."

"Well, we'll have to let Johan have his surprise," said Rip. He turned to the engineer, who just shrugged, smiling a little.

"Whatever you have put together, it's not going to be easy. The timing is really tight. With the Floaters lurking around during daylight hours we can only mine at night, and only on nights with two low tides. That happens only every six days or so, and the increase in sunspot activity has really revved up storm activity, which further limits them. With all the delays, much of the ore has been carried away by the sea by the time they can go collect it."

"And they had to stop going out when they ran out of meds and Parkku needed constant care."

Ali whistled.

Rip said, "They did the best they could, but they hadn't known what to plan for until they surveyed the site, any more than we had. As we'd guessed, their ship was to return with a better refining kit—along with all the other things they needed, including new supplies."

"They low on food?" Mura asked.

"No. Corliss, their steward, had insisted on leaving double what they thought they'd need. She was apparently an old hand, and had convinced them that she'd seen her theory proved out too many times to stint now. They're fine on shelter—thanks to the trees, and their own metabolisms—and food, but except for the flitters, they're low on everything else."

Dane quickly finished eating and jammed his plate and utensils into the recycler. "I'm going to get my winter gear. Sooner I'm there, the more we can look around."

"Just what I was thinking," Johan Stotz said, and handed himself down the ladder with his old quick, unthinking speed.

Of all the Terrans he'd probably recovered from the grav the fastest. Dane wondered if it was all those years he spent during his youth, playing null-grav sports. He adjusted between gravs with little apparent discomfort.

Dane followed a little more slowly, remembering to duck his head. Once again he was too tall for his surroundings.

A few hours later they were in the flitter, fighting their way through fierce winds as they headed for the meet point. Stotz was at the controls, a frown of concentration on his

long face; the flitter bucked and wallowed, the engine scream-
ing, as he fought to keep it level.

At the meet point, a short distance from the Traders'
camp, they saw a tall, bulky figure and a short, thin one waiting in the lee of an outcrop of volcanic rock.

They'd agreed to take the flitter now assigned to the
Queen's Traders, as they had more fuel. Stotz brought the flitter to a stop, and the engine whined as the craft settled gently
to the ground despite the wind doing its best to flip it end
over end.

Lossin climbed in, his weight making the flitter jerk and
sidle. He wore a shrouding jacket of Trader brown, but the
scent of wet dog filled the small space inside the flitter. Dane
hid a grin. Siere swarmed in, his movements quick and fluid,
hardly disturbing the balance of the flitter at all.

"I will take controls?" Lossin offered, pointing. "I know
this battle." The deep voice held a distinct note of irony.

Stotz slid over into the next pod, indicating with a lift of
his chin that the Trader should pilot.

Lossin dropped his bulk into the command pod, closed
the hatches, shutting the wind out. The engines keened up the
scale, and then, with a swooping rise that reminded Dane of
a raptor in flight, the flitter lifted and veered.

Now the wind was no longer an enemy. Instead, it pushed
them; Lossin jetted them in a long circle, dropping them over
some thousand-meter cliffs before he brought them around to
their destination. Cut off from the wind, they proceeded in relative peace; Dane looked out at the fantastic rock formations,
lit by the powerful lamps of the flitter. The cliffs were striated
with a rich variety of colors, silent testimony to the violent tectonic history of this planet.

Large, webby-looking seabirds circled and floated on this
lee side of the island. Huge, veined breakers loomed with deliberate, slow power and smashed against the rocks, and the
birds dived down toward the foaming waters as they receded
out to the choppy black sea. As another breaker formed the

birds darted here and there among the brilliant variety of pebbles washing down the steep shoreline, and then zoomed upward just before the next wave came smashing in like a vast hand.

Lossin sped along the cliff walls; the birds darted out of the way, their beaks open, their eyes reflecting angry crimson in the lamplight. Dane wondered what their voices sounded like, but of course all he could hear was the hiss of the air circulator, and the steady spin of the engines.

Stotz, Dane noted, scarcely afforded the outside view a glance. His attention stayed entirely with the constant readouts above the controls.

They rounded a promontory, and quite suddenly they felt a gust of wind, and Lossin's big hands worked swiftly on the controls, stabilizing the flitter. They were in a small bay; as the flitter dived toward the choppy water, the wind subsided again as they came into the lee of the natural breakwater that sheltered the cove.

The flitter dived into what looked like a cave, so dark that the high-intensity lamps on the flitter did not penetrate far. The flitter slowed, the engine whining up the scale as the jets cut out and the ducted fans' beams took over, balancing them on columns of air. They moved over mossy rock and settled on a blast-smoothed platform next to a huge craft bobbing next to a dock. One glance at it and Stotz's serious face lifted; he leaned forward slightly in his pod, as if he couldn't wait another second to get at this unusual-looking piece of equipment.

For, as Dane had learned to expect by now, it didn't look like anything a Terran would design. In fact, it resembled nothing so much as a huge, almost-teardrop-shaped gourd covered with a scintillating layer of pearlescent overlapping scales. A large elliptical viewport gave the appearance of an eye on the side Dane could see, and a faint bluish luminescence glowed from it, hinting at a shadowy interior punctuated by the more familiar twinkle of status lights.

"Another gastropod, right?" asked Stotz.

"Yes," Lossin said. "Tath grow cargo reentry pods from the same seed-plasm; very strong crystalline structure."

That was enough for Johan. As Lossin set the flitter down, and they climbed out, Stotz fired technical questions at him. He was fascinated by the problems of interfacing machine tech with biotech.

Dane half listened, his attention absorbed in the surroundings. The shellboat was anchored to the cave walls by more of what Dane thought of as living catch-tab, which enabled it to lift and fall with the tide. Above he saw a thick mat of something else, where apparently the shellboat snuggled when the sea filled the cave. It was obvious that it spent parts of each day underwater; scattered small barnacles and other undersea creatures were affixed to it from top to bottom.

Lossin showed them how to activate the egress controls from inside the flitter, then he put that vehicle in park mode, and they all climbed out. Bitterly cold, briny air smote Dane. He followed the silent medic into the bigger craft.

There the Tath picked up a hoselike tube with cilia around its opening and briefly groomed most of the water- and windborne debris out of its fur. Then, as he led them to the control center, past machinery that looked half-familiar and half-organic, Dane watched Stotz look around intently and fire even more questions at Lossin.

Finally, the engineer asked: "You seem to have so much control of the growth process; why not grow some or all of the circuitry using similar methods?"

"Silicon systems faster and more precise than organic," rumbled Lossin. "Unless you make organic intelligence, which we do not do."

Stotz looked like he wanted to ask more questions, but something in the big Tath's tone seemed to deter him.

Lossin brought the shellboat's systems up and soon they were hydroplaning out over the water at high speed, flatten-

ing the water below them in a wake which stretched out behind.

"This flight will take almost a Standard Terran Hour,"
Lossin said as he lit the control panel. The engine came to
life, and the life support. Last thing, Lossin fired up the
weather scope.

Stotz, seeing this, frowned slightly, and then his face
smoothed out. Dane scanned the screen, wondering what had
caught the engineer's attention. There appeared to be nothing
amiss—this was just a standard weather scope, tracking storm
patterns around the—

Around the planet.

Which meant that their ship had seeded the atmosphere
with comsats before landing these Traders on the surface.
Their ship . . . now in orbit under the command of Captain
Jellico.

Which meant that the *Queen*'s Traders could have been in
contact with the other ship at any time.

And these Traders had not told them.

12

"**Dane is reporting,**" Ali said. "Sounds like a nice, tidy little craft—though I wonder why he thinks it necessary to natter on about everything on it. Does he think we're buying one?"

Rip didn't answer the question. He could feel Ali's sour mood as if it was his own. In fact, it was rapidly becoming his, the navigator thought wryly.

Rip was going to be glad when the Traders finally arrived with their flitter; he didn't know what was taking them so long. Jasper and Ali had their scanning equipment stowed in the outer lock, awaiting the Traders' arrival so they could depart for the ore site.

Rip had been busy with the logfiles, so Ali offered to watch the com. Rip had accepted, if only to give the restless engineer something to do—and he'd been regretting it ever since.

"Hold." Ali's voice sharpened. Then he laughed, and tabbed the mute as he swung around on his seat. "Fascinating."

Rip distrusted the arch to Kamil's mobile brows, and even more so his sardonic smile. "You mean troubling."

"How perceptive of you, my good pilgrim," Kamil said in a falsely congratulatory tone. "Or are you merely reading your mystery beams?" He tapped his skull.

Rip ignored the rhetorical question with the stolidity of long practice. Because it *was* a rhetorical question, meant merely to be goading, to make Rip as angry about the psi business as Ali himself was. Rip knew that Kamil did not for a moment believe that any of the other three were suddenly adept at reading minds.

"Thorson will be out of range soon," he said, glancing at one of the com-readouts. "Is there a problem?"

"Yes, but there's nothing we can do about it," Ali said, his tone changing to business. He tabbed a couple of keys, and a number came up. "Two minutes and forty seconds until the helmet coms are out of range. Short of getting our blasters and hijacking a flitter to go after them, whatever Lossin and his accomplice are planning shall be carried out."

"Accomplice? What's this?"

Instead of answering, Ali keyed the com-log, and played a short portion. Dane's voice filled the *Queen*'s cramped control deck, describing the shellboat's controls. Rip listened, puzzled, as Thorson went on to talk about the weather scope they had, and how it was tracking a gigantic storm on the other side of the world. He rambled on a bit on how the Coriolis effect seemed to interact with continental features on this world—then Ali cut him off mid-sentence. "Got that?" he asked, goading again.

Rip ignored him, thinking rapidly. "Planetwide scope . . . Comsats! And of course we wouldn't necessarily pick them up on our equipment." He indicated Ali's console.

"Not unless we were looking. Which we haven't been, lest we alert those pirates."

"But the *North Star* should have found them," Rip said, rubbing his chin. "Tang Ya's one of the best comtechs in Trade—he wouldn't miss something like that. Particularly as the sats have to be tuned to one of *North Star*'s pre-set frequencies."

"But they've kept radio silence," Ali said.

Rip shook his head. "Damn. I wish I knew what all this meant. Just one talk, one straight talk with the Old Man, instead of all this indirection and second-guessing—and now, with those pirates up there listening to every word, we won't even get that."

"Jellico plainly doesn't trust our Traders, so he hasn't let on about the comsats," Ali said, restless again. He got up and paced back and forth in the tiny space, making the control deck seem even more cramped. "But we're not dealing with Jellico or the pirates. We're dealing with these Traders, with a ready-made planetary com-system. The question here is, why didn't we find this out right from the start?"

"Did Tooe find out?" Rip asked, trying to think back.

Ali started to speak, then hesitated, his lips parted.

"Don't," Rip said. "Whatever went on in that conversation with the Tath, I will guarantee there was nothing important that she didn't report. Thorson vouches for Tooe. We have to trust her, at least."

Kamil smiled unwillingly. "I guess I'm becoming too habit-bound in my old age. We twelve were a stable unit for so long that my first instinct is not to trust the motives of anyone new. First Rael Cofort, and now Tooe. So what does that leave us with?"

"Questions only," Rip said firmly. "We've already learned that we can't trust our interpretations of their motives. They think too differently from us. When Tooe gets back from their camp, I'll brief her."

"When she—" Ali paused, looking down at the console. An insistent light blinked. He tapped it, then the speaker connection.

"Tazcin here." The leader's deep voice rumbled.

Rip keyed the exterior port-screen, and saw the flitter waiting outside, well within the perimeter of the floodlamps.

Jasper Weeks popped his head through the hatchway a moment later. "They're here," he said. "Want to help me get the equipment outside?"

"With you," Ali said, casting a strange smile over his shoulder at Rip.

In silence Rip watched the two men, now clad in their winter gear, carry out their scanning equipment to the waiting flitter. Tooe appeared briefly, hopping out to offer her help. Rip saw Tazcin—or what he took to be Tazcin. The Tath were too hard to tell apart, unless they were standing in their customary row.

Row. It tugged at a memory.

Ali had first responded negatively to that impassive row of Tath standing shoulder to shoulder, as if they were hiding something—or confronting someone. Rip's mind flickered to their bunkspace in the camp, all four crammed together, and then he had it.

They lived in an artificial environment, a habitat in space, with its finite living area. Hadn't he read in some drab history text somewhere in his youth about early Terran experiments with living in habitats, and how artificial environments tended to either drive people crazy or else cause them to alter their perceptions of personal space?

That was it. Terrans needed room around them. Tooe obviously didn't, judging from how close she used to stand, until she herself learned to keep herself at a comfortable distance. But the Tath, habitat-dwellers all, naturally required little personal space. In fact, they probably felt more comfortable standing close together. It had nothing to do with threat or defense, any more than the Terrans' standing at arm's length from one another had to do with threat or defense—though someone not used to it could be excused for surmising that the arm's length was a necessity for freedom in drawing and firing weapons.

And if they saw our sleeprods that first night . . . Rip knew he was onto a real insight.

This very well could be the main impetus behind the mutual wariness.

He wished all the others were there to discuss his ideas with, then he shrugged. Soon enough.

Meanwhile, he could get them recorded in his log. Keying his console to life, he flexed his fingers and started typing.

Dane and Johan stared in dismay at the forbidding low rock dome harsh-lit in the mining boat's lights.

"Fourteen islands only," Lossin said. "Most so close to the limit that conditions must needs be ideal before we go out to them. This one is Number Two. Work there is still yet to do."

Stotz shook his head slowly, his mouth grim. The evidence was clear: mining cielanite was tougher than they'd figured.

No, not mining, Dane thought. The mining-slugs were largely autonomous. What did they look like? Various horrific images flitted through his head, remembered from the trashy tri-D vids he'd watched so eagerly in his youth. Doubtless they were some sort of organic machines, something Terrans rarely saw, except depicted as monstrosities on vids. But Dane remembered the engineer's earlier reaction. Stotz wouldn't just grin about them if they were really terrible.

No, it was getting the ore they produced that was hard. The only ore the Tath mining devices could reach was in these volcanic domes, forced up by magma. Some domes were too far away to be reached except when the moons' complex cycle reached its longest between high tides. The mining-slugs needed the very tidal scouring that tended to carry away the ore, but too long a high tide would carry away all of the ore brought up by the biomechs, which made scheduling even more complex.

That was if the weather stayed relatively calm. And if no one was sick.

"No trees on any of these dome islands?" Stotz asked abruptly.

"None. We assume cielanite content in the extractable range inhibits their growth, for the trees are thick on islands with no useful ore, or with ore content registering only in deep layers."

"And you don't risk setting up camp on an island with no trees?"

"We know only that the Floaters move around trees, but never go among them. There is rarely fog in the trees. The Floaters stay near land. We assume they spend their nights out here over these islands, where there are no trees."

Siere spoke. "We haff recorded thisss fog moving rapidly over the watersss as the sssun setsss, before our inssstruments loossse sssight of them."

"Don't show up on infrared, eh?" Stotz murmured.

It was a rhetorical question, Dane knew, nevertheless Lossin grunted affirmation, and Siere said, "Yesss. Thisss isss true."

Stotz glanced at the time—they all did. The engineer gave a soft grunt, and Dane saw his brow clear, as if his mood had changed.

His manner was one of anticipation as he said, "All right, then. Let's unstow the ore-bots and get to work."

They pulled on their heavy-weather gear. Dane worked quickly; he hated the way the cold got into his clothes and chilled his flesh.

But when he got a glimpse out the viewport of the shell-boat, he forgot about the weather. He'd never seen anything like this before. The boat seemed to be crawling up on the beach, like an amphibious landing craft. The motion was strangely smooth, and Dane could hear no hint of an engine sound now. Instead, there was a strange rhythmic hum as the shellboat moved out of the surf and beached itself. Peering back out of the huge viewport on his side, he could see a long track of strangely patterned sand extending behind the vessel back to where the wind-whipped waves obliterated it. Finally the craft stopped moving, and the only sound was the wind.

The back of the shellboat lowered, like a ramp. As they got out, Dane looked around to orient himself and saw that they were facing the sea. Chill wind buffeted his face, and in the distance was the flicker of lightning—something that he hardly noticed anymore, so familiar was it.

Dane's boots sucked and squidged in the mucky sand as he walked around to the side of the shellboat, leaned forward, and peered at its underside. The scales on the underside of the boat were moving slightly, in unison. He reached out to touch one.

"No!" Lossin's voice boomed. "The motor scales are very sharp!"

Dane pulled back his hand. "It moves like a snake!"

"Snake?" Lossin repeated. "Good for short distances only."

"Thorson?" Stotz waved an arm, and Dane mucked his way back to the door of the shellboat. He looked in, and a sudden laugh shook him when he saw—

"—haggis on legs." Stotz grinned.

The bots were standard eight-legged motivators—like the guy-bots that had moored the *Queen*—with a universal machine platform on top, but where Dane had expected some sort of complicated digging equipment to be mounted was a huge, brightly colored bag flopping over to one side, with an articulated flexplas snout jutting from one side.

"The tartan plaid of the collector bags is in honor of your duel with the Shver on Harmony, Dane," said Stotz. He chortled at the reaction his surprise had caused, then looked up as an especially severe blast of wind buffeted them. "But we'd better get to work."

Quickly he demonstrated how the ore-bots worked. The snout was actually a powerful vacuum tube, with a Tath-supplied cilia fringe that helped it dislodge the ore eggs from where the mining-slugs deposited them. A small camera in the tip of the snout relayed an image to the operator, who walked behind the ore-bot and worked from the image on-screen to guide the snout.

They walked the bots over toward the dome, which Dane recognized immediately as exfoliated granite flaking off in big chunks.

"Must look upward," Lossin said. "Rock falls often, and workings of the mining-slugs accelerates the process."

Just then Dane caught sight of something bright yellow glistening in one of the cracks in the dome. He stepped away from his bot, which automatically went into idle mode, and approached it cautiously. It was moving!

He looked up to see Stotz grinning at him. "Behold the fabled mining-slugs!" he said.

Dane leaned over to look closer, then pulled back abruptly as the thing raised one end as though to look him over. It was a giant slug! At least four feet long, it had no eyes, and glistened all over with an oily sheen.

"Touch not," Lossin said, coming up beside them. "This outer substance is great corrosive, which makes it possible for miner-device to bore through rock."

As he watched, there was a clanking sound, and something rolled away from the other end of the slug.

"There you go," said Stotz. "Cielanite ore." He pointed at the familiar joined-sphere shape of the ore-bodies they'd first seen at the Trader camp.

"Ore eggs!" said Dane.

"Pretty much," agreed the engineer. "So you know what that makes these," he continued, waving at the ore-bots.

Dane started laughing. "Egg collectors." Then he sobered quickly as Lossin looked down at the chronometer strapped to his furry wrist.

"There is not much time," the Tath said. He looked around. "Much of the ore has been washed away—we will have to climb higher."

As they walked on, Lossin described the difficulty of finding ore. Dane noted that that was the only slug they saw, and Stotz explained that most of the ore lay deep in cracks. Lossin nodded emphatically as the engineer demonstrated with his ore-bot.

The next period of time was highly unpleasant. The wind ripped at them, never steadily, but in sudden gusts and jolts that made it even more difficult to maneuver on the wet, rocky ground. Dane nearly lost his balance several times, and that was before they began climbing behind the bots, which nuzzled into the deep crevasses and cracks in order to sniff out ore eggs left by the Tathi mining devices.

When they had reached the mass limit for the speed and fuel required of the return trip, Stotz and Lossin called a halt. Dane said nothing, but his reaction was pure relief as they returned the bots to the shellboat and boarded it.

The wind was slowly rising to gale force, Dane noticed, as they began to pick up speed. The ride became rougher and rougher, making him wish the shellboat was a ground-effect vehicle, despite the fact that would have reduced its payload considerably.

Heavy rain smote them abruptly, a watery stream that made the ports impossible to see out of. Lossin was guiding entirely on radar by the time they neared their island, but all too often the entire screen went white as a series of lightning bolts ripped through the sky. In haste—no one needed to speak it—they closed the boat down, got it anchored, and piled into the flitter.

The tide, whipped up by the storm, was heaving just behind the floor of the cave. One good wave, Dane thought as he threw himself into his pod, and they'd all be swept out onto the rocks. No one could fight that force.

Lossin hit the flitter controls, and the little ship rose and jetted out of the cave, just as below them a great dark swell surged into the cave and smashed against the walls, washing around the secured boat.

The next time they came, precious hours would be spent in transferring the ore to the two flitters. No mining could be done until that was complete.

Dane's thoughts narrowed to the viewscreen ahead as Lossin fought steadily against a shrieking gale. The flitter shuddered and shook, its Tath pilot fighting for every meter of distance.

The fuel gauge dropped rapidly as the engines howled in protest. After a time, Dane began to wonder if the weather or the fuel gauge would get them first.

Visibility was near zero, so Dane watched the console

readouts as Lossin fought the little craft. Directly ahead of Dane sat Stotz, his back tense with his silent concentration on Lossin's hands. Dane spared a glance at the medic, who sat quietly, his eyes half-closed. Of them all, he seemed the least ill at ease. Though he might be misreading, Dane thought to himself. He'd already learned not to trust his second-guessing.

"Nunh." The grunt came from Lossin.

And seconds later light shone on the slanting rain, highlighting the individual drops until they looked like liquid fire. A moment later the *Queen* herself appeared, first gleaming wet and silver in her own lights, then glaring brightly in a flare of lightning far overhead.

The flitter nosed directly up the *Queen*'s ramp and lurched inside.

Someone closed the outer hatch just as the flitter settled to the deck.

The engines spun down to silence, which was deafening after the continuous pounding their hearing had taken. Dane rubbed his ears as he climbed out behind Stotz.

The engineer said to Lossin, "We should drive you back to your camp."

Lossin shook his shaggy head. "Not needed. Storm is worse, and you will not be able to avoid trees." He pointed outside. "We go directly to trees, where the storm is less. We will be fine."

They left immediately; dawn was less than an hour away, though the storm made it impossible to tell.

Stotz disappeared immediately in the direction of his lair. Dane heard him yelling for Jasper and Ali.

Dane stopped at his cabin to shed his wet winter gear and put it through recycling, then he climbed up to the galley deck in search of something hot to drink—and news.

There he met Tooe, Mura, and Rip Shannon. All three were silent and tense.

Dane had been about to offer a report on the mining excursion, but he felt the words slip from his mind. "Problem?"

Rip jerked his chin up sharply, his usually pleasant face uncharacteristically grim. "Compiled a suitable report for the *North Star,* something that could be read by the pirates."

"Right. And they came into com range, and . . ." Dane prompted.

"Nothing."

"What?"

"That's just it," Rip said. "Nothing. They should be here—" He got up and pointed to a dot blinking on an orbital path called up on the computer screen. "But there's no sign or signal. Nothing."

13

***

"**What's this?**" **the** voice came over the open com—it was Ali Kamil.

"Pirates attack?" Tooe asked, her voice shrill.

"No." Rip's voice was flat, an enforced calm. Dane felt a sympathetic twinge at the back of his neck—and without warning he sensed Jasper and Ali pounding up the ladders from deck to deck.

The momentary sensation of being in two places at once gave him a moment of vertigo—like snapout. Dane shut his eyes, breathing deeply.

"We would have seen it if they'd been fired on." Rip pointed at the screen.

"Unless it happened on the other side of the planet," Dane said.

Rip's dark eyes flicked his way, a distracted glance, then back to the screen. Dane noted fine beads of sweat along Rip's hairline, and knew with a sudden but intense conviction that Rip had felt that same moment of vertigo. Which probably meant that Ali and Jasper had also felt it, only reversed—sensing the two of them seated in the galley. Unless Ali was full of his drug. But no, he hadn't had time to take any drugs, Dane realized. Ali and Tooe and Jasper had returned just ahead of them, and had been busy working ever since.

Further, the connection between the four wouldn't have been so clear. The drug, it seemed, muted the psi effects for Ali, and at the same time diffused it in a strange way for the others.

Dane braced for more of Kamil's temper.

Rip, meanwhile, was drumming his fingers on the console. He hit the buffed metal edge of the table with his flat hand, and said, "I'm going to ask Lossin about that."

And without further speech he hitched out of his chair and clambered up the ladder to the control deck.

Jasper walked in a few seconds after. "Ali went up to the com," he murmured, going to the jakek dispenser.

Craig Tau and Johan Stotz were just behind him.

Mura said, "Dead Dog Billiards."

Everyone looked over at him.

Tau gave a crack of laughter. "By the Holy Nose of Ghmal! I'd nearly forgotten."

"What's this?" Dane asked.

Both the older crew members swung around. Mura said with his faint smile, "Before your time. Before any of you, in fact." He pointed at Jasper, then waved upward toward the control deck, and Ali and Rip. "We were involved in a complicated five-way trade out in the Asteroid Belt around Viper III. Rough part of the starlanes, but you can get some good deals—Terran goods bring high prices. Anyway, we found ourselves boxed in by pirates. But Jellico had worked us deep into the gee well of a gas giant with dozens of moons. We cut power to everything but life support and passive sensors, and used gravity-sling maneuvers to randomize our course."

"You've never seen Jellico play billiards," Tau put in. "We got clean away. And all four of those scumslinkers were armed like Patrol cutters."

Mura sat back, frowning slightly. "That was before colloid blasters." Then his expression lightened, and he shook his head with a slight grin. "Doesn't matter. Short of a report of an explosion, I'll just bet that Jellico is up to his old tricks."

"Cut power . . . but what that means is that we're cut off, then, too."

Rip's voice came over the com. "That's exactly what it means. We can't even use a tightbeam, even if we wanted to, since we've no way of aiming it."

"What's the word?" Tau asked, facing the com.

"Lossin reports that the *North Star* has changed orbit and gone dark. No evidence of fire or foul play."

"Dead Dog Billiards," Mura repeated with satisfaction. "He's using the EM pulses from the storms to cover his drunk-walk course changes."

"Except this means that for the duration, we're effectively cut off from communication," Rip's voice came. Dane heard the strain under his calm tone.

"That's all right," Tau said, smiling. "We're doing fine. We seem to be establishing a working relationship with the Traders here. We have a job to do, and we know how to do it."

"What's more," Mura said, rising from his chair, "Jellico is letting us know as clear as if he was on the comlink himself that *he* thinks we're doing fine."

"I suggest we shut down, then, and everyone get some rest," Tau added. "Sun's coming up—we'll have a full night of work ahead, if the weather cooperates."

"Sooner we're done here, sooner we can leave," came Ali's wry voice. He passed by the mess cabin and continued on his way down.

Jasper rose without speaking and walked out, his steps soundless as usual.

Dane got up to follow, noting Tooe's huge yellow eyes moving from one to the other of them, her crest quirked in question mode.

He wondered if she suspected there was something going on. Then he remembered that day aboard the *North Star*—

she'd been there when Tau had called the four together for that conference. He'd also promised to debrief her when they were done, but Dane knew that because of Ali's reaction Tau had dropped the subject, except for his report to Jellico and Dr. Cofort on their decision, as far as the other crewmembers were concerned.

Which meant Tooe couldn't know. Or could she? Dane knew how inquisitive she was—yet she had never asked him about that private conference with the medic.

He shook his head tiredly. Well, he couldn't discuss it with her. That would break the promise they'd made with Ali. So he might as well put it out of his mind.

"Anything to report?" he asked her.

Her crest flicked upright into what he thought of as Tooe-pleased-with-herself mode. "I get foods I like," she said, happily. "And we Trade some seeds, some cuttings. Frank has new cuttings, new data. Kamsin, steward for Traders, get seeds, data. Parkku better, wants to help with ore, engineer with Ali. Bioengineer new ideas, Ali happy."

"So it was a good work session," Dane said.

Tooe nodded vigorously. "Not so good, mining?"

"Difficult. Now I know why they don't have much ore stockpiled."

Dane went on to explain his trip out to the island. Tooe listened intently, her pupils expanding and contracting with disconcerting fluidity; Dane knew this was a more subtle reflection of her emotions. This was her Rigelian heritage.

At the end, he said, "Tomorrow—if the storms don't pen us up—we can't mine, we'll have to spend our time refining and loading. But maybe with more hands at work we can speed up the process."

"Stotz refining machines. Not needed?" Tooe asked.

"Oh, yes," Dane said. "They're not set up to refine all the way up to fuel—no reason to be, especially since it's somewhat more unstable that way."

Tooe said, "Tomorrow, I help with refine and store?"

"Yes," Dane said. He hesitated, then said, "Tazcin. You spoken much with her?"

"Some. No Terran, only Tath, and language of Parkku, Siere."

"Do you see any rank problems ahead?"

"Rank. Like Rip." Tooe's crest wriggled through a complicated pattern, a little like fingers waving.

"Yes. I'm trying to think ahead, study. Be ready for further trading." He paused between words, not sure how much to say—or if anything should be said.

Tooe merely looked inquiring.

Dane shrugged, gave up. "Let's hit the rack."

Tooe bobbed her head and took off, swarming down the ladder. Dane grinned, and followed more slowly.

It was nearly two weeks later when Rip Shannon walked back to the *Queen* from the Trader camp.

He'd been away for what he thought of as forty-eight hours—though more correctly it had been thirty-nine, two days' local time—caught by a sudden, exceptionally vicious storm that had raged without cease for nearly the entire period.

He and Jasper had been visiting the Traders, monitoring the refining process, which required frequent tuning, as the composition of the ore eggs varied wildly. He hadn't intended to spend the night there—though as yet he was the only one who hadn't. He'd felt that duty required him to stay at least part of each day with the *Queen*, lest something occur that would require him to be on hand.

The others had slowly but surely begun mixing more freely back and forth. Particularly during the past six or seven days, any given sleep period one could find at least one Trader bunked down in the tiny passenger cabins, and at least one of the *Queen*'s crew high in the Trader camp among the trees.

Rip was glad that he'd ended up staying there. He'd

learned more just by watching and listening than he could have done reading a datafile, or even by asking questions. Too much occurred that one never thought to ask about. For instance, he'd tried to compile a list of the Traders' official functions. As the days went by, it became increasingly clear that they changed their titles to fit their audiences.

"Are you the engineer?" Tooe had asked Kamsin, instructed by Stotz.

"Yes," Kamsin had said.

Tazcin had admitted to being comtech, and Lossin navigator—but then, not five days later, Stotz returned from a long, apparently satisfying work session building one more egg scooper—all they had parts for—and reported, quite casually, that Tazcin was one hell of a biochemist.

"I thought she was the comtech," Rip had asked.

Johan shrugged—this was not his area, which meant he shut it out of his mind. "Schooled in biomech," he said. "Read translations of Dzay'yi of Riez's doctorate on quantum effects at the intracellular level in school, just as I did. But came at it from a different perspective."

He shook his head. "Still can't *like* it . . . not exactly. But she's modified a slime mold to lay down a biosuperconductor mesh inside our biohaz suits, to protect us against EM much the same way the Taths' fur does." Unconcerned with questions of job definition, Stotz had then disappeared down to his engine room to grab some needed tools.

The same thing happened when Ali got to talking to Parkku, who, now fully recovered, turned out to be able to communicate in Terran. She also claimed to be a trained comtech, at least to Kamil, and in truth, Ali said, her help in designing the EM ore-egg detectors he was working on had been invaluable.

Rip finally realized that the Traders were in fact trained to cover whatever job was needed. Some apparently preferred different kinds of work or had talents in specific jobs. But unlike Terrans, who were most comfortable when each had his or her professional niche and understood placement within the hierarchical status, the Traders were just the opposite. Tazcin had been forced into position as final arbiter on the grounds of her age. The captain and the cook-steward had been the only fixed positions on board the *Ariadne*. Everyone else had served in rotations at each job.

While staying in the camp, Rip had learned that Parkku and the other Berran, Irrba, were life-mates. There were other kin connections: Tazcin was Kamsin's mother, and unfortunately, Vrothin had lost a kind of cousin to the pirates who had killed the *Ariadne*'s crew.

Vrothin had been the most affected, but not the only one. Kinship was important to the Tath, and they were all connected in some way. Vrothin's cousin should have stayed, but had been lured to go with the *Ariadne* by the prospect of the bright lights and fun spots of Exchange—and since the ship needed an extra hand, the kin-group had been split this way.

Before sleeping the Tath performed a memorial ritual for the lost one. Rip, falling asleep on another platform, had listened to the deep voices rising and falling on droning notes that reminded him of some kind of ancient Terran wind instruments, their voices augmented by the eternal wind in the trees, and the steady plash of rain on the leaves. A strange experience, he thought as he bowed into the icy wind. So alien, and yet strangely familiar in unexpected ways. It called up an old memory, the sad voices singing at the memorial for his grandfather, killed in a freak accident when Rip was very small.

The *Queen* was just ahead, flaring in the occasional flares of lightning. The discharges seemed to be getting longer as the days passed and the sunspot cycle neared its peak; during storms the thunder was often continuous for hours, varying only in pitch and loudness, like the drums of a senseless symphony. Rip keyed his helmet com, and the lock slid open. Rip fought his way up the ramp, leaning against the wall in relief when the wind and weather were closed off. His ears popped as he yawned rackingly. Tau said the fatigue might be from the pulses of energy pouring through them from the rocks below, flexed by the tides and the deep-plunging roots of the trees.

Jasper Weeks appeared in the hatchway above.

"Anything to report?" Jasper asked, pulling off his gloves and working his cold hands.

"No coms," Jasper said. "Dr. Siere is in the lab with Craig. Tooe didn't come back with you?"

"She stayed behind. Playing some kind of computer game with Kamsin. He's apparently just about her age, and they are both addicted to hologames."

Jasper smiled. Rip noted the carving knife in Jasper's hand, and was glad. Craig had reminded them of the importance of remembering rec time as well as sleep and eating. Apparently the hardworking Jasper had taken some time out to work on his carvings.

"I'm for food, a mindless action-packed tri-D vid, and sleep, in that order," he said to Jasper as they climbed up to the galley deck. "Anything else?"

"There's apparently a lull coming in this storm series. Not much of one—but enough for them to try another mining run. This time we're going to really load up the shellboat—the comsats show it will be calm enough to up the payload almost fifty percent. And we'll transport additional crew in the flitters—with the extra egg scoopers we should be able to really clean up!"

Rip felt his good mood slipping away. "Think it'll work?"

Jasper grimaced slightly. "Slow coming back, and the bigger the load, the more unstable. If something blows up, we might have to jettison it. But they feel the pressure as much as we do. We don't have enough ore yet. We have to get more before these storms become constant."

"Will they?" Rip asked.

"Simulations all say so, but how long that'll take is anyone's guess." Jasper shrugged. "Just chance, really."

Rip nodded. "Who's going on this expedition?"

"Biggest crew we can take. Gleef sent over the report on the weather, and we just set it up, while you were on your way back from the camp. From our people, Dane, Ali, Stotz, myself. That's all the modified haz suits we've got. Both medics will come, but stay on the boat and the flitter. Tooe will watch com from the camp, and Frank here—unless you want to take that on, in which case Frank can lend a hand at the camp. From their side, all the Tath—they're the strongest—and Shoshu. The Berrans and Gleef are going to keep the refiners going. And Frank, if you take the com here."

"Nothing easier," Rip said, thinking of Shoshu, the thickset oldster from the desert world Aelsaven. He reminded Rip strongly of Karl Kosti, the big bear of a jet man now up circling round the planet with the *North Star*.

Gleef was a tall, weedy hybrid from the old Terran colonies of Stanislaus World. His skin was even darker than Rip's, his people bred for a much harsher sun than Sol, and apparently he had grown up in a place where there were harsh seasons. The EMP appeared to affect him not at all. He was even quieter than Jasper, but a fine musician on the complicated instrument peculiar to his world. When played right, it sounded like a choir of wind instruments.

Rip, satisfied with the plans, climbed up to follow through on his stated plans. He was confident that they would have some success at last.

14

★

Aboard the *North Star,* Rael Cofort drew a deep breath, then immediately felt guilty. She watched her breath cloud, the vapor blowing into the leaves of an air-rooted tomato plant. At least here, in hydroponics, her carbon dioxide recycled quickly, as plants converted it back into oxygen. The problem was, it took too long everywhere else in the ship. The emergency fans weren't efficient enough—the Traders of the *Ariadne* had evidently been adapted to higher levels of CO_2.

They'd also been adapted to lower temperatures; at this distance from the sun, with the engines down, the *North Star* was getting steadily colder. Kosti had rigged some DC heating elements, but they could use them only at the high points of their caroming orbit.

So she and the rest of the *North Star*'s crew pretty much lived in the hydro lab now, venturing out only for work forays, until the CO_2 buildup and searing cold in the cabins forced them back to the hydro again.

She adjusted her datapad on her lap, feeling the twinge of

headache fading as she moved. It always did, here in the jungle at the center of the ship. Elsewhere, as carbon dioxide levels built up, so did their headaches, along with lethargy and rapid breathing. She'd warned the others of what to expect when they first cut power, and though nobody complained, she knew the others surely suffered as much from the symptoms as she did.

It helped to have work at hand. She was combing through their planetary survey data with Jellico's and Ya's help. Her datapad was linked to the ship's computers via low-energy infrared transmission; very low power operation of computers, like hydroponics buried deep within the ship for safety's sake, was undetectable. Her medical education had led her to question the effect of the extreme EM levels of Hesprid IV on the *Solar Queen*'s crew, which in turn had led her to build a model of the storm systems.

The work was slow, and she frequently rechecked the data because it seemed what she was getting was impossible. Yet it seemed to checkout; they were in real danger. Despite her present physical discomforts, she wondered how the crew on the planet were functioning. And what was going on with the *Ariadne* survivors? Were they part of the pirates after all—or not? But mostly she wondered how the EM had affected the *Solar Queen* crew? They'd been there over two weeks.

There was a muffled snort from one of the other sleeping harnesses rigged around the perimeter of the lab. Rael turned her head in time to see Steen Wilcox sit up and rub his eyes. His coat bulged and rippled; Rael smiled as she watched him unfasten it, and a black-and-white cat leaped out.

The cat bounded expertly off bulkheads, floor, and ceiling, then disappeared out the hatchway with a twitch of its tail, bent on its own errand.

"So much for keeping warm," Wilcox grumbled.

Silently Rael reached for the pack of jakek tubes and tossed him one. With a nod of thanks the navigator caught it, tabbed the heat mechanism, and opened the tube. His eyes closed as he sipped.

"Ahhh," he said.

Rael knew from Jellico's earlier report—he had been especially complete—just how cold the control deck was. Its central position in the ship, the high moisture content, and the presence of the humans and cats, kept the hydro relatively comfortable.

She was just settling back to force her mind back to her task again when there was a blur of movement and the captain reappeared from his latest check on the control deck. Since the ship was blind except for brief glimpses at safe parts of their orbit, there was no need for a constant watch. And if the pirates found them, they couldn't power up fast enough to escape.

So far, the pirates had not found them, ricocheting as they were, just like a billiard ball, from high orbit to low, around the moons, out and in.

Rael looked forward to their next run in close to the planet, only so they could flush the air again, regulate the temp for just a while, and take care of other necessities.

She scanned Jellico's face, saw nothing there to alarm her.

It had been a very long two weeks—sometimes in her sleep it seemed they had been tumbling about this system endlessly and would forever after. But on their last check Jellico had been sufficiently happy with the complex course that he and Steen had worked out that they had needed only one correction so far. Again, it had been done close to the planet, so the EM would mask their presence.

Jellico settled into the harness next to hers—she saw then how his jacket bulged, and she laughed, this time out loud, as he unzipped it and the second cat emerged.

Jellico's eyes glinted with humor. "Made it an order. No one does control deck duty without taking a cat. Can stand the cold a lot longer—in fact, it was the cee-oh-two that drove me out, not the cold."

Alpha (or was it Omega? the two cats looked exactly alike) flipped off the bunk, purring loudly, and vanished out the hatchway.

"How's your work progressing?" he asked her.

Unspoken among all of them was the need to communicate, to use the seemingless endless time to keep their minds busy. She could have answered in a very few words; instead, she said, "Tang has been giving me help. He's rigged some elegant matrices for me, to compensate for the lower power. The model I'm building takes into account solar energy, the sunspot cycle, vulcanism, ocean currents, and all the rest."

"Using data from the comsats?" Jellico asked.

"Tang copied the latest data from our last power-up," she said, nodding. "It's a fascinating—if frightening—picture. I have an idea that there is going to be significant interest in the scientific community over this data."

"Which ought to bring us significant profit," Jellico said. "Well, we've earned it."

If we live to spend it. She didn't say it, but Rael could tell from the sudden narrowing of his eyes that he'd shared the same thought.

"I think I'll tour about, see if Kosti needs a hand in Engineering," Steen said.

Rael appreciated that the others tried to leave the captain and his wife alone from time to time. They all lived crowded in this little area, making each hyperaware of the others. Rael had noted, without commenting, how much care each of these men took to accommodate the others. She did her own part, leaving the men alone from time to time, so they could change their clothing in relative comfort—or just indulge in some male talk, without the politeness they felt due to the captain's lady.

A politeness, she'd noted, that disappeared when she was called on to function as a medic. Then she seemed to transform into a faceless, genderless medical figure—an alteration inspired by respect for her training, another human quirk that she secretly appreciated.

Jellico was squinting at the datapad on her lap.

With difficulty she dragooned her scattering thoughts back to the work at hand.

"Those readings correct?" he asked.

"They are indeed," she said.

Jellico's face tightened, and Rael realized his thoughts had gone beyond the scientific data to the eight crewmembers caught down on the planet underneath that spectacularly building ion storm.

"They don't lift off in, what—" He squinted at the data again.

"It looks like about ten days. If I were down there, I'd set it at eight for a safety margin," Rael said, her innards tightening as she tapped at the keys. "Ten days."

Jellico drew in a slow breath, then rubbed his temples. His eyes opened, their blue gaze strained. "Rip will wait until the last minute, to get as much ore as possible."

Rael looked at the numbers and shook her head. It was only marginally comforting to know that Craig Tau was also with the *Queen* and thus must have the same data that she had—which could be dinned into Rip's ears. But what other problems was Rip dealing with?

Míceál was thinking on about strategy. ". . . because that's the only way the two ships can synchronize without communication—an obvious rendezvous time."

His expression brightened, and he smacked his fist lightly into his open palm. "That's it. That's what he'll do. Which means now we can plan intelligently."

He launched himself off his sleep harness, and disappeared with a speed and grace that reminded Rael of the cats.

"The first question that comes to my mind," Van Ryke said a little while later, "is whether or not the pirates have also come to the same conclusion."

They were all gathered in the hydro lab.

Kosti grunted. "They have to have good scan gear. And they must know about the comsats."

Rael said, "Assuredly. But they might not know how to interpret the comsat data—if they're even reading it. Pirates put their money into weapons, not science officers."

Tang Ya nodded agreement. "They have to be watching the light show down there. An idiot could guess that it's building toward something. But I agree with Rael; they probably don't have the data to project a deadline."

"If they don't know, we've got an edge," Steen Wilcox said, cradling a tube of jakek in his hands.

"Whether they know or not, we've got to do what makes sense," Jellico said. "I am just about certain that Rip is watching this model down there, or one like it, and is going to push up against the deadline as close as possible. For one thing, the ion storm will give him some protection."

Steen said, "We can watch the pirates' orbits as the time approaches. That ought to tell us if they're onto the same idea."

"So where does that put us?" Karl Kosti asked.

Jellico jabbed his finger toward the planet. "Waiting right where they'll least think to look for us—synchronous right over the *Queen,* masked by the EM. Maybe we can shake them up a little when the *Queen* lifts."

Karl frowned, then his craggy face altered. He laughed, and slapped his knee. "Thereon's Shadow! That's a sweet idea."

"Sweet and damned dangerous," Steen said. "If these Shver are armed with colloid blasters, we have absolutely no protection. And if we're sitting right above the *Queen,* and they figure it out, we won't have to paint a target on the side of the ship."

Kosti pointed with his chin toward Rael's datapad, which had been positioned in a place so all could see its small screen. "The building solar storm is distorting the electromagnetic field around Hesprid, so the blasters will have erratic aim. Charged particles wreak havoc with tuned plasma jets."

Rael nodded in realization—Steen and Míceál had both been down in the jet area helping him to retune the jets for the tremendous magnetic storm raging around Hesprid IV. It was the worst space weather, said Kosti, that he'd ever seen. The blasters would be especially hard to aim in the magnetopause of Hesprid or the moons—at the edge of their magnetic fields—where the flow of the solar wind was turbulent and unpredictable.

"That's what makes a fight possible," said Jellico, grabbing the datapad. "We know where they'll have to be to have a chance of hitting us."

He, Steen, and Van Ryke began a dense three-way tactical discussion over Jellico's datapad. Rael, looking over Jellico's shoulder, watched the plots changing as they ran simulations of possible pirate tactics. This was an area she had only the sketchiest knowledge of—and she could see Ya watching intently, probably thinking the same. Computers and communications gear he knew to an extent that was almost frightening. The vagaries of human action and reaction seemed to be beyond him.

Human beings had been her study. Not human beings at war—she knew best how to patch them up afterward, or how to deal with the terrible emotional consequences when patching didn't work. She loathed war, the mindless destruction, the horrible fallout. There was no purpose to war in her view. Though she had tested extremely high in all subjects in childhood, she had never had any difficulty turning down offers to train in the military.

The discussion ended abruptly, and she realized she hadn't heard the result as her mind had been wandering. Not that it mattered. Whatever decisions needed to be made had been done; Jellico moved with characteristic speed as he flicked the datapad back to Rael's program and then launched himself out of the hydro.

"Course changes?" Rael asked, looking up at Jan Van Ryke.

"Yes indeed, Doctor," the cargo master said, looking pleased. "He'll be going to lay up the course changes necessary over the next few days to put us in a position to take up synchronous orbit without using a lot of energy, which would make us more detectable."

Steen's thin, dour face wore a peculiar smile as he handed

himself up to his sleep harness. "Damn, but he's fast," he said
quietly. "I ran high scores in nav school on tactics—it was like
a game to me—but he can outthink me every time. Not that
I would have anything different, but I wonder why he didn't
go into the military."

"Our captain was raised in a military family," Van Ryke
said, and Rael nodded. Míceál Jellico seldom talked about his
past, but every so often he'd make a comment, or an obser-
vation, that seemed to draw on past experience, and a close
listener could put these together into a fairly coherent picture.

"And he has a long memory," Ya said. "Probably another
family trait, besides the smarts and the honesty. All it would
take is one bad command from some crooked or self-serving
brass, and that would be that."

"Free Trader captain is his own man—or woman," Steen
said.

"The gift of command," Rael said softly.

"Which Rip might discover in himself," Jan murmured,
reaching for the jakek.

A sudden sobriety gripped the others, and Rael, sensitive
always to atmosphere and mood, wondered if they were
doubting the young man—not his abilities, but whether or not
someone so new to command could cope with a set of circumstances that would be trying even to an experienced captain. Would he follow through on his end, or was Míceál just
projecting himself into the younger man, and hoping?

They wouldn't know until the last minute.

Fighting the headache that eternally threatened to return,
Rael decided she'd speculated enough. It was time to bury
herself in work, hoping the time would pass faster.

15

Inside the *Queen,* Ali dropped his hazard gear on his bunk, and stared down at the medicine case on his desk.

"It might interfere with quick thought," Craig had warned. "Not to mention your reflexes. If you feel you have to take the drug, at least use the smallest dose possible."

Ali did not want to jeopardize the others. Of course. On the other hand, a man with half a brain could make certain he took jobs that guaranteed risk only to himself.

In the meantime, there was the prospect of being penned up with Dane and Jasper in a very small space for long hours, while all were under tremendous stress.

Defiantly he bent down, grabbed a full dose of the medication, and swallowed it. Then he jammed his way into his winter gear, hating the bitter taste of the meds, but angrily welcoming the sensation of an invisible cotton blanket settling over his mind. Or at least over the part of mind that insisted on bleeding over into others' minds.

It did fuzz the speed of his thoughts, but he knew his

thought processes, and for that matter his reflexes, were much faster than most people's.

The annoying thing was that though the others might not be as fast, they were not stupid. They sensed the diminution in his speed—he knew it just from the occasional glances, the tightened mouths. No one discussed it with him, which was just the way he wanted it. Nor, from everything he could tell (and he had exerted himself to find out), did they talk around him. They didn't talk at all, not about *that*.

Good. Don't talk about it, mask the effect, and it would go away. Wither and die, like an unwatered weed, or a muscle that was never used. Made perfect sense.

Perfect way to handle a subject that made no sense at all.

Ali thrust it from his thoughts, impatient with himself for permitting it to creep into his mind even for a few seconds.

He hustled up to the mess cabin, where the others were gathered.

"Any change in plans?" he asked.

"Let's move," Dane Thorson said, pushing a half cup of something hot into his hands.

Ali swallowed some jakek, ignoring the slight burn. He welcomed the fierce heat inside. It would help him to fight the cold longer.

He drank down the rest, blinking against the burn-sting in his eyes, stashed the cup, and followed Dane's impressive bulk down to the cargo bay. When all suited up, the Viking looked almost like one of the Tath, except he wasn't furry and didn't smell like a rain-soaked mutt.

Ali climbed into the flitter. None of the Tath were with them yet, but the odor clung to the craft from their previous visits. Ali breathed through his mouth to avoid smelling the stink. It didn't seem to bother the others—even Sinbad, the ship's cat, seemed to like the Tath, and one would think a cat would instinctively recoil from their distinctive aroma.

The drug seemed to help with that, Ali had noticed. It muted all sensation a little. He closed his eyes, trying to get his nose to adjust. He really liked the Tath as individuals, and in their camp, with the constantly moving air, they were more bearable. Of course one couldn't ask them to shampoo their fur—the natural oils in it that would wash away were the ones that protected them against the extremes of temperature and humidity.

Ali opened his eyes again as Stotz eased the flitter out of the cargo-bay door. He strongly suspected that there was one other who also had an aversion to the Tath smell, and that was their refined feline medic. Of course Siere would never say anything, but Ali had noticed the silver fur around the medic's slender neck ruffling when the Tath suddenly entered a closed space, accompanied by the inevitable odor.

As they reached the rendezvous point, Ali sat up straight and made himself focus on what the others were saying. The bad side of the drug was how, if he hadn't eaten recently, it had a tendency to make his mind wander down odd paths. He winced inwardly. What a waste of time, castigating the Tath for something they couldn't help.

". . . so the tidal scouring has been minimized," Stotz said. "There should be a lot of eggs here, although, again, be prepared for some climbing. You'll plant these"—he held up a small luminescent greenish yellow cone, another Tath barnacle device—"where you find ore eggs, for Lossin, Tazcin, and Vrothin running the egg scoopers. It's tuned to the frequency of Ali's eggfinders. The flash is pretty bright."

"Got it," Dane said, sounding—as always—as unperturbable as an ice floe.

On Ali's other side, Jasper just nodded quietly.

Ali wondered if Weeks was also taking the drug. Not that there was any sign of slowness or any kind of insufficiency in the jet man's work. He was just quieter than before, if such a thing were possible. Was his mind wandering as well, because of that blanketing effect of the drug?

Ali gave a mental shrug. He wouldn't ask; that would be breaking the promise—worse, letting *that* take hold of his thoughts again.

He tried to relax, watching intently out the viewport next

to his seat. Overhead stretched a fleecy ceiling of gray cloud, but far to the west a greenish belt of clear sky beckoned, fading as the terminator swept ahead of them, bringing night, and safety from the Floaters. Occasional flickers of lightning from high above them threatened soundlessly, briefly washing out the running lights of the shellboat almost a kilometer below them.

Ali craned his neck, but the source of the high lightning—quite rare, according to the databanks—could not be seen. It had started quite suddenly, and increased in frequency almost daily. And the comsats reported that the aurora borealis of the planet had stretched over an increasing area of the strange world as the particle storm from the uneasy sun lashed Hesprid IV with growing intensity.

A blinking light caught his attention: a com request from the Trader camp. The interruption was welcome. He leaned forward to tap the link.

"Here speak Gleef," came a musical, accented voice. "Inform all, developing squall, possible tornadoes. We warn you, watch weather scope." He clicked off; he didn't speak Terran—had probably gotten the words from Tooe—so he wouldn't understand an acknowledgment.

"Tornadoes at night?" Stotz slewed around to stare at them.

Jasper looked up from his work on his hand comp. "Gleef knows weather. He's been predicting this, just didn't know when. There's an extensive rift system east of us, lots of heat energy pumping into the seas, which are shallow there." He help up his hand comp. "I just ran some numbers based on the barometric and wind-direction readings he flashed us on the screen. If there's any more velocity from the south, or the barometer drops here"—he tapped his screen—"then we'd better move out."

Stotz nodded. "I'll get Lossin on the com, see what they think."

A few moments later the Tath's voice rumbled into the flitter's cabin: "We have seen this pattern before. Very common on Gleef homeworld. Here, normally only in winter. Bad change for us."

"But we should go ahead?" Stotz asked.

"Yes. We think. Must get ore. But if barometer change, wind change, we return."

Stotz looked around at the others. Ali saw Dane nod agreement, and he also nodded. Weeks did as well.

"We're with you," Stotz said.

It was completely dark now, the shellboat only a minute pattern of colored lights far below. No stars could penetrate the thick cloud cover, but Ali thought he could detect at least two faint patches of light, one much larger than the other, that indicated the presence of two of Hesprid IV's three moons. He tapped at the little miniconsole in his seat arm, and the screen obligingly delivered a simple graphic of the tidal bulge sweeping toward them. Even if the storm was slow, the tides would chase them away eventually. Ali looked up again, wondering if any of the occluded stars were ones he knew, suns whose light had once bathed him on a planetary surface, secure in gravity's embrace.

Rip would know, of course. Ali contented himself with leaning back in his seat, very aware that this brief hour's respite was the only rest he was going to get for a long time.

"Got the signals straight?" Johan asked abruptly.

Ali said, "Want a repeat?"

And together he, Dane, and Jasper recited the various emergency signals they'd concocted, all in case the winds were so bad that there was interference on the com—or they just couldn't hear voices.

After that Johan and Jasper went on to discuss contingency plans for the boat. Ali felt his attention slipping again, but this time he didn't mind. Jasper, as the lightest man, was to stay on board the boat and man the com there and work the controls.

Ali found the time disappearing faster than he'd thought; suddenly Stotz said, "Here we are. Get your stuff together. Let's make every second count. You know the Tath will."

Ali paid close attention as the flitter settled to the sand. He could see the shellboat approaching through the surf. He watched, fascinated, as the biodevice crawled up the beach— through the outside pickup he could hear the scrunch-slither of the motive-scales on its underside. When it came to rest, Dane and Stotz hopped out and began to unload the egg scoopers; Ali felt his ears pop as the wind eddied coldly into the flitter in the few seconds the hatch was opened. Their task finished, the two motioned Ali and Weeks to come out.

Ali obediently settled his helmet tightly onto his head, checked to make sure everything was in working order, then pulled his gloves on. Weeks did the same, and they popped the hatch again and sprang out.

At once the terrible wind did its best to flatten Ali onto his face. Despite his gear, cold leeched in, making his extremities ache. He resolutely ignored it and followed Dane as they began work.

It was probably the worst four hours of his entire life.

He found it hard to concentrate, and wished he'd eaten something. The increasing lightning to the east was no help, tickling his retinas from his peripheral vision and adding to his sense of danger—of something not right.

He fought that off, telling himself it was just his body re-acting to the increased static in the air. But the wind smacked at them with cruel force, and distant thunder muttered fairly constantly, reminding him that just being there was dangerous.

After a couple hours of hard labor, many slips, and tire-some climbing, he paused to look up, and became aware of long, silent flares of light overhead, streaking through the clouds like meteors. No one else spoke, though, so he kept silent and turned his attention back to his work.

The only satisfaction he had was that the handgunlike sen-sors he'd designed for finding the ore eggs functioned properly—but his satisfaction was considerably diminished by the explosive belchlike squeal they emitted when triggered. The ore eggs, like the ore beds, responded to the sonic burst with pulses of light, which a sensitive detector could pick up. Unfortunately, the sound was in a frequency range that made it feel like knives being pushed into Ali's ears.

Before their searches took each of the members of the team out of sight of each other, he noticed that Siere's fur was standing on end along his backbone and cheeks, and his ears were flattened. The ear plugs didn't seem to help any of them except the imperturbable Tath, who gave no sign of discomfort.

But the effort of bracing himself against the repeated sound, of slogging through muck that sucked at his boots and made his feet feel as if they were in triple gee, soon began to exhaust Ali. Worse was when he had to climb the slippery rock, sheeted with runoff from pools of rainwater in the pitted rock dome. Occasionally, exfoliated sheets of stone rocked under his feet. Ali fell down painfully several times.

He was falling more often, now, he noticed hazily as he rose from the last. Was the wind worsening, or was it the physical stress? He went on, moving painfully in isolation, for so bad was the interference from the sunspots that their coms were almost useless, so nobody really talked except for terse reports of egg deposits on the common channel.

He didn't even have the long trip to make, he realized, straightening up and peering as best he could into the darkness. He clicked his helmet light into high intensity, and saw a vague shadow moving about in the distance. The Tath had all taken the outside perimeter, and left the inner area to the lighter Terrans.

The problem was, their territory had virtually no more ore eggs.

A shadow loomed on the edge of Ali's vision; he turned his head. His light fell on Johan Stotz, nearly buried in his gear, his gloves blotched from the thick mud.

Ali's com lit, his own frequency, and Stotz's voice came into his head: "Wind's rising."

"It's getting harder and harder to find more eggs, though

I'm sure there are more," Ali replied. "The pulses are getting too close to the noise level for direction-finding. We'll have to go out farther—"

Jasper's voice overrode them: "We've got a problem." And then came the signal for everyone to clear their coms. Ali clicked over to the frequency they'd agreed to share with the Tath.

Jasper said: "Barometric pressure dropping, winds veering southerly. On the scope it looks like we've got a bunch of funnels forming about an hour east. Go ahead, Lossin."

They heard Lossin translating for his fellow crewmembers. There was a swift exchange, then Lossin said, "How much ore in the hold?"

"We're at about sixty percent of our goal."

More talk—Ali looked around as he listened. There had been faint responses in this area on his first pass, but he'd ignored such in favor of the stronger pulses. There might still be a few eggs to find. He said so, and Stotz agreed.

"Let's keep working for half an hour, then pull out," the engineer suggested.

Again Lossin translated, then his deep voice came: "Is agreed."

A surge of adrenaline made Ali's mind flicker—as if reaching—but it reached the cotton barrier, and he laughed to himself. Foiled, esperite, he thought, picking his way over a jagged section of broken rock.

Careful triangulation finally yielded a sizable cache of eggs deep in a water-filled crevice. When Stotz arrived with an egg scooper, he helped him manhandle the bot up the slope to the crevice. Even with eight legs, the machines maneuvered with difficulty around those domes that were too broken and steep in approach.

The half hour elapsed in what felt like half a day of throbbing bruises and cloudy mind. Then came the return journey, slowly and carefully, the complex eightfold clicking of the egg scooper's feet on the rock an odd counterpoint to Ali's fierce concentration. He was nearly crawling; he didn't have the time to fall on his face and have to retrieve everything once again. Stotz and he didn't speak, for the wind was so strong now that it was impossible to hear without shouting. He sighed in relief when he finally saw the ore boat. He reached it at the same time as Stotz. Stotz ran the egg scooper into the hold of the shellboat and put it in reverse mode. As it began unloading ore eggs into the storage bin, Stotz came back down the ramp and said, "There's about two men's worth just down that rise. Did you find anything bigger?"

"No. I got most of it—all that was left were little nuggets. Must have fallen on a rock and broken." Behind them the rapid clank of ore eggs spitting from the proboscis on the egg scooper dwindled and ceased. Stotz retrieved the machine and steered it back away from the boat.

"This way."

They started walking.

"Where's the Viking? I haven't seen him," Ali commented.

"Went out further afield, with the Tath. With the interference, we probably won't hear from him until he comes back into range. But there's some big stuff out there—more than the scoopers could handle."

"We need a dozen more scoopers."

"We need scoopers and carriers and an extra ship, and while we're at it, some good weather and sunshine and beautiful women who like nothing better than entertaining a bunch of scruffy Free Traders by lolling around beside a hot mineral bath and feeding us peeled grapes."

Stotz rarely descended to sarcasm; Ali enjoyed it when he did. They moved as quickly as possible—Ali once shooting out his hand to steady the senior engineer when he stumbled. Another time Stotz caught Ali by the back of his coat just after Ali's foot slipped on a rock that had seemed steady, and he nearly pitched into a muddy pool.

They reached the deposit site.

"I'd say we've got at least three loads here," said Stotz. "There's a batch in the crevice over there." He steered the scooper over, and as it began to nuzzle into the crevice, the eggtube stretching alarmingly, Ali turned and began to load his shoulder bags with eggs from the pile that had formed in a V-shaped pocket of stone. He filled four pairs of shoulder bags before Stotz returned with the egg scooper, its bag bulging with eggs carefully balanced on top.

Stotz sent out a general call. "Anyone near us? We've got at least two extra loads here."

Ali half listened as he bent to lay down the last pair of shoulder bags. A movement in the corner of his vision made him straighten up.

"Johan, look!" He pointed at the barnacle lights the cache had been marked with. They were flickering: not the flash of response to the eggfinder guns, but a faint stutter of light.

Suddenly the shoulder bags and even the tartan collector bag of the egg scooper glowed as all the ore eggs lit up inside them, but before either of them could react the ground jolted underfoot and a grumbling roar built up as the terrifying accelerated jerking of a violent quake shook the island.

Ali fell heavily, but the flash of red through his head had nothing to do with the pain in his knee. Although the mental flash registered as pain, it didn't hurt, and then the cotton smothered it. He realized then that it wasn't his, and his anger drove out fear even as the rumbling died away. The ground gave one last admonitory jolt, then stilled. Ali glanced up— and was nearly blinded when a vast sheet of lightning ripped across the entire sky.

Ali blinked the afterimage away and cursed, fluently and with as much descriptive invective as he could command, not caring who heard. He stopped only when he fell, and gouged his hip on a rock so sharply it drove the breath from his body. As Stotz bent to help him up he became aware that the com channel was full of questions zinging back and forth in at least three languages.

After a few minutes, Ali realized he'd sorted the voices. Dane and one of the Tath had not been heard from, which meant they must still be out of range. Meanwhile the others had decided to get on with the job of getting the extra ore back to the shellboat while waiting for those last two to report in.

As Lossin clicked off, a huge shape loomed out of the darkness, and into the light of Johan's helmet lamp. "Tazcin here."

She bent to load up, and grabbed twice what Ali could carry. Ali winced silently, wondering if the Tath thought the Terrans no more helpful than children, and when it was his turn he grabbed more than was comfortable.

The next twenty minutes were grim. He placed each foot carefully, walking bent over in a crablike position, knowing if he fell he'd not be able to break that fall—and of course his ore would scatter in four directions. His thighs soon ached with an insistence that overrode the drug in his system, while the wind howled over the rocks and battered them, cruelly and sublimely indifferent.

They finally reached the boat, with twelve minutes left of the half hour—not enough time to go out again. Ali, whose legs were trembling, was secretly relieved; he knew he would not last through another journey—not without rest. And even then, he thought, as a sudden vicious blast of wind slammed him into the side of the ore boat. Even with the helmet taking most of the impact, his head rang, and for several seconds he was unable to understand the voices now speaking over the comlink.

But the urgency in the voices penetrated the haze, and Ali realized something was wrong. With a flash of guilt, he realized he'd forgotten about Dane and the other Tath.

Then he saw the light indicating Jasper wanted to talk to him on a private channel. Ali tabbed the accept, and Jasper said: "Did you feel that mental flash, during the quake?"

Ali gritted his teeth. This was breaking the promise— giving in. "What are you talking about?"

Jasper sighed. "Then it was just me? I'm afraid Dane's in trouble. It was pain that I got, the sharpest ever."

Ali looked around, but Thorson's tall form was not among the Tath moving around the loader.

"Didn't you hear? He's not answering."

Ali tabbed Jasper off and keyed Dane's frequency. Nothing. He tried it again. Still nothing. He looked up, scanning slowly in all directions. Lossin and Dane Thorson were missing. Alarmed, he contacted Jasper again. "He hasn't reported in?"

"No. Vrothin lost sight of him about ten minutes before the quake. His com was damaged, and he couldn't report."

"Do they have a location for him?"

"Didn't send one. I have his location at the time of the contact. Lossin is on the way there now—hang on."

Ali clicked into the common channel and heard Lossin report.

"Lossin report now. I have reached Dane's last position. Nothing there. No answer."

Ali switched back to Jasper's private channel. "What do we do?"

Ali heard Jasper draw a harsh breath, then the jet man said, "Did you—can you—get a location?"

Ali was about to snap that he didn't have any instruments, but he knew what Jasper meant. And the situation was too dangerous to be squawking about promises now. "No," he said. "Can't you?"

"I don't get location," Jasper murmured apologetically. "Emotions only."

I do, Ali thought. *Thorson and I both get location. Damn, damn, damn!* He squeezed his eyes shut, for the first time trying to open himself to the connection. Except—how? He tried to imagine where Dane was, and his mind obediently produced various images—Dane falling into a pit, clinging to the side of a cliff, buried under rock. But Ali knew it was all imagination, sparked by fear.

He tried to empty his mind of all thought and just wait . . . but all he was aware of was the soft cotton blanket over his mind, muting everything.

"Ali?" It was Jasper. "I apologize—"

"No. It's all right. But I can't get anything."

Jasper clicked off.

Lossin appeared a minute or so later, bent almost double against the shrieking wind.

Tazcin went up to him, spoke. Ali saw Lossin wave back, and they talked animatedly for a time, then Tazcin turned to Stotz and waved a hand. Ali realized he'd keyed off the general com, and quickly tabbed it on again.

". . . risk search? You must decide."

Johan's voice came, tight and grim: "I don't think I can walk in that wind. Look, can we sweep over his last reported location with the flitters?"

"We shall do that."

"All in," Stotz ordered. "Fast."

They piled into their flitter, mud and wet forgotten. The shellboat began crawling back into the surf as the Stotz activated the flitter controls. The craft's wings were drawn in hard against the hull, presenting a minimal surface to the winds. Even through the muzziness of his mind, Ali could see that in this configuration they had very little fuel to spare. In tense silence the two flitters sped across the island, then circled around. Again they circled, wider, and then a third time— though by now the fuel gauge was flashing red.

Finally Stotz said, "We can't risk all our lives. We have to return."

No one spoke.

Jasper pulled out of the circle and began the long, dangerous flight back home.

Ali pulled off his helmet and gloves, and dropped his head into his hands.

16

★

The roar of jets startled Dane.

Get out of the way! Get off the launchpad . . .

He couldn't move. "Get out . . . the ship is about to launch . . ."

Ship? He was a child, having sneaked out to watch the great Trader ships launch out toward unknown worlds—

No, it was the *Solar Queen,* his home—

North Star was now his home.

The images splintered and spun away, leaving darkness—and the roar, and awareness of cold, and pain.

Dane opened his eyes, saw the faint glow of his helmet controls. Reflected in them, in running green and red and yellow streaks, was streaming water. What had happened? He'd been unconscious, and was grateful he'd kept his faceplate closed. He tried to read the time, but the only result was a lightning stab of pain as his eyes tried and failed to focus that close.

Now to assess the rest of the damage. He keyed the helmet

light, which flared obediently, then died down to a faint glow. He reached for his auxiliary power pack, then gasped as pain wracked his body. He fell back, fighting for breath. Head— moved side to side. Ached, and his neck ached. Concussion? Had to have hit his head pretty hard on a rock for it to hurt through the helmet. Hands—right, left. Arms. Shoulders. Back—though there was a twinge from—

Right leg. The left moved fine. Right foot intact, but again there was a warning winge from his knee. Dane realized he'd fallen, twisted his leg, and hit his head. He was hurt, but alive.

So now to report, and let them know where he was.

He tabbed the comlink on the general broadcast frequency. "Jasper?"

He waited. The light glowed orange, but there was no response.

He clicked over to Jasper's personal line, and when that did not work, he tried Johan, and then Ali.

No response.

His head ached, making clear thought hard. The power measure showed that the helmet was midway in emergency-power mode, which meant it ought to be strong enough for the comsignal.

Nevertheless he levered himself up carefully, making certain not to move his leg, and detached the aux power pack from his utility belt. Some quick fumbling and he had it hooked up to the helmet.

Now he could tab on the helmet light. He scanned the area, found that he had fallen in the lee of a huge outthrust of rock—which also had probably saved his life. He became aware of the roaring again, a combination of wind and rain. A glance out and he saw the rain falling in sheets, blown almost vertical. He was on a slight rise, so the water coming round either side of his rock ran down and out of sight.

He wedged himself with his back to the rock and, centimeter by centimeter, straightened his leg. The effort left him shaking and bathed in sweat. When that was done he tried once again to alert Jasper on the boat.

Again, no answer. It was then that he thought to check the time. For a moment he stared blankly at the readout, wondering if the low power had cut out the time, then he realized he had only an hour until dawn.

An hour until dawn. He knew what had happened: the others had been forced to return to the camp. He'd been left for dead.

And in an hour, when the sun came up, and the fog drifted over the island, he would be dead.

He sat back and closed his eyes.

"I'm going back."

Ali's voice was soft, uninflected, but Rip took one look at those glittering, angry dark eyes and realized with a nasty roiling in his guts that he was about to face yet another unbearable decision.

There's no winner here, he thought in despair.

Out loud, "You can't."

Ali flung up a hand, his tendons rigid. "I'm not asking for orders. Or permission. I'm telling you where I'm going."

Rip waited, one full breath in, one out. When he spoke, his voice was even, not at all angry. "You can throw your life away. This is not the military—your life belongs to you. But you can't throw away that flitter."

He saw the impact of his words in the suddenly narrowed dark eyes, and then a flush of rage ridged Ali's cheekbones.

"You don't think I can bring the flitter back safely?" he asked, his mouth curving derisively. "Watch me. I can fly any atmospheric craft made, and if it takes damage, make it better than it was originally designed."

"I know your credentials," Rip said. "You don't need to list what you can fly and where you've flown it. That's not the point; the storm is subsiding, and any of us could fly there. But we don't know that those damn creatures out there can't kill you through the flitter. If you're fried inside it, you can hardly fix it when it crashes, right?"

"I'll avoid 'em—"

Now was the crux of the matter. Rip struck fast, before Ali could think. "And rescue a dead man? You'll be in a flitter. Dane's on foot."

"Thorson is not dead," Ali shot back. Then his lips parted, and he laughed, a ragged, unwilling sound. "He's *not* dead. Can't you feel it? I've known it ever since that damn drug wore off five hours ago. He's not dead, but he's hurt."

"Yes," Rip said softly. "I can feel it."

Ali turned, stepped, slammed his fist against the bulkhead of Rip's cabin. "Hellfire! It's my fault. I hate this cursed thing that's twisting my brain, hate it so bad I . . ." He shook his head violently and turned around to face Rip, his mouth pressed into a white line. "I could have found him. Jasper apparently doesn't get location. Tau even warned me to take a minimal dose, but I ignored him. Of course. I could have found Thorson—" He stopped again. "I want to go now."

"Dane's alive, but there's a good chance he won't be by the time you can get there," Rip said. "Dane himself would not want to risk lives and equipment—you know he wouldn't."

"But he's alive," Ali said. "And while there's a chance, I have to take it—or have his death on my conscience for the rest of my life."

Rip sighed, feeling pressure building behind his eyes.

"I can find him," Ali repeated. "I suspect I'll also know if he suddenly isn't alive."

Rip knew that was true as well. He rubbed his eye sockets, then looked up. "All right. Go. But don't tell any of the others. Jasper in particular. He'll want to share the danger, and we can't afford to lose more people. I'll control the cargo bay from here."

Ali whirled around and disappeared through the hatchway.

Rip dropped down at his desk and activated his computer. The control-deck main controls had been slaved to his computer, complete with alarms should anything happen while he was asleep.

Now he called up the lock controls and put the external

viewscreen on. Dawn had arrived, and already the storm was lessening. There was no sign of fog—but that could change with frightening speed. Tau was certain that the Floaters didn't actually generate the vapor, but they manipulated it somehow.

"I'm up and running." Ali's voice came, private signal, from the flitter.

"Fuel?" Rip asked.

"More than enough to make it there and back."

Rip didn't answer; he could feel Ali's mood, volatile as magma below the surface. Better to let him take action. *As if I could have stopped him.*

He tapped the lock control, wondering bleakly how Jellico would have managed to stop him—and how he was going to report this to the Old Man when the time came.

Then the flitter zapped out, banking in a flashy roll and disappearing in a tight curve round the trees.

Rip closed the lock, shut down his console, and got up tiredly to head for the galley, and hot coffee. Hot, strong, and lots.

When he got there, he found Jasper waiting silently. One glance at the pale little man's face, and he knew that Jasper had figured it all out, or enough. Jasper silently held out a steaming mug, twin to the one he held in his right hand.

Then, still in silence, they climbed up to the control deck, where Rip activated all the com signals with one quick, angry chop of his hand. Then he sat down, and Jasper dropped into the com pod.

It was going to be a long watch.

The storm subsided rapidly, and a little after dawn the clouds broke and disappeared in a sudden, dramatic line. For a brief time Dane stared with mild pleasure at the beauty of the shafts of sunlight illuminating the moisture in the air, like pillars of white-gold that ethereal creatures could climb.

The rock around him was black and rusty red and various

shades of brown. Here and there craggy outcroppings thrust upward like hands reaching for the distant sky. Marbling striations marked each, striking in their alien beauty. The ground was uneven all around, barren of any growth except some low, scrubby plants with spiny leaves. Pools of water glistened in the bright sunlight; as Dane watched, steam rose gently from them, making the air shimmer.

He took a small sip of the emergency water on his belt, then leaned back. As the sun mounted higher, the temperature rose. Soon he was roasting in his haz gear.

Wishing he was in a temp-controlled space suit, he began the long, painful trip round to the other side of his rock. What he'd do at noon, when there was no shadow—

Maybe the Floaters would be there by then.

No, don't think. Just move. Hands, then foot. Hands, foot.

He crab-walked backward, dragging his damaged leg.

It took a long time, but he had nothing but time to spend. At last he was well into the shadow, and with the last of his fading strength he took off his coat and draped it over a couple of jagged pieces of rock to make a kind of tent. The air on his neck made him feel vulnerable, but he knew that the presence or absence of a coat would not hinder the Floaters, if they came.

He smoothed out the wrinkles in his tunic, resettled his utility belt, and leaned back, closing his eyes. Slowly the throbbing in his leg subsided, enough that—almost imperceptibly—he became aware of another sensation: cool air.

He opened his eyes, felt a zing of shock when he saw the tendrils of fog snaking with dreamy laziness round the distant cliffs. Behind them, white and puffy, a white cloud glistened softly in the sun.

Dane's heart thumped against his ribs.

Instinctively he tightened his helmet over his head— knowing it wasn't going to do any good. Maybe it would hurt slightly less, he thought, amused at his own cowardice. As if anyone would ever know.

Leaning forward slightly, he scanned the landscape once again, this time for possible hiding places. None. So he leaned his head back and tried to make himself as comfortable as he could. Death was inevitable, he told himself. It was one true prediction made for each human being at birth. Now, after all his adventures, his time had come. He tried to relax, to think over his past. His mind darted from memory to memory, moments of beauty, of insight, of surprise, terror. Of anger, of justice, of humor. He tasted every strong emotion again, savoring them like the fine wines of Deneb-Gloriath. Only his heart, tapping rapidly under its steady infusion of adrenals, moved. Dane himself was still, contemplating how much of the automatic fear washing through him was question. Great question. The greatest question.

Now the fog lifted over the far rocks; in a few moments it would block the sun. Trails and curls of vapor wreathed the cliffs, like necklaces of warm-lit cotton.

Where? A sudden flash, and he sensed Rip and Jasper far away, like distant stars, their focus bright and steady. Ali was a comet, arcing across the sky.

It was just a moment's vision, then it was gone.

And so was the bright, beating sun. The white cloud drifted overhead, and Dane lifted his face to stare up into the mesmerizing whorls of silver, gray, white.

And then there it was, directly overhead, a great white bowl, gleaming with muted rainbow colors. Delicate ripples ran round its fabric, making the colors shift and glimmer. It grew; Dane realized it was coming closer. Now he could see a subtle tracery of reddish green all over the upper surface of the creature.

His heart thrummed, but he did not move. A weird calm seized his mind, shutting out his pain, fear, worries. He was alone in the universe with a being of awe, of beauty. He would die seeing beauty; he would not mar the moment by cowering against the inevitable.

The great bowl lowered. Now he could see interstices like

lacework in it, patterns of veins, all faintly glowing with rich color. Just beyond the great bowl was another, and higher still, another. A colony of them, gathering.

The great bowl rippled like a tent under the drumming of the wind, and with visionary slowness white-gold tendrils, lit softly from within, rolled down and dangled just overhead. Then, soft, gentle, they caressed his face.

A moment of cool touch, then fire exploded through his brain. He was still looking up, in question, in wonder, as the fire lit his neural pathways.

The fire was cold and hot, pain and not pain, a terrific load that his brain could not process, and he felt consciousness slipping even as his body seized. Still, thought persisted right over the edge into darkness. Thought, memory, awareness of that question—which had not come from him.

A sudden flash of white-hot pain blinded Ali. His hands flexed convulsively on the flitter controls; far away, to the northeast, he felt an echoing flash from Rip and Jasper. Then it was gone.

Cursing softly, steadily, he smacked his hand down on the speed control, and the flitter obediently surged forward. Ali thought fiercely, wishing that he could control the accursed psi link. He didn't sense that Dane was dead, but was afraid that was just his own guilt-laced fear refusing to acknowledge the truth.

He glanced at his navscreen, saw that the island was near. Shifting his eyes to the viewscreen, he saw a bump on the horizon. He guided the ship lower, and sped up even more, until the engines screamed. The deep azure of the water below rippled and boiled beneath the powerful fans as he jetted toward the island.

Now it was larger, and he saw the glow of white. He bared his teeth, hoping the fog was still there, so he could rip the flitter with savage deliberation right through it, killing as many of the damn Floater things as possible.

But the fog was drifting high and eastward, a thin blanket, and his sense of Dane's presence was growing stronger.

Ali slowed, skimming over the rocky shore and the splashing waves, up across the great red rocks. The ground blurred beneath him; then the sight of a single figure lying prone against a rock arrested his gaze.

Ali threw the flitter into a sharply banked dive. The engines whined in protest, sending vibrations through the craft. He dropped it down twenty meters away, sparing Dane the spray of gravel from the fans. Almost before it was fully settled he'd slammed the hatch open and vaulted out, taking only a quick glance upward to see if the fog things were coming after him.

Five, six strides. There was Thorson, his helmet lying beside him, his yellow hair ruffling in the breeze, his face contorted and his limbs lying at angles as if he'd been picked up and shaken by a giant hand. Seizure; Ali knew the signs.

He bent down, then paused, staring, at the tunic stretched across Dane's chest.

The man was still breathing.

Dane rose slowly out of a well of red-hot pain.

Unwillingly. Dizzy. Thirst, heat, cold . . .

He opened his eyes, to stare into a pair of dark eyes. Familiar eyes. He knew those eyes. He tried to point this out, and to observe that he seemed to be alive, but his tongue seemed to be frozen.

The eyes crinkled. "It seemed a crime against the universe," a familiar voice drawled, "to let die a man who would fight a duel using a bagpipe."

Dane tried to laugh, and fainted instead.

17

★

"He's going to recover."

Rip leaned back against a bulkhead in the passage outside of sickbay. He hadn't permitted himself to hope, not even when Ali brought the flitter in, its fuel nearly gone and its engines steaming, and they brought out Dane's breathing body. Breathing, but deeply unconscious. Thoughts of coma, brain damage, neurological disasters had chased through Rip's mind as he helped Mura carry Dane up to the sick bay.

Ali had followed right behind, still dirty from the disastrous mining expedition the night before, his face set, his eyes daring anyone—anyone at all—to speak to him. Jasper had trailed them, walking with his accustomed silent tread, speaking to no one, but Rip suspected that the emotions that he hid were much the same as his own. Right behind Jasper walked Tooe, her posture drooping, her crest grayish and limp.

The entire crew gathered outside the sick bay, spilling into the hydro for lack of room, as they waited for Tau's verdict.

He'd just emerged, and he smiled and repeated his statement: "He's going to recover."

Then Johan Stotz said, "Why?"

Ali's quick brows rose, and Frank Mura gave a short nod. "We're glad of that. Of course. But I thought these creatures killed on contact. Was he hit by one, or wasn't he? And if not, what happened?"

Craig Tau paused, then said, "I may be able to answer those questions, and others, after I run some more tests. We're all overdue for rest—I suggest you all get busy on that. When you wake up, I'll have a full report for you."

Stotz looked from Tau to Ali, then grunted. "I'll wait. And I certainly need the sleep. Though it's going to be a while before any of us goes anywhere, sleep or not."

Rip thought of the data squirt that Gleef had just sent over, showing a massive black weather front moving in from the west. From the looks of it, they'd be battered by gale-force winds for at least two days. There'd be no mining for anyone.

As the crew started to disperse—Tooe lingering longest, with several backward glances—Tau said quietly, "Ali. Jasper." And he flicked a look Rip's way, bobbing his head back toward the lab.

Seconds later the three of them were gathered in the lab. Rip collapsed into a chair. Ali lounged against the hatchway, his shoulders betraying his tension. Only Jasper seemed impassive as he bent and stroked Sinbad's notch-eared head.

"Dane is alive only because of whatever it is that has changed his biochemistry," the medic said without preamble. "His neurological system was just barely able to handle whatever kind of zap these creatures gave him, and his brain also survived—"

"Did he speak?" Ali cut in.

Jasper's head lifted.

"Yes." Tau glanced Ali's way. "I knocked him out again so I could start the repair work on the ligaments in his knee. He said that the Floater thing contacted him. No words. But he was definite about it. He said he sensed question, and he thinks it sensed his pain, because it withdrew very suddenly. All this within a second or two's perceptions, as he was in the midst of convulsions, but I am inclined—considering all the evidence—to believe him."

"Contact?" Rip repeated, and as his exhausted mind grasped at that, he said, "Sentient?"

"Possibly. But that's for later. The thing is, the rest of the crew, and the Traders, are going to want a report. It would be a mistake to let them believe they might survive a contact with this being, sentient or not. I am afraid, gentlemen, that the time has come to brief everyone on what has happened to you."

Rip nodded without speaking, and Jasper also gave a quick inclination of his head. They all turned to Ali, who stared down at the deckplates, his one visible hand white at the knuckles. Then suddenly he looked up, his smile twisted. "If we're going to be freaks—"

"Not freaks," Tau interrupted sharply. "Never that. Would you call Tooe's clan-mates freaks? The Zacathans?"

"Freak humans—or are we human?" Ali asked bitterly.

"Humanness is an open set, haven't you learned that by now?" the medic shot back. "You grow, you change, or you petrify and die. The Tath, the Berrans, Siere, Tooe—all these are mammals, and could be called human; the greatest asset of our species is its endless adaptability. You are individual, but you are not alone—unless you choose to be."

"Alone. I wouldn't mind my dreams staying in my own head."

"We can work with that. There are techniques—I've been reading. But you'll have to work with it."

Suddenly all the tension went out of Ali's slender frame. He looked up, serious for once. "All right. Tell them what you want. I'll do what you want—I'll flush the drugs down the recycler. But promise me I can keep my own mental borders, sometime, somehow, or I can't live with it."

"I promise," Tau said steadily.

Ali swung around and left.

Jasper nodded politely to the other two, and slipped out behind Kamil.

Rip lingered. "I promised Lossin a report."

"I'll com Siere," Tau said. "Tell him what I told the others. Go get some sleep. You've got enough facing you. I suggest you try to be awake when you deal with it."

Rip nodded and went out, heading for his cabin. His mind slid from Dane to the other problem—getting ore. Despite all their plans, and heroic efforts, both teams of Traders had only managed to accumulate seventy-five percent of what they had hoped to net. And it was obvious they would not be going out soon.

Rip thought about the *North Star* as he stretched out on his bunk. Incommunicado—in danger?

Ali wanted to be alone. Rip could have told him he was welcome to this feeling of isolation.

He closed his eyes, and drifted into uneasy dreams.

"All right, let's try again," Rip said, trying to control his own impatience. It was three days later—three frustrating days full of interruptions, questions, three emergency trips to help the Traders repair things broken by the ferocious series of storms that had been battering at them.

Ali made an impatient gesture. "This is—"

"We've heard," Dane cut in curtly.

No one smiled. Ali had been fluent and profane, especially as they all got tired. But the connection worked—or could work, if everyone concentrated. If they closed out other thoughts. If they focused. If they kept up their energy. They'd been working at it whenever possible for three days, and Rip knew it was not nearly enough.

"Once more," Rip said. "We have to get some kind of control if we're even going to attempt it with these Floaters."

"Assuming they won't just decide to annihilate us outright," Ali muttered.

"It was question I sensed," Dane said in a patient voice.

"Not maliciousness, or anger, or irritation, or any other human emotion." He paused, then spoke more slowly. "And urgency, too, I think."

"You can jettison the subtle hints." Ali gave them his twisted, derisive smile. "Admit it—this is like trying to skate in oils with your eyes blindfolded."

Jasper spoke suddenly. "It's more like trying to wrestle lightning."

They were all silent, each thinking out the implications. Rip knew that what maddened the engineering mind (besides the question of privacy barriers lowered) was that there were no instructions, no predictable results for the work they were attempting. For the engineer, this was intolerable; even when presented with an engineering problem which required modifications to what existed, or even new technology, tools, machines, physics all performed according to specs. There were laws, rules, measures.

But not now.

Rip knew it was easier for him and Dane. Dane had been trained to accept the fluidity of interaction as part of Trade. Motivations, expectations, goals, all could change from moment to moment. Navigation was a blend of the two ways of thought: there were rules, but space could—and would—surprise you. Adaptability was a survival mechanism in a good pilot.

"Again," Rip said, gathering their attention. "We know that we can't do anything unless we are in physical contact." The others nodded. This was one of the few givens. At least in this situation. The Floaters had to make physical contact, and the humans had found that their own connection was much less erratic when they were in contact.

They were crowded in Dane's cabin, around his bunk. Rip and Jasper had stools. Ali perched on the edge of Dane's fold-down desk. Each man now grasped the wrist of the man to his right. Immediately Rip became aware of . . . of what?

He made a conscious effort not to map onto the others his own expectations. What exactly was he aware of?

Emotions—like colors—were vivid from Ali. Fire colors. The reds and oranges of anger and impatience, the yellow of curiosity, the white light of his intense energy. Dane was blues and greens, like an ocean. One was aware of his focus, his interest, his regrets concerning his current physical limitations— the mining problems—the lack of contact with Jellico—the prospect of communicating with the Floaters. Dane was afraid they'd fail.

Jasper was pale colors, muted silvers, beige, ivory. His emotions were so distant one could sense only a whisper of them. The greatest sense—the only consistent one—was a profound reluctance to commit (or permit) trespass.

Rip, knowing that the jet tech would not like being first, said "Jasper."

The colors intensified for a brief flicker, blended—and Rip felt the sharpened focus of the others, waiting.

Jasper's concentration was a muted burn to Rip's nerves, then—slowly—an image took shape in Rip's mind: the *Solar Queen*, seen in the dock inside Exchange, glowing in the reflected light of the primary Mykos. Rip's own mind seized the image, then lost it when memory triggered his own flow of thoughts. He felt the others' focus disintegrate in the same way, and once again they got scattered.

Rip felt the grip on his left wrist loosen, and he dropped Ali's bony wrist and opened his eyes. "All right. We had it again—almost."

Dane said, "I think we need something more than a single image."

"But thinking words at each other didn't work," Ali said. "Or mostly didn't work."

"How about a sequence? Not a memory." Dane frowned in his effort to articulate new concepts. "But some kind of sequence that we can learn to follow while keeping our own thoughts from taking over the focus."

"Your turn," Ali said. "Do it."

Again they gripped one another, and waited. Rip felt that at least that much was becoming . . . not habit, but part of a building process. The image, when it came, was sudden—a piece of machinery. Rip tried to hold his thoughts and expectations at bay, but not with such concentration that he closed out the image. The machine flickered out—but he reached for it and got it again, and then as he watched it, a cog started turning, coming away from the parts it held together. Rip held his concentration, held it—felt the others holding, too, and excitement rippled through him—

And he lost it. But waited. Once again the image took focus, and another part turned, as though being loosened by an invisible tool, and separated itself from the machine. Then the machine turned over, presenting itself from a different angle. Rip wondered if they were all seeing the same angle—and lost it again.

This time they all lost it.

"That was you, Shannon," Ali said crossly. "Dammit, this is like juggling water balls."

"Heard you," Dane said. "Not in words, but you wondered if we saw it in three dimensions, each a different view, right?"

Jasper's expression lightened; apparently he'd caught that as well.

"Yes," Rip said.

"Then we can count that as progress," Dane said. "Now. My turn. It'll be a memory, but not an experience. See how long you can stay in it, and try to look at everything, because I think we should go round the circle and you try to image it back to the rest of us."

"Good idea," Jasper murmured. "But you'll have to work on not providing your own view when it's our turn to reflect it back."

"Right." Dane nodded.

Once again they took hold. Rip felt the familiar tightening in his temples, a headache threatening. He ignored it.

Again he waited, and a weird room took shape in his mind. The dimensions were not square, and there was no up/down orientation established by furnishings standing on floor and fixtures on walls and ceiling within reach of inhabitants. This room had furnishings on all walls, and the space was further bisected by catwalks crisscrossing at odd angles.

Rip made himself observe, without thought, first one wall, then the next. He was trying to absorb the catwalks when he felt the others withdrawing, and suddenly the room was his own memory.

"Ali?"

The room came back—and for a few seconds Rip saw it with double vision, his own version and Ali's. He could not reconcile them, and dropped out. Cursing, Ali gripped his wrist tighter. "Again."

This time Rip worked on holding his own image at bay. He worked so hard that Ali's vision did not come through—and all three sensed it.

"Come on, Rip, concentrate," Ali snapped. "This is like having someone dragging at our ears."

Rip shook his hands free, rubbed his palms down his trouser legs, then once again connected. Then he closed his eyes and tried a mental exercise that Tau had given them from his research, the floating-on-the-sea. The image Ali sent replaced the sea, but this time Rip managed not to superimpose his own memory. He let it stay there, noting how Ali had managed to see the cabled catwalks as some kind of engineering gestalt; the furnishings were almost nonexistent.

Jasper then sent his image—they all felt him doing it. This time the focus was the computer complex that some unnamed person had constructed in one area. The consoles could be approached from several angles, something weird to gravity-accustomed Terrans.

Rip then sent his own image, noticing the others reacting to his own perceptions of the furnishings, and how they must be adapted to this or that being.

Put them together. The thought arrowed in from Dane— one of the rare moments they were all so attuned, without their own internal chatterers going, that they "heard" the words.

Rip worked to blend his image with the others, and for a moment they had it—then it crumbled.

Frustration succeeded, and awareness of mental fatigue and tension. Ali was cursing again; Jasper was, of course, silent.

Dane shifted on his bunk, then said, "We're getting it. Slowly."

Ali grimaced. "This could take years."

"We don't have years." Dane said the obvious. "I've been thinking—nothing else to do sitting here—and I believe if we're going to have any luck at all with those creatures, it will be in not trying to project, but to receive. It's Craig's floating image we need to use."

"You mean we wait for what they might send," Rip said.

Dane shrugged. "All I know is, I didn't send anything during that one contact—of course. But the Floater did, which makes me believe they're used to communicating that way. Who knows? Maybe those times we saw on the tape were nothing worse than attempts to communicate, and not attacks at all."

Ali grunted. "Makes sense. What if there were sentient spiders that communicated by exchanging toxins? We'd be facing the same kind of problem."

Jasper said quietly, "So what you're saying is, we should try soon?"

Dane nodded again. "I don't know. I just don't think we're going to be much better prepared if we wait a week."

Rip said, "The next question is, whom do we permit them to touch? The obvious choice is Dane—obvious except for the fact that another seizure like that might do permanent damage—"

The com blinked, and Dane reached to tab it. "Thorson here."

"Report from Lossin." It was Johan Stotz. "He and Irrba ran a standard comcheck with the shellboat. Didn't get a reply. Went out to check."

Rip braced for bad news, thinking of pirates secretly landed—or one of the Traders turning on the others.

"And?" Ali prompted.

". . . sorry, Craig was talking. The boat's gone, along with the cave and the entire cove, buried under a multimegaton rock slide. Along with much of the ore we got on the last trip, which we hadn't transferred yet. So the ore we've refined so far is all we're going to get, and it's not enough."

No one said anything for a moment.

"But there's more," said Stotz. "Craig says there are Floaters outside the *Queen*—I just pulled up the external view, and you can see 'em. They're almost pressed against the vidcams."

Jasper stood up. His bleached skin was paler than ever, something Rip would have thought impossible. "If we're going to do it," he said, "let's do it now. I'll let them touch me."

18

★

Craig Tau's voice came over the ship's com: "Siere reports that their camp is surrounded by fog, and they can see the Floaters hovering just beyond their trees."

Dane pulled himself up impatiently. He was heartily sick of not being able to move about with any kind of ease. "Put the external on, Ali?" He pointed to his console.

Ali tapped at the desk-computer console that he was leaning against, then shifted his weight so they could all see the screen.

"First lull in the weather for five days," Rip Shannon said, from his perch on Dane's snap-down cabin stool. "And right before that Dane had his encounter. Seems significant, doesn't it?"

"Except I wish we knew what kind of significance." Ali folded his arms. "They could be crowding around waiting to zap us. Maybe we're vermin to them!"

Tooe spoke up from the hatchway, where she was peering

over Rip's shoulder. "They think question at Dane. Not 'Danger.' " She tapped her smooth skull. "Not 'Go Away.' "

Jasper had laced his hands tightly together and was staring down at them. Dane glanced at the short, weedy man, feeling a surge of sympathy. Funny—he didn't feel at all sorry for Ali. Kamil, despite his struggles with the reality of the shared bond, had proved that he was a survivor. Jasper, the one who never complained, who never got in anyone's way— he was the one who was taking this hardest, Dane was convinced.

But it was Jasper who looked up suddenly, and said, "They could be waiting for us. Let's get it over with now."

"Now?" Ali repeated.

"You think we're ready?" Rip asked more quietly.

"I don't think—" Jasper started, then he looked down again. "I'd rather know." His voice was so low Dane almost didn't hear him.

For answer he grabbed hold of the side of his desk and swung himself off his bunk. Being upright again made him giddy for a few seconds.

The others moved out of his cabin, making the small space seem a lot less crowded, and Dane hitched along behind, moving fairly quickly for a man with one leg immobilized.

They filed out to the cargo-bay lock. Tau met them there, and in silence fitted each with sensors. Tooe hovered just inside the cargo bay, and Dane knew that the others were watching from the vid-links on the upper decks.

Rip looked around at them. "Ready?"

Ali shrugged, his brows raised, a challenging gleam in his dark eyes. Dane gestured with one hand; Jasper edged up next to the lock, his shoulders tight with tension. But it was clear he expected to be the first one out.

"Wait," Ali said. "How are we going to do this?"

"I'll go out," Jasper said. "Maybe you'd better hold my shoulder from behind. In case I can't use my hands after they touch me."

"We'll line up like Blind Man's Walk, then," Ali said, moving into position. And, with his customary drawl, "This will be one for the vids."

Dane knew that drawl for the bravado it was, and ignored it as he stepped up to clap his hand on Jasper's shoulder. He felt Ali right behind him, and Rip took a step nearer to Ali so that he could reach him as well as the lock controls.

"Tooe control lock?" the little Rigelian offered.

Rip nodded his thanks and stepped back.

Now they were in a row, their backs to the bulkhead. In case. Dane didn't need a psi link to know that all four of them were thinking of convulsions—and worse.

Tooe stretched up on her toes, looking an inquiry at Jasper, who gave her the thumbs-up.

The lock slid open.

Vapor puffed in, smelling of greenery and mossy rock and damp soil. Dane saw a huge Floater hovering directly outside the lock, and inadvertently sucked a breath in. His nerves tingled almost painfully, a reminder of his encounter.

Jasper did not falter. He stretched out his free arm, and Dane saw the Floater move slowly, gently, over him.

"Concentrate," Rip murmured.

Dane closed his eyes. He could see the contact on the vid record later—if he lived. Now, he tried to clear his mind of memory, of fear, expectation, and called up the familiar image of the vast ocean. Not Hesprid's angry gray sea, but the beautiful blue Terran ocean he remembered seeing in his childhood. He was floating on a raft. Ali appeared near him, not visible; it was more as if he were just behind, but Dane was aware of him. Rip and Jasper were also there. Dane concentrated on the warm air, the mild sun, just floating, drifting—

A silver flicker flashed across his inner vision—almost painful, certainly intense. Instinct almost forced him out, but he held on to his image, and then suddenly new images flooded his mind, powerful and vivid and rapid, a tidal wave of sensation that overwhelmed his mind.

Again he nearly lost his place in the bond, but fought to

hold it—*swimming* he sent the thought out, *treading water*— and the images slowed.

Now he was high in the sky, looking down at the island from above.

With an exultant surge of energy he realized he was seeing the island from the perspective of the Floaters. Yes—the trees were there, and so was the ship.

And he realized he felt exposed, in danger from—what? All around the island the sky glared at him, unfriendly, dry—

The perspective dissolved into a complicated series of images having to do with the trees but all Dane got was searing heat—

Flames. That was Jasper. *Lights in the sky.*

Another silver flash, almost painful. Dane now sensed many awarenesses, like sentient stars watching above the ocean. The images came rapidly again, then slowed; now all four felt the effort of the stars' attempt to keep the flow of imagery at a sustained pace.

Quakes. That was Rip. *Why would Floaters be concerned with quakes? Let's concentrate on that. There's something important here.*

At the stream of words Dane felt a ripple of reaction go through the stars. It was impossible to assign any kind of emotion to that reaction, only magnitude of intensity. He realized that the Floaters did not use words—of course! They had no mouths and could not speak!

His thought speared to the other three; he felt their reaction. Then he tried to reach for the image of the trees.

Again the images came, so fast Dane felt his brain unable to cope with them. He wished suddenly that he had not fastened on to the image of swimming, for now the sensation that he was drowning was so overwhelming he staggered, gasping for breath—

And was out of the bond.

He fell back against the bulkhead, to find Craig Tau at his elbow. "Here. Sit." The medic guided Dane to a storage crate and he sank down gratefully, cast-bound leg stretched before him. He was surprised to discover that his good knee felt watery, and that he was soggy with sweat. The cargo bay swam unpleasantly before his vision, and he closed his eyes, drawing deep, slow breaths.

"They are sentient," Rip said wonderingly. "But so different."

"What was that about lights? And the quakes?" Dane asked, his voice hoarse.

"And flames," said Ali.

Jasper said slowly, "The End Times." His pallid face was beaded with perspiration. "The End Times are coming. That's what I got. First lights in the sky, then quakes, then the flames."

"And no escape," Ali said. "Just like the legends of ancient Terra."

"Of every world," said Jasper.

"They are related," said Tau suddenly. "Stotz and I tried programming some new parameters into the weather simulator. What seems likely is that the piezo effects in the rocks not only generate EM, but, of course, respond to it, so as the sunspot cycle builds, you get tectonic events occurring with increasing frequency. The high lightning may be tied in as well."

"I caught the storm images," Ali said. "Have we gotten ourselves into some religious conflict? With the other species? I couldn't see them."

"No," Jasper murmured, still in that odd, dreamy voice. As if his mind was only partly present. "They all fear. Something has changed, something that will affect the others undersea."

"Undersea?" That was Craig Tau.

Jasper turned toward him, his eyes curiously unseeing. "Lives . . . lives undersea. They were all there, listening. First the Floaters—whole colonies, and then these others joined—"

"That's why I felt I was drowning," Dane exclaimed, sitting up again. "I kept getting *place*—"

"Undersea!" Ali snapped his fingers. "Me too! I thought

they were dragging us underwater by some weird psi method."

Craig Tau looked from him to Jasper. "Go on, Weeks."

Jasper shook his head slowly, then winced. Dane felt dizziness hovering on the edge of his own perceptions, and again had to steady his breathing.

"Never mind," the medic said abruptly. "All four of you. Orders now—get some rest. We can debrief later."

Ali left without speaking, and Rip started after, rubbing his temples. Jasper took a couple of steps, then turned around slowly. "The entire planet," he said. "Floaters, swimmers. Trees. They're all connected." He touched his head, and then walked slowly out.

Dane felt as if a puzzle had suddenly fallen into place. "That's it," he said. His head throbbed. "That's it—and there's something desperately wrong."

Rip Shannon watched with sympathy as Dane Thorson wedged uncomfortably into a corner of the weird little elevator box behind Ali and Tooe, then braced himself as the lift lurched upward.

It was ten hours later, during five of which Rip had slept. When he woke up, he'd been told by Craig Tau that the Traders were full of questions about what had happened, and so he and Siere had suggested a meeting of all the Free Traders. Because the *Queen* had no cabins that would comfortably hold seventeen, they were meeting in the tree-camp.

First, though, he and Dane, Ali, and Jasper had held their own debriefing. Each found that they retained vivid images of what they had experienced, though those experiences did not always match completely. As Dane said when they finally broke, "We discovered that when we send each other images in three-D, we all see it from the angle the person projecting it sees it. But with the Floaters, it's as if we're getting different angles—only not of an object, but of a gestalt."

Gestalt. It was not a word most navigators had in their ready vocabulary, Rip had thought with a weird tickle of humor, as they all parted to don their winter gear—Tau helping Dane.

Ali ferried Dane over in the flitter; the rest walked in the pouring rain. At least the winds were not as bad as they had been, but the temperature was just above freezing. Rip thought about trying to mine in ice—and then remembered the lost boat.

He shook his head, resolving to set those thoughts aside for later.

Just then the lift reached the main level, and they stepped out and sent the lift down for the remainder of the *Queen*'s crew.

The Traders waited for them above, on the biggest platform. Rip saw Stotz talking earnestly with Irrba and Tazcin, and the two medics went off to another corner to talk. Kamsin brought out a great brass urn and poured out cups of some drink whose aroma reminded Rip of the scents of apples and cinnamon and pears.

Rip noted Dane regarding his cup with satisfaction; the handle was big enough even for his hands. Tooe looked like she was holding a bucket, but she didn't seem to mind. Just gripped it in both fists and slurped enthusiastically. Kamsin made pleased huffing noises, and Rip realized that again the Terrans had missed a cue. The Tath ate quietly—he'd noted that before—but they apparently drank noisily.

When he got his, he experimented, slurping the hot liquid up so that it cooled before it reached his lips. Kamsin huffed at him as well, and Rip smiled.

Then Tazcin said, "We here, all. Begin."

Tau said, "You saw the vidrecording of Jasper's encounter with the Floaters. Why don't we start with any questions you have?"

A quick riff of comments went round the Traders, then Lossin said, "Floaters speak?"

"No speech," Rip said.

"Images—pictures. Here." Ali tapped his head.

"Dr. Siere has the data I took from the sensors," Tau said slowly, looking from face to face. "The Floaters function with roughly the same kind of neurology as we have—though their synaptical charges are enough to trigger seizures in humans. The Floaters seemed to realize this, and made an effort to dampen the effect of their link."

"Need all four Terrans?" That was Gleef's reedy voice.

"I think so," Dane said. "Maybe we could handle their touch alone—if they damp the effect. But it takes all four of us to process the images. We each seem to 'hear' something different."

"But there isss a messsage?" Siere asked in his raspy voice.

"Yes—though we don't know what it is yet."

"Evidence is clear, they are sentients?" Lossin asked.

"Yes." That was Craig Tau.

Jasper Weeks had sat quietly, holding his cup. Now he said, "The Charter. It is null—or will be as soon as we report to the Federation, or the Patrol, that there are in fact sentients on Hesprid IV."

"The ore." That was Lossin. "It is not ours, then. We trespass."

Ali looked up, and Rip knew without any psi connection what he was thinking: *if we say anything.*

And it was tempting, that could not be denied. Without the ore they had refined, they could lift the Traders only by abandoning several tons of equipment, which would break them.

They had only to load what ore they had onto the ship and depart, and within months the Charter would expire. Who would stop them?

But Ali did not speak. The child who had survived the Crater Wars had grown up learning—painfully—how to be trustworthy before he could trust. This much Rip had discerned from the vivid dreams Ali had perforce shared with the others. None of this had been discussed, or would be discussed, for it was still personal trespass. The bond between the four was no more than a truce; they shared what touched them all, but ignored, or pretended to ignore, what touched them singly.

"We Trade!" That was Tooe. She whistled happily. "We are Traders. We Trade."

"With a species that does not use words, and may not have understanding of the concept of Trade?" Johan Stotz rubbed his jawline. "I'm for it—if we can manage—but do you four think you can communicate with these Floater things in a way that will convince the Feds that we are really Trading? The last I heard, the Patrol—and the Federation Diplomatic Corps—don't include psi training for their agents."

Dane looked up from the depths of his drink. "I don't think we can worry about how the legal mind will approach our records once we lift. But I do think the Old Man would insist we do right by the inhabitants any way we can. Even if that means endless hassles with bureaucrats later."

"Which is nothing new," Craig Tau added, grinning.

While they spoke, Tooe and Lossin both were busy translating in an undertone to the others. Now Tazcin spoke, her low, mellow voice definite in tone.

Tooe said, "They want only honest Trade."

Rip looked at the other three. "I guess that leaves it up to us, then, doesn't it?"

Ali crossed his arms, lounging back. "Us and the Floaters—and if by some miracle we can manage to come to an accord, we have our pirate friends waiting up there." He glanced at the cloud-torn sky.

19

"Kamsin! Tooe! Get out of here!"

Dane stumbled forward, nearly fell facedown in the mud, and caught himself against a boulder.

Jasper Weeks ran forward, waving his arms, and the Floaters descending toward the tall and the small figures floated upward again, vapors swirling around them.

Tooe and Kamsin ran back up the ramp into the *Queen*, and Rip moved with a kind of painful slowness to Ali Kamil's prone form in the mud.

Dane sat up against his rock, gasping for breath. He looked up at the swirling gray mist, shot through with threads of fervent light from Hesprid's increasingly uneasy sun. It was five days after the conference in the trees, two days since the comsats reported a vast bubble of gas rocketing out of the sunspot-riddled sun toward the planet. The effect of its impact on the magnetosphere, now only two days off, couldn't be predicted—their computer models delivered nonsensical answers.

Dane, remembering the glaring brightness of the aurora they'd seen during a brief period of clear sky, shuddered at the thought of what such a magnetic storm would do to the weather. And communications. Already, even if the *North Star* broke radio silence, they'd never hear it.

He levered himself wearily to his feet. This was the third try the four had made to continue the contact with the Floaters. Two days of storms had kept the fog and Floaters away; three relatively quiet days had seen the four coming out each morning, to find thick fog and an ever-increasing number of the strange beings.

Dane looked up now. The fog made vision difficult, but he estimated at least a hundred of the things. But they hovered, instead of descending.

He transferred his gaze to Rip. "Passed out?"

Rip gave a short nod. "Again."

Jasper reached Rip's side, and in silence the two slid their gloved hands under Ali's armpits and lifted the unconscious engineer. They dragged him up the ramp and into the ship. Walking slowly, Dane followed.

His cast was off, which meant he could bend his knee— but sudden movements of any kind were agony.

The cargo-bay hatch slid shut behind them. So far, the Floaters had never tried to get inside the ship. Obviously Tooe and Kamsin had been watching this latest attempt at communication, and when they saw Ali fall, and the others initially frozen, they'd come out to help.

Luckily Jasper, Rip, and Dane had broken out of the contact fast enough to see them coming.

Dane looked across the cargo bay at the two, who stood at the inner hatchway. Tooe's crest drooped, her huge eyes intent.

"Don't go out there," Dane said. "I know you wanted to help. Just because we've lived through contact doesn't mean you will."

"But they know you four by now, do not they?" Tooe asked. "You say they don't want to kill us—"

Rip said tiredly, "Tooe, I don't think they can tell any of us apart, any more than we can tell them apart."

Something flickered at the back of Dane's mind: Rip's words were important. Why? He tried to examine them, to focus, but his head ached in counterpoint to his knee.

Then he forgot both as Ali groaned and sat up, rubbing his temples. "Damn." He dropped his hand and winced. "Me again."

All three times it had been Ali who broke the contact. Not voluntarily, which made it all the more frustrating, Dane thought morosely.

Rip said, "Recap. Where did you feel yourself dropping out, Ali?"

Dane could have told him, but he kept his lips closed. Instead, he remembered the bond the four humans made, now always connected through the mental image of them floating on their rafts atop a calm sea. The Floaters worked hard to keep their images limited, but Dane strongly suspected that this was unnatural for them—the equivalent of trying to hold an important conversation with a two-year-old. Or with someone who knew just a few scattered words of a foreign language.

"I can't hold the image of us all when the images get to a certain level of intensity," Ali said, his voice hoarse. He rubbed his hands through his fine hair, then looked up, his eyes bloodshot. "Look, how long are we going to keep at this? It's not working."

"We have to know why," Rip said, his manner detached. His dark eyes turned Dane's way. "What have you observed?"

"Same thing Kamil says." Dane rubbed gently at his knee. "We're trying to do two things—hold on to the bond, and concentrate on what the Floaters send us. It's too hard, like reading two screens at once."

Rip turned to Jasper. "Weeks?"

The Venusian had laced his fingers together, and was studying them as though the answer lay there. Now he glanced up, and said, "Just as Ali says."

"And?" Rip prompted.

Jasper shrugged his thin shoulders slightly.

"And?" Rip said again. "Jasper, you know something. I can tell that much. If I could read what it was, I'd say it myself."

Jasper Weeks went very still, so still he seemed to have stopped breathing. Dane sensed his deep reluctance to speak, and so to break the tension he said, "Shannon. What you told Tooe. Repeat it?"

Rip shrugged slightly. "It's nothing profound. I don't believe they can tell us apart—any more than we can tell them apart."

Dane got to his feet and hit the comlink. "Craig?"

"Right behind you." The medic appeared, carrying a tray of gently steaming drinks. "Something to fortify you. Drink up."

"Coffee," Ali said. "I want coffee. Strong, and lots. Not one of your vile medicinal concoctions."

"You're getting a concoction, but I hope it isn't vile. Frank infused it into a good strong soup he's had simmering all day. Or what passes for day. Drink."

As he spoke he went around to each of them. Dane took his and sipped. The flavor was a blend of various vegetables—the fresh tomato of the hydrogarden being most prevalent—with an overlay of spice. He drank a big swallow, and then finished it. Almost immediately he felt energy flowing through his veins again.

Craig grinned at him. "You look less like a month-old corpse now."

"And more like a week-old croaker, eh?" Ali murmured. "That's what I feel like."

Tau ignored him. "Dane, you had a question?"

"You ran tests, right, on the Floaters? Infrared, sonic, whatever you had—have you discovered any distinguishing characteristics for telling these things apart?"

"Nothing," Tau said. "I can't even tell you if the ones you touch are repeat customers, or are completely new."

Dane felt again that impulse that this was important, but

when he tried to think, the impulse dissolved. Then he looked down at Jasper and felt it again—this time with a sense of urgency that made him say, "Weeks, you know something. What is it?"

Rip hunkered down next to the jet tech. "Jasper. We have to solve this. You know that. You've worked hard—at least as hard as any of the rest of us—"

"No I haven't," Jasper said in a low voice.

The interruption was so uncharacteristic that everyone was silent.

"I beg your pardon," Jasper said promptly.

"No. Speak." Rip stayed next to Jasper. "You haven't worked hard?"

"I have," Jasper said slowly—and then glanced over at Ali, who was gazing at him over the rim of his cup. "But it's not the right work. I—I know it."

Ali Kamil hit the flat of his hand against the bulkhead. "Identity," he said. "Damn it! It's identity, isn't it?"

Jasper dropped his gaze again. "That's it. I think. We lost the contact because we're working so hard to maintain our identities."

Dane drew in a deep breath, conviction making him almost giddy. "That's it. That's *it*. The Floaters don't have identity. Not in any way we understand it. And that's what's holding us back."

Rip stood up, rubbing his jaw. "Identity. But that's so basic—" He stopped, frowning. "When we're conscious, anyway. We've already learned that bleeding over into one another's dreams happens when we're unconscious. The identity barrier seems to drop then."

"So we're supposed to do this contact thing when we're asleep?" Ali queried, then he rolled his eyes, and added derisively, "Wonderful news. This gets better all the time."

"I don't think that's possible," Dane said, working not to let Ali's sarcasm make him angry. "It takes too much focus to hold it. In our dreams we're all over the place—past, present, weird combinations of both."

Rip said, "Jasper?"

Weeks looked up again. "Image," he murmured. "If—if we change the image. Not us. On rafts." He licked his lips, and Dane felt a suffusion of pity. The discussion was obviously crossing some kind of ingrained privacy barrier that upset the Venusian deeply.

"I see!" Rip exclaimed, looking enthusiastic. "You think, then, that the image of each of us on our rafts symbolically sets up the identity barriers?"

Jasper nodded, his lips compressed.

Again Dane felt a spurt of pity. The Venusian was visibly upset—a rarity that ought to have warned Ali. Jasper just never showed emotion. Dane suspected that, given a choice, Jasper would rather be required to trade among the Sky-Born cult on Sarabbi II—where clothing of any kind was outlawed—than to be exposing his inner self even to crewmates. Maybe especially to crewmates, people he knew and had to live with.

Dane thought about the ribbing he'd taken from one of the inhabitants of Xecho, who thought it crazy for the *Queen,* which was not by any standards a spacious ship, being further divided into tiny cubicles. But Dane had explained how humans needed the illusion, at least, of privacy. How much more profound a change would it be to lose those mental barriers?

Rip said, "Look. We've run out of time. Either we solve this, or lift."

No one spoke, but Dane saw that the other two were listening.

Rip said, "We've already proved that we can't do much on our own—that we all have to work together. If we use that image and let the Floaters drive our thoughts, it should minimize the . . . personal trespass."

Dane said, looking from Ali to Jasper, "We don't have any more time. Let's do it fast—and let's do it now."

Ali hit the bulkhead again, then wrung his fingers. "I suggest, my pilgrims," he said in the grand manner, "that we rejoin our waiting friends?"

Rip's relief was apparent only in the way his shoulders relaxed slightly. His voice was as calm as ever as he said, "So our image now is simply ocean. We're no longer going to make mental images of ourselves on rafts. We'll be in the ocean—not fish, or creatures, but part of the water itself."

Jasper jerked his head in a nod, and activated the outer hatch.

The fog was now so thick that Dane couldn't see the end of the ramp. He glanced up, and his nerves sang painfully. Despite the fog the Floaters were visible, or visible enough to hint at an incredible number.

At the ramp the four sat down in a square on the platform they'd laid out earlier, and clasped one another's shoulders. Dane closed his eyes, trying not to think about the touch of the Floaters. So far they'd avoided him; the others had not shown the effects, which meant the Floaters were aware on some level of the damage they'd done, and had worked to control it—but the body remembers pain, and his muscles tightened unbearably.

He forced himself to breathe deeply as he obediently called up the mental image of the ocean. Or tried. It was too hard to just imagine himself in the ocean, so he pictured his familiar raft, but this time visualized himself diving off and into the water. Deep blue water, cool and pleasant, with waving fronds . . .

He looked ahead, tried not to see the others. He knew they were there, but it was that sense of someone standing at your shoulder. No image! His mind said, and he steadied the blue of the water. . . .

And with a sudden surge of terrific energy, his mind dived down not into the murky depths of his imagination, but into a vision so real he was utterly mesmerized. A tiny part of him watched the process—likening it to starting a ship on manual, one system at a time, until the autopilot takes over and lights up the control deck, launching the ship at the same time.

Control was now out of his hands, but it was right to be so. He closed out that last part of his identity, and—

—And he *was* the ocean.

The bond between the four men had been a faint candle to the sun of this worldwide awareness. For that was what he was now part of. Dane saw it, lived it, felt it. He was the Floaters, drifting between the islands in the short summers, sifting the pollen of the trees from the air, raining the metabolites like silver threads to the sea far below, nourishing the vast kelp beds which were farmed by the other sentient species, arthropodal bottom-dwellers.

And then the microscopic seeds of the vast trees through the rest of the years, as the pods burst at long intervals between storms. For with those seeds came a lichen that proliferated in each Floater's upper skin, staining its vast upper surface reddish green, the energy thus extracted from Hesprid's glaring sun enabling the creatures to float as natural aerostats through the night. They avoided the worst of storms by flattening out on the smooth rock atop the rock-dome islands, where the Traders would, of course, never see them.

Exhilaration slowly damped, to be replaced by the sense of wrongness pervading the world. Not a human wrongness—the humans seemed to have made about as much impression on the world's consciousness as harmless microbes did for Terrans.

The wrongness was in the sea, and the air above it. The Floaters didn't know why the currents had changed, slowly shrinking the belts of fog they lived in. Ordinarily that was not a problem, but the End Times were indeed coming.

Guided by the consciousness, Dane saw the growing fury of the planetary elements as Hesprid's sunspot cycle reached its fervid peak, watched as quakes and the howling winds toppled vast trees in windrows, shrank away from the sky-spanning lightning that ignited the islands into the flaming hell of heat that was the only trigger the seeds knew for growth.

The forest was reborn in fire, while the Floaters waited far out at sea in their protective fog bank.

But not this time. The Floaters did not know the precise data—and their sense of time was difficult to grasp. But the humans knew, and the impact of that knowledge shook the bond that linked them for a moment.

For a moment Dane's mind lifted back into individuality. *Two days to doomsday. Doomsday for us, too, unless we trade.* Then he felt ashamed. The Traders faced only financial ruin; the Floaters faced extinction. With an effort, he let himself fall back into the sea, become one again with the water, with his friends, with the Floaters.

The aliens accepted the knowledge of their time of death without emotions—at least none that Dane could discern—but in fact, with them all sentience on this world would die. Without the Floaters and the pollen metabolite, the kelp would die, and the sea life that it sheltered—including what the Floaters thought of as the singers-of-the-water—and the arthropods would starve.

Singers-of-the-water? Another sentient race? Dane thought, and he felt the question echo through the other three.

It was the tragedy of Hesprid IV that sentient life was confined to the archipelago rich in cielanite, and the piezoelectric emissions that underlay the ecology of the trees.

Now he felt emotion, knew it to be the very human reactions from his three crewmates.

Becoming aware of their reactions made him more aware of them. The image of the world changed again, this time showing in a weird blending of time the *Queen* and the *Ariadne* secured to the island. But the images did not include humans or humanoids—it was as if they didn't exist. The images focused on the ships, more specifically the vapors given off by the exhaust vents.

Salutary, came Ali's thought, wry and clear—a kind of rusty red. *We seem to rate the importance of the grass we tread on at home—*

Through that came Jasper's thought. *Vapor! They want the vapor.*

And Dane felt his own emotions radiate out, like golden sunbeams. He could have laughed aloud, for suddenly he knew what was needed.

Jan Van Ryke had told Dane often enough that a good Free Trader traded with whatever was at hand—even if, as had happened once, the item wanted was nothing in the cargo hold, but grew in abundance in the hydrolab for the delectation of the ship's cat.

Now facing him was perhaps the greatest challenge for a Trader—to work with beings who did not speak, who did not seem to know the concepts of ownership or possessions . . . but who had a need.

He projected his own images, strong and sure, and felt the other three sensing his direction and backing him up, quick as electric current. Perhaps the intensity of the connection aided him; he saw, clear as a vid, the mining slugs following veins of cielanite, shown in the image as a blue-glowing stone in a dark matrix. He watched them excreting the cielanite eggs, the crews of the two ships working hard to gather them, the tide washing them away. Dane tried to convey their need, not knowing if even that emotion was clear.

He then visualized the crew picking up the ore and stowing it on the ship—and last, he formed images of the ships making vapors that stayed in the air.

At once a kind of electric current zapped through the bond.

Dane felt it as a physical shock, recalling the trauma of his initial contact, and he felt his consciousness dissolve.

But as he faded out he felt the triumph of the other three, and Rip's inner voice, green and clear:

They got it!

20

Dane was dreaming.

He swam in a storm-lashed sea, but the water was warm, and sunlight shafted down through the waters. He wanted to dive down, and keep exploring, but he knew he needed to return to the surface. More air? No, he had air . . . he had gills . . . he looked down, about to dive . . .

Suddenly there came the sense that he was not alone. Ali! Where's the comlink?

Dane looked around, sure that Ali Kamil had called him, but there was no other figure visible in the water. A weight anchored him, curiously comforting.

Again the call, and he looked toward the surface, saw the bright sunlight—

And woke up. On his chest Sinbad sat curled up, his eyes slitted, his body vibrating gently with his purring.

"Come on, man," Ali said with heartless impatience. "On your feet. You have a lot to see before you get to work."

Dane worked his mouth, which felt like the inside of a shoe after a fifty-kilometer hike. "Unh," he said.

Ali's brows lifted. "Cogently spoken! Was that an interrogative? What happened then, is Craig gave you something to sleep after you woke up from your faint. What's happening now is that your trade is going on—and this is one for the record books. Where, along the coast, and just outside. When, now. How you get there is on your own two feet to the flitter, but it had better be fast, because the scope shows a storm line that looks like the end of the world, approaching fast."

Dane started up, his heart hammering. "Is this it?" Confused, apocalyptic images swirled in his head.

Ali shrugged theatrically. "Floaters think so. Gas cloud was projected to hit the magnetosphere several hours back. Seismics show a lot of little sub-1 and -2 quakes, EM is up, and the aurora looks like a nuclear explosion. We're lifting off soon's we finish the Trade, but it's even money if we're out of the atmosphere at show time, the speed this storm is moving."

"Lifting . . ."

"Off. Jets firing. Zoom. Six hours." Ali thrust a hand skyward. "You have three minutes. I'll be out here, counting. If you're not ready, you go just as you are." He lounged the short steps to the cabin door, then turned to smile. "Coffee on your console there."

Dane realized that that was the aroma he'd been smelling, and he stopped mentally cursing the heartless-sounding engineer. Instead, he gently set the cat down and got to his feet, the threat of onrushing doom mixing oddly with the excitement of the trade—and of leaving Hesprid—to infuse him with energy.

When he stepped outside his cabin, tabbing the fasteners on his clean tunic with one hand and holding his mug with the other, Ali straightened up from wall-propping. "Two and a half minutes—not bad."

Dane laughed. The air felt cool on his wet head, and his stomach growled. But he ignored those things as he said, "Stotz came up with something, then?"

"Stotz and Tazcin and yours truly." Ali flourished a hand. "Also Jasper and Vrothin and Shoshu and whoever else was at hand. The Tath didn't have time to grow the whole things, so Stotz cobbled up some of the varitubing from Craig's medtech and figured out a way to interface it with the saltvines from the camp. What we have created, my friend, are spritzers."

"Spritzers?" Dane almost choked on a swallow of coffee.

"Yes." Ali led the way through the cargo hold to the outer lock, but to Dane's surprise, he walked around the waiting flitter, its fans already humming in neutral, its wings folded against its body. "Your coat is here." He pointed, shrugging into his own haz gear. "Sun came up an hour ago. And the Floaters are waiting." He poised a thumb over the lock control. "Suit up."

When Dane was ready, Ali motioned him forward and opened the lock. Dane stopped in the hatchway and looked out, confused. Around the ship towered the vast trees, their branches swaying in low gusts of wind, but the air was empty of presence.

"Look on the ground."

And there, like greenish red warts, on the rocks and on hastily laid plasweave tarps on the muddy ground, lay the Floaters, each almost empty of air, looking as helpless as a jellyfish on the beach. Crumpled in on themselves, they were far smaller than Dane would have expected.

"They don't even need sunlight to loft now," said Ali. "There's so much EM."

"I guess nobody needs to worry about psi-contact, then."

"Not now. But after you faded, Jasper and Rip and I did our best to try to show them what their touch did to us. We couldn't hold the bond long, but they seem to have picked it up. At any rate, at least they have eyes, and can see: they understood that only the beings who thrust their arms in the air should be touched."

Dane leaned against the hatchway, sighing with relief. "I don't know if I can take any more of this psi-link work."

"You won't have to," Ali said with a strange smile. A triumphant smile. "We're out of here."

Dane eyed the engineer. "And? You can't be gloating about that."

Ali lifted one expressive brow as he turned away from the lock and sauntered back to the flitter. "I learned yesterday in the process of opening the door how it could be closed," he said as they strapped themselves in.

"Door . . ." Then Dane got it: Ali had somehow learned how to mentally shut the others out. Could Dane do it as well? He realized he didn't want to try. Though physically he was as well as he could expect to be, he felt mentally fatigued. He did not want to experiment any more with psi powers, at least not now.

And in a way it didn't really matter. If the others could shut him out, then he didn't have to worry about whether or not his own thoughts disturbed them. Privacy was extremely important to Ali; now that he had gained it, he might even be willing to work further on the bond.

Someday.

If they managed to get off Hesprid IV.

And past the pirates.

Moments later the flitter leapt from the ship and bolted up at a steep angle. Dane gasped as the trees fell away beneath them, revealing the sky in its entirety. Eastward, above a distant line of darkness the sun lofted, and even with his unprotected eyes Dane could see the sunspots marring the glaring disk. Overhead small clouds in serried ranks marched toward the west; above and between them the sky flickered, pearlescent, like lightning reflected in an oyster shell.

"The aurora," Dane said, unable to keep momentary disbelief out of his voice. "In daylight."

"Right," said Ali. "You don't even want to know what the

instruments are saying about the amount of energy building up in the ionosphere. The whole planetary electrical field is beginning to ring like a bell."

"Don't tell me," said Dane, danger signals singing along his nerves. "We're at one of the nodes?"

Ali nodded grimly. "Rip says if the amplitude keeps growing on its present curve, this spot is going to be the center of a short circuit the likes of which we can't even imagine."

"The trees," Dane said, remembering. "They'll burn—"

"And reseed themselves," Ali finished, ramming the controls. "Frank Mura is calling them the Phoenix Trees, from some kind of dragon in his ancestors' mythology."

As he spoke he caused the flitter to dive down over the cliffs, and they skimmed along the coast, buffeted by gusts of wind. Peering again at the far horizon, Dane thought he saw vague flickers of light sheeting across the darkness, warning of vast thunderstorms hidden by the planet's curve.

Ali nodded over to the right. "Look at that."

Dane looked away from the coming storm—and then forgot all about it.

The long, rocky coast was flat and wet-looking as the tide went out. What drew his attention was the churning of the waves as thousands of strange, spiky crablike creatures emerged from the water, each carrying in its pincers something which they then dropped onto the sand.

Four crew—Mura, Tooe, Parkku, and her mate Irrba— were sweeping back and forth along the shoreline with bags, picking up the rocks, then hurrying up the beach and dumping their contents into makeshift ore-carts. Not just rocks; as Ali swooped even lower, just above the waves, Dane realized that most of those rocks were ore eggs. Something bothered him—something was not quite right about the scene. He frowned, trying to identify the source of his reaction.

"This has to be the stuff swept into the ocean by the tides and storms," he said.

Ali nodded. "Retrieved by these critters. Oh, but you haven't seen the big stuff yet. When the sun came up, Vrothin called us on the comlink. He was sent to scavenge what he could from the mining-launch site, and found . . . this."

They lifted suddenly, veering round vast cliffs to which ancient trees clung. Ali jammed the speed forward, and the flitter vibrated in the heavy winds as it sped to the south. Then he abruptly pulled up, and Dane gazed in amazement at the sight below.

Huge loads of ore lay along the pebbly beach. As Dane watched, a mighty creature with black, rubbery hide and massive webbed feet emerged from the water, waddling up onto the shore. Were these the singers-of-the-water the Floaters had hinted about?

Arms ending in tentacles dragged a load of muddy material on what looked like gigantic kelp leaves. The tentacles laced together in a kind of net around the leaf. As Ali circled around, Dane watched two creatures pull their tentacles away, shake off their leaves, depositing on the beach a huge mound of the ore eggs.

"That's got to be from quake-caused cracks in the ocean bottom," Ali said.

As they circled again, Dane saw Gleef and Shoshu zoom their flitter down next to the piles, and begin loading the eggs into the back pods.

"Where are they taking that?" Dane asked.

"The *Queen*. Soon's you see the spritzers, your job is to supervise getting all this stowed for liftoff, cargo master."

Was that the nagging feeling that something was amiss? But that was just his job; already a part of his brain was totting up possible numbers and trying to calculate mass and storage. Then he realized the Traders would be bringing all their equipment—or as much as they could—and he whistled softly to himself.

Ali's brows slanted. "Thinking of storm versus weight? I thank the lords of space daily that I never chose piloting for my career," he commented breezily and pulled up with a sudden lurch. No one could call his piloting soft, Dane thought, smiling to himself as Ali added, "Time to see our people in action."

Dane looked up, realized they'd reached the *Queen* again. The craft settled near the ramp to the ship's cargo bay, and as the two emerged, one of the Traders ran down the ramp and waited.

"All yours," Ali said, and he and Dane took off at a swift walk north of the *Queen,* threading their way among the quiescent Floaters, vast mounds of wrinkled flesh festooned with lichen and even small flowering plants. Dane noticed movement in the floral pelt of a Floater as he passed it, saw insects and even what looked like a furry worm—there was an entire ecology there!

And its continued existence depended on the Trade.

He looked up at Ali, a question forming in his mind. The engineer's lips quirked sardonically. "Tau says there's no way the Floaters can get away now without our help. And without the Floaters, sentience on Hesprid IV will die, and the planet will be just another hunk of rock and swarming mindlessness."

Dane shook off the feeling of impending danger. Action— the need to take action gripped him with invisible claws.

When they reached the last of the Floaters at the edge of the forest, they found Stotz and Tazcin waiting at the head of a long line of what looked like small piles of translucent red spaghetti. Stotz's face, glimpsed through his helmet, was taut; it was impossible to discern what Tazcin thought of the nearness of the creatures that had, however inadvertently, killed some of her crewmates.

Then Stotz picked up the first pile of spaghetti and shook it out. Now it resembled a squid's sac, its surface warty and gourdlike, with many long tentacles made of surgical varitubing trailing the ground.

"We figure that the Floaters live partly off the EMP sent out by the piezoelectric cielanite ore matrix," Stotz said. "They use this energy to help heat their internal air space and generate lift—works nicely, since they get more energy just when they need it, to flee the End Times."

He and Tazcin walked over to the nearest Floater. Stotz tossed the sack onto the center of the deflated creature; the tentacles unrolled and then, eerily, began to stretch and quest, like snakes, toward the edges of the Floater.

"Their ability to modulate this energy makes it easy for them to control the varitubing, since the surgical tool that sizes it uses similar electrical fields."

Now Dane could hear a kind of muted belch coming from the creature as ripples coursed through its lichen-covered pelt. Its upper surface began to swell as it took in air. Stotz and Tazcin moved gingerly to opposite sides of the Floater, and Ali and Dane, following the big mechanic's directions, arrayed themselves along the other quarters of the Floater. They began pulling down the tubes all the way to the edge, where small pseudopods sprouted to hold the ends, which curled up and back, ending in small limpetlike shells.

Stotz stepped back and motioned them away from the Floater, which now had swollen to a height of over a meter.

"The moisture is needed for the EM conversion, evidently, although we can't quite figure out all the reaction pathways, as well as protection against the heat of the fires that regenerate the trees." He paused dramatically. "Thus . . ."

After a brief pause, the Floater's pelt twitched, and the squid-sack began pulsing visibly and emitting a droning hum. Dane smiled as Johan grinned broadly at him. The sound was very like one of the drones on Steen Wilcox's bagpipe.

"What, couldn't you grow it in tartan?" said Dane.

To his surprise, Tazcin spoke. "Would not. Not esthetic."

And suddenly Dane realized the Tath was making a joke; the first he'd ever heard from the taciturn Trader.

Slowly fog boiled up over the Floater, issuing out of minute holes in the shells at the ends of the varitubing tentacles of the hybrid creature/machine Ali had called a spritzer. And the swelling of the Floater accelerated.

Dane stepped back; he could feel the heat as the creature radiated its internal space with modulated EM from the approaching storm and the aurora blazing overhead. The ground shook suddenly, then again, more strongly, and the Traders leapt into action, carrying the spritzers to each of the quiescent Floaters and shaking them out, two people to each creature. As they worked, members of both crews joined them, and the work went more and more quickly. At first, some of the others flinched away from the Floaters as they drifted overhead, but soon urgency possessed them and they no longer noticed them.

For there were many more Floaters than Traders, and the eastern sky was rapidly filling with clouds as they worked, the sound of thunder a jaw-aching background to their every move. High lightning flared more and more often, picking out the shimmer of the Floaters clustered overhead and the glistening slickness of the Traders' haz suits and the water beading on the Tath fur from the spritzers.

Now the entire clearing was filling with fog; they waded through white mystery that swirled slowly about their waists, for the wind had fallen, and an eerie stillness possessed the air around them despite the growing electrical fury above. The only sound was the growing drone of the spritzers, like a hive of enormous bees. In the darkness between the trees, branches and leaves glowed with coronal light, eerie ghost flickers of the flames to come.

"I hope that's enough to see them through the fire," Stotz said as the last of the Floaters drifted up from the ground. He watched them; Dane suddenly noted the red light blinking on his helmet and realized the engineer had been recording their work with a vidcam.

For a moment the vast creatures hovered overhead, and Dane felt a pressure in his head. He was intensely aware of the other three Traders in the psi link, though no one spoke.

Then the sensation abated, and the Floaters drifted higher, letting the wind blocked by the trees take them away westward like scudding clouds, the lighting and auroral discharge lighting them with nacreous colors and highlighting the vapors trailing from them. Slowly the drone of the spritzers died away, leaving only the rustle and slap of leaves in the rising wind and the growl of distant thunder.

"We'd better get to work," said Dane. "Lots of stowage."

Rip merely nodded—Dane was in charge now. As cargo master, he had the responsibility of deciding what they could take on board, and what must be left behind, and how to stow the former to avoid disaster during the acceleration of liftoff.

They followed him back to the *Queen* at a run, and for the next several hours Dane was busier than he'd ever been in his life.

The Traders couldn't help, for they were used to calculating storage for the *Ariadne,* whose design was completely different. Dane sat at his computer in the cargo bay, where Jan Van Ryke had reigned for so many years, and calculated masses to several decimal places—a couple of orders of magnitude beyond what he thought might be safe. Mass storage had to be exact, with the center of gravity along the long axis of the *Queen*'s needle shape.

First came the ore, close to the axis, and when it was loaded, then the Traders' belongings farther out. Everyone worked like demons, even Tooe; her little blue body seemed to be everywhere at once, stowing, measuring, sealing, lifting far beyond her spindly strength.

As the Traders kept bringing their equipment aboard, he grimaced; and an hour later he reluctantly summoned Lossin and issued a mass cutoff.

"Ten kilograms more per person," he said.

The Traders did not argue. They had loaded the material in order of importance, except for personal belongings. Silently, they went out to the staging area and began sorting through their keepsakes, deciding what would have to be left behind, and what taken. This tacit acceptance of his decree made Dane feel all the worse, and he worked hard to compensate, helping to rearrange things as items were brought on board to gain an additional mass allowance.

Rip kept sending queries over the comlink. Dane had ignored the last couple of them, meaning to get back as soon as he finished this or that chore—which always led to another, and another. At length Rip came down in person. Dane realized the navigator had been standing there for half a minute before he comprehended his presence, and looked up.

Rip said tersely, "It's now."

"But—"

"Or never."

It was then that Dane realized the vibrating of the ship was not from the transfer of cargos, for they were down to smaller items now. Thunder roared, racketing seemingly endlessly across the sky behind a flare of purple-white light that glared through the lock and the silver rain now falling with increasing force.

He shook his head and closed down the computer with a swipe of his hand. The other hand activated the general com, and he said, "Everyone to stations and strap in for liftoff."

He and Rip made the rounds, seeing that everyone was secured, and then Dane went back down to the cargo bay. He checked on Tooe, who was unwontedly solemn as she strapped herself into the apprentice couch. He brought up the control deck on his vidscreen, strapped in, and waited.

On his screen he saw Rip strap down, run his hands once down his trousers, then look over at Lossin, who was running the com. They had all decided earlier that this liftoff required both engineers and their jet tech to be on hand for emergencies: Ali, Johan, and Jasper were in the engine compartment.

"Stand by to release cables," said Rip. They'd decided to sacrifice the guy-bots in the interest of both mass and a fast liftoff. "On my mark, in fifteen seconds." As he spoke his hands flashed across the console, and the ship trembled as the side thrusters came to life.

"Ten seconds." A puff of smoke came out from under the ship; Dane had his side screen tuned to the external vids. The jets muttered softly; Dane could visualize Johan hunched over his displays, alert for any sign of trouble as the pressure built.

"Five seconds."

Now a great gout of smoke and steam sprayed out from beneath the *Queen*. Dane could see good-sized rocks bouncing and shattering as they rolled away from the blast. Beyond, abandoned equipment began to smolder, flaps of plasweave blistering and fluttering away like flaming bats. Dane saw what he thought was a musical instrument among the abandoned personal effects flare up and crumble into embers fleeing ahead of the shock wave as the jets coughed again. The *Queen* trembled and creaked, the jets thundered and then screamed, the sound winding up,

"Two . . . one . . . Mark!"

There was a triple-stutter explosive crack as the cables blew away from the ship and the *Queen* leaped into the air. Rip slammed the jet feeds forward; for an agonizing moment the ship seemed to hover, then slowly—Dane felt it through his body—continued lifting.

Vibrations shuddered violently through the ship, and Dane hunched unbreathing over the computer screen, watching his sensor readings lest anything shake loose, or shift, which could be disastrous under acceleration.

The lights stayed gold, though the shuddering increased to a drumming, as the side screen showed Hesprid IV rapidly dwindling below, lightning flaring and lighting up the clouds from beneath. Air screamed past the hull like a mad organist's toccata—then the shuddering intensified for a moment, and abruptly stopped. They'd gone transsonic, outpacing the sound of their flight. Dane imagined the double boom of their shock wave slapping at the Floaters, now far below as the *Queen* clawed for space.

21

★

Dane felt a little of his tension ebb, and he drew in a deep breath while twisting his aching neck from side to side— without removing his gaze from his console. Liftoff was usually when something broke Murphy's Law, especially when the loading had been done in haste.

But his relief was short-lived.

Suddenly, the exterior view on his screen was webbed with crawling streamers of light, and the image began to break up.

"We are entering the ionosphere," came Lossin's voice. "Activating sand shields."

An armored shutter, designed for regions of space heavy with micrometeorites, snapped across Dane's external view, which then went black. Moments later it was replaced by a graph of the planet's electrical fields, and Dane stared at his screen in disbelief—the *Solar Queen* was only twenty-five kilometers up, less than half the normal altitude of the ionosphere's lower boundary!

"Stotz! Tau! You getting these readings?" came Rip's taut voice.

"Affirmative." Stotz's voice was flat with tension.

Dane felt his own stress increasing again, like an invisible vise clamped round his skull as he tapped a query into his computer. The answer that popped up made his jaw tighten: the wild fluctuations of the planet's geomagnetic field were beyond anything reported on any planet listed in the ship's library computer.

Dane windowed up a view of the bridge. Rip Shannon looked as tense as Dane felt. His profile was severe, his hands moving swift and sure over the command console as the *Queen* struggled to gain altitude.

As Dane watched, for a moment he felt an echo in his mind—Rip watching him watch, and the flicker of vertigo this caused made him shut his eyes. He then felt an answering sense of displacement from Jasper—but nothing from Ali. For that, Dane thought grimly, he was grateful.

Then alarm thrilled through him as Lossin's console bleeped for attention.

"Retrofire detected, ten mark thirty-two, nine hundred kilometers—" The Tath Trader's report ceased for a moment. Lossin bent over the com console. "Exiting ionosphere," he said then. "Trace lost." Dane could hear his puzzlement.

Over the com came a quick exchange. "We're still lifting at max, aren't we?"

"Yes, then how—"

"Belay the chatter," Rip said curtly, his rudeness, so rare, underscoring the tension.

Silence.

The *Solar Queen* shuddered, then seemed to slow, as though she had hit something; but at their speed, Dane knew, a collision with anything more solid than rarified gas would have destroyed the ship.

The sand shields snapped open again, and the external image flickered, shifting dizzily until it came to rest on what looked like an elongated tornado of flame twisting up into space across the cloud-wrapped, lightning-webbed surface of Hesprid IV, dwindling to invisibility near a gleaming point of light.

"Blaster fire, two-ninety mark thirteen, ninety kilometers out." Lossin's voice sounded odd—almost thin.

Was it fear, excitement, Dane wondered? The sweat popping out on his own brow argued for the former.

"Ninety!" Stotz exclaimed over the comlink.

Dane realized they'd not known just how powerful colloid blasters were; that information was heavily classified by the Patrol. Now they had a good idea, and it was far worse than anyone had assumed.

"Closer, we cook," Tooe murmured, her voice high.

Dane looked over, saw her huge yellow eyes watching him, her crest stiff. He nodded reluctantly; if they could feel the effects of a miss ninety kilometers out, a near miss would leave little more of the *Queen* than vapor and droplets of condensing hull metal.

Dane turned his gaze back to his screen and stared at the dissipating flare of the pirate weapon. What chance did they have now?

"It won't be so bad if we can get farther out," Stotz said suddenly. "Less atmosphere means less shock wave and radiation normal to the beam."

"Can't yet," Rip said, his voice tense. "Higher means slower, more time for them to lock onto us. I'm taking us at least one orbit around, so I can try to lose them in the EM glare over the cielanite islands. Anyway, the beams can't be very accurate with this hellish magnetic storm going on."

Then as Dane and Tooe watched on their screens, he matched action to words and throttled back the jets, adjusting them to just match the tenuous grip of the atmosphere, keeping the *Queen* in a low, fast orbit.

Dane's harness creaked as acceleration fell to zero. They were in free fall. An atavistic part of his brain gibbered in terror for a moment as two ancient nightmares awoke together: a predator's chase, and falling.

The sensation intensified briefly as the psi link woke. Now all four of them were there, but almost instantly they disappeared again.

Another flare of light erupted from the pursuing ship, still only a point of light, now closer to the limb of the planet below as it fell behind the *Solar Queen*. But this time the deadly beam twisted up and away from the planet. And at its terminus, the point of light faded out.

"Dane, what happened?" Tooe demanded. "Pirate blow up?"

"Intruder entering magnetopause," came Lossin's laconic tones.

"No," said Dane, as his heart slowed and understanding came. "He flew into Hesprid's shadow."

And Jasper's voice came over the comlink, the calm voice of the teacher: "The particle shock wave near the terminator deflected his beam."

"Conductivity rising," Lossin cut in as, once again, coronal discharge crawled across the external view and the sand shields snapped shut. The Tath had apparently linked them to ship's sensors.

To distract himself from the growing sensation of helplessness, Dane explained to Tooe how the flood of particles from the restless sun bent around the planet, creating a kind of bow wave in space.

Tooe seemed equally glad for the distraction. She listened carefully, her sensitive crest flickering, then she gave a quick nod, and said, "So pirate beam hit that and was deflected?"

"Yes," Dane said. "Unfortunately we can't rely on that happening again."

"Sections, confirm condition reports," Rip's voice interrupted.

Dane welcomed the new distraction as he listened to the terse reports of the others, and scanned his instruments as he awaited his turn.

"Jet temperature at sixty-three percent and holding," Jasper reported.

"Engines at ninety-eight percent," Johan Stotz said. "Still within parameters."

"All secure," Dane reported when his turn came. "No breakage detected."

And all the while, furnishing a bass harmony to the quick interchanges of the crew, the jets hissed and rumbled, keeping the *Queen* aloft against atmospheric friction, almost orbit, not quite flight.

"Hull temperature seven hundred fifty-five degrees and holding," said Tau from his station in the dispensary. "Refrigeration at fifty-five percent capacity, two hundred fifty minutes to discharge at this rate."

There was nowhere for the heat building in the hull to go—the refrigeration system would store it in pressurized tanks for another four hours before it had to be expelled through the jets, which would cut their efficiency in half during the discharge cycle. But they'd be away from the planet long before then. Or dead, Dane thought bleakly.

And again he felt a ripple of reaction from the three others, sharper this time. Ali was first to cut it out, then Jasper; Rip was so preoccupied his focus functioned as a kind of shield.

Dane shook his head to free it of the inevitable vertigo that accompanied those links, and he looked at his screen. The sand shields were open again, and ahead of the ship, Dane could see a light glowing over the nightside curve of the planet, about twenty degrees off the port side of the *Queen*. Unlike the violent lightning, diffuse circles and chains of light like negatives of bacterial cultures that flickered in constant crawling motion underneath the clouds far below, this glow was constant.

When the ionization rose again, cutting off the external view, Lossin suddenly reported, "Retrofire, one-seventy mark eighty, four hundred kilometers."

"Intruder's trying to get under us," Rip said.

"Can they?" asked Tau over the com.

"Depends on their hull and coolant capacity," replied the navigator. "Lossin, can you get a mass reading on that ship?" In the window he'd set to the bridge, Dane saw the Tath shake his head. "Too much fluctuation in the magnetosphere." At that moment the shields snapped open again, and the Tath's neck fur fluffed out. "Trace lost. Can you not fly us in the ionosphere, above the reflecting layer's fluctuations?"

"That would take us too high," Rip replied. "Do what you can. No luck with the comsats?"

"Ten minutes to lock-on," reported Lossin, his neck collapsing to its normal size.

"Comsats?" Tooe asked. "Gleef could not reset?"

Gleef's voice came from the engine room. "We haff reset the comsats for tactical monitoring, but they were not all reoriented yet—"

"Must to wait for takeoff," Irrba put in from the jet department.

Dane murmured, "To avoid tipping off the pirates."

Tooe nodded, her pupils slitting. "Now I see, me."

"And the images will be slow," Lossin added, from the control deck. "Too much noise."

"Planet's ringing like a bell," came Stotz's terse voice. "Frequency dropping, amplitude increasing. But the rate of change is down."

"Good thing, too," Jasper said. "It's playing havoc with the focus of the jets."

"Just like it is with their blaster beams. And we'll be past it before the big show," Rip said, "if the computer projections are accurate."

"Good thing, too," Ali cut in, drawling as if this were just a sim-run. "When the ionosphere hits ground level, all hell's going to break loose."

The implied warning shut everyone up.

For a time they flew unpursued, or so it seemed, but Dane knew there was another pirate ship out there, tracking them, waiting for its opportunity while the other two accelerated into higher orbits until the *Solar Queen* had come around the planet again.

He rubbed his thumb against the webbing of his acceleration couch as he frowned at the numbers flickering on his screen. What was Jellico up to on the *North Star?* It had no weapons; what could he do?

"Any sign of the *North Star?*" he asked.

"No," Lossin stated.

"Bad sign—" Stotz began.

"Not necessarily," Rip said in a slow, almost meditative voice. Dane saw him working at the control console; his hands never ceased moving. "I think I know where he was—hiding in plain sight—"

A sudden exclamation came from Craig Tau, quickly silenced.

"—where the pirates couldn't afford to be, when we took off," Rip finished, as though there had been no interruption. *Which he probably didn't even hear,* Dane thought, watching the navigator-pilot on the screen. Rip almost seemed to be in an altered state of consciousness. No longer did Dane feel stress from him; his focus was too strong for that.

"Where's that?" Tooe asked.

"Right over the *Queen*'s landing spot, in synchronous orbit—worst place to begin an interception," Rip replied.

Now Craig Tau laughed, a triumphant sound. "You're thinking like him now, my boy! I'll bet my next year's leave time you're right."

"But what can he do?" asked Ali.

There was a momentary silence, broken by a bleep from Lossin's console as the sand shields snapped open again.

"Whatever it is, we'll see soon," Rip said. "We're coming up on our first orbit, and that is where we took off."

He didn't need to point, for the light Dane had seen had rolled up over the horizon, revealing itself as an almost mandalic pattern of light, like a vast pinwheel with an intricate internal structure centered on the island they'd blasted off from. And the *Queen*'s flight was taking it just past the center of the maelstrom.

"I sure hope computer is right, me." Tooe's voice held bravado, and a question.

Dane tried to force a reassuring smile. "With Frank on it, we don't need to worry."

And if it wasn't right, Dane thought, we'll never know it.

Rip felt a mild wash of bleakness from Dane, and instinctively pulled back from the sudden link without severing it. The sense of background presence seemed to steady him, but he didn't need discrete identity. There seemed to be a level where the others' thoughts felt like his own—the safe thoughts, of facts and hypotheses. Almost like more windows on the control console, but inward ones. And—he reflected wryly to himself—he needed every advantage he could get.

"Comsats coming on line," reported Lossin suddenly. "Nine-minute lag."

Rip studied the fuzzy orbital plots intently. There was still no sign of Jellico and the *North Star,* but now he was certain of what the captain was doing. He would have jetted out in the opposite direction while the pirates chased the *Solar Queen.*

And if he was right, Jellico was racing toward them at this very moment.

But Ali's question still beat on his mind. What could an unarmed ship, or even two, do against the overwhelming force of three ships armed with colloid blasters?

The pinwheel of fire over the island loomed ahead, now filling the cloudscape far below

And then acid burned through his nerves as Lossin reported, "Retrofire detected. Ten mark twenty-five, nine hundred kilometers and closing."

Rip cursed under his breath, not caring if the sound carried over the comlink. He'd hoped to lose the third pirate in the noise from the cielanite islands. It hadn't worked.

Rip triggered the retros and the roar of atmosphere across the hull grew louder.

"Hull temperature rising," Tau warned. "Refrigeration at seventy-five percent and rising. Two-point-five hours to discharge."

Lossin boomed, "Intruder at fourteen mark twenty-two, seven hundred forty kilometers and closing."

Despair flooded Rip. The pirates had them boxed.

22

Aboard the *North Star,* Rael Cofort held her breath as she watched the growing pinwheel of fire on the big screen in the survey lab. She was subliminally aware of fresh air wafting against her cheek, smelling slightly astringent; she'd added some biotic scrub to it, to make sure that they didn't catch some disease after the long days of stale air. Power use was safe again, here only forty thousand kilometers above the hell building below them. That amount of EM and particle flux could mask the output of a far larger ship—now their worry was the ship's shields.

She sucked in a deep breath, appreciating the sweet tang of fresh air. It would be a long time before she took it for granted again.

A long time *if—*

She stopped the thought, and ran another scan on the spectacular evidence of the magnetic storm tearing at Hesprid's atmosphere. Somewhere, under the center of that maelstrom of ionization, was the *Queen.* Had been, for a month.

She touched a control; false color spilled across the display. Rainbow brilliance symbolized the intensities of the EM fields and particle fluxes lashing the archipelago where the ship had landed. She shook her head, her mind racing now to figure what kind of damage this might have done to the *Queen*'s crew, right down to the cellular level. She and Tau would have to begin a course of treatments for them all, as soon as—

If they—

No. She turned her thoughts firmly back to the medical lab, and the full range of treatments that every ship carried for all types of radiation damage. She was glad that she and Tau, while they'd had the chance on Exchange, had run data surveys on the latest techniques and treatments and had laid in those as well.

As she watched the astonishing light display over the planet, she firmly kept her mind on those new medicines and the syndromes they treated; this led her to wonder what effect, if any, the heightened EM over the planet had had on the mysterious bond between the four apprentices.

When she ran out of speculations, she leaned down to tab the intercom to broadcast. Better to listen to the talk of the others than to be left alone with fruitless worries and fears.

". . . how long the Patrol will take to arrive?" Van Ryke was saying.

"If we were lucky enough to be heard at all, way out here," came Kosti's gravelly voice.

"Oh, we were heard, I'll guarantee that. Issuing a Nova Class Alert would just about assure that they arrive ASAP and in force; the Patrol is known for its efficiency," Van Ryke retorted.

"We can guess when they heard it," Steen came in to say. "Unless there's a Patrol base we don't know about that's closer than the one on Sarmege II, a response would take a minimum of fifteen days until we could expect a response."

"So they could be here already."

"Or a week off," said Kosti gloomily.

Rael thought soberly, *And even if they get here in time, then we get to worry about whether or not they'll consider our problems here to be Nova Class Alert in size—and if not, the Charter we strove to protect will be revoked by people on our side.*

Stop it. *Stop it.*

"... don't know if those Shver constitute 'unfriendly alien contact,' but I think what's going on below will qualify for planetary-scale disaster," Ya said with dry humor.

"Except there don't happen to be any sentients in danger—"

"Except ours," Jan said with a chuckle.

"Rip and the others?" Rael heard herself speak.

"And us, if we don't get moving soon," Jan added, still with high humor.

"We wait," came Jellico's voice. "Until the *Queen* lifts off, now no more than an hour away if they expect to make it."

"Wonder if the down crew saw the gas cloud," Tang Ya said. "I'm sure they'll have accessed the comsats by now."

They were chattering, something ordinarily the captain tolerated only minimally unless they were either docked or safely in hyper. But he knew that the strain of waiting for something that might not happen would be the worse if they were all isolated with little to do except listen to the gibber of internal voices.

"We'll assume then that they are about to lift off."

We'll assume that they are still alive.

She must have spoken the thought, because Jellico said, "The pirates are acting as if they are."

Then Rael heard a short intake of breath, and Ya's voice, tight with excitement: "Signal—they've lifted off."

A short time later, a pinprick of light materialized from the center pinwheel of light on the big screen and raced outward, seeming to move with agonizing slowness against the bulk of Hesprid IV below.

Rael tapped into the main computer, and an orbital plot windowed up, glowing lines showing two pirate ships, the first on an interception course. The third, Rael knew, was waiting on the other side of the planet.

"Their courses show they haven't seen us," Steen said, as Rael struggled to make sense of what she saw.

Jellico spoke a terse agreement.

Jan Van Ryke appeared in the lab and silently joined Rael. In this battle the two of them had nothing to do but wait.

And watch.

And hope.

A flash appeared on the vid.

"Intruder firing," Ya said.

Rael held her breath, her gaze locked onto the glowing green line representing the *Queen*. It did not wink out, or glow into a sudden light burst, indicating a hit. Slowly, steadily, the point of light lifted away from the planet, its velocity seeming to fall. Rael realized that was an illusion.

"He's staying low," Ya said. "Problems?"

"More likely he's going for an entire orbit to lose his escape course in the EM from the islands," Steen responded.

"And we'll be in position by then," Jellico said. "We'll dump some coolant between them and the pirate—that and their own jet exhaust cloud will divert the blaster beam from the *Solar Queen*."

"Ah," Jan said, smiling at the screen. The brilliant colors washed over his face and glowed weirdly in his white hair. Rael smiled a little, feeling comforted by his presence.

"It will only work once, so it will have to be enough," the captain added.

They watched until the *Queen* disappeared over the limb of the planet, followed by the pirate ship. Then Jellico triggered the jets. Weight returned, reached 1.0 gee, passed it.

"One-point-six gees," said Steen. He grinned. "Seems appropriate."

Jellico permitted himself a faint smile.

"Just so. Now, unfortunately, we have a bit of high-gee cargo-wrangling ahead—Jan? Rael, help him—let's spread a little trash in their way."

"Trash?" Rael said.

Van Ryke mirrored her surprise, and then they both laughed.

"Come, let us essay a creative gesture," Jan said. From the timbre of his voice, Rael guessed that the man was delighted to be able to take some action at last.

Moving with amazing speed for a man of his size and bulk, he zoomed down to the cargo area, Rael propelling herself after him at a breakneck pace. Once there, he grabbed a guidehandle, propped his other fist on his hip, and surveyed the neat rows of crates. To Rael the display meant nothing, but of course he knew what was in each.

Then suddenly he launched himself forward, and for an unmeasurable space of time they hastily unsealed crates and packages, ushering an amazing variety of objects to the locks, where Kosti had jury-rigged a number of message torpedoes into trash launchers. While they worked, Van Ryke kept up a continuing stream of comments, some of which had Rael laughing so hard her middle ached.

". . . they've been teasing me about these Norsundrian noserings for years," he said, brandishing a fistful of gaudy objects with glitter-decorated trailers of plasweave. "So it was a bad buy. A very bad buy. I thought there'd be some race somewhere that might start a new fashion. Never admit a bad buy to the apprentices, of course. They have to think me omniscient, or they won't listen. Noserings!"

The noserings joined the jumble of other weird objects now piled in the cages that Kosti had welded to the torps.

". . . now, here's a valuable lesson. Never, *ever,* trust a Myrkwudi Trader when he, she, or it—you know they have a taboo about revealing their gender—offers to translate at the Emporium of Universal Congeniality on Durgewarth Five. Thought I was getting rare gems, and what I discovered in the crate after liftoff was Pipli toe molds. Of course I've told the others these are ritual items known all over the Rigelian frontiers. Not," he added with a laugh over his shoulder, "that they believed me. But they pretended, at least. One has to think of one's self-respect . . ."

Never had she had so much fun while in so much danger! It seemed only minutes later—though her body ached from the unaccustomed exercise, after their days of inactivity—Jan tabbed the com, and said, "Locks full, Captain, and I'm about to seal them."

They retreated into the hatchway, the cargo master sealed the locks from the outside, and they retreated to the survey lab.

When they got there, Jellico's voice came over the com: "You in the lab. You won't want to miss your show."

"We're here and ready."

"Trash first," Steen said. "Fire One!"

Rael watched the torp drift out of the lock, attitude jets flickering as it oriented itself. Then its main rocket flared and it abruptly vanished. She smothered a laugh at the idea of throwing crushed jakek tubes at a pirate ship armed with colloid blasters.

Except at the speed the pirates were traveling, those tubes could be as lethal as a laser strike on the hull—

"Fire Two."

Another torp drifted out, oriented to a different course, and vanished. Jan heaved a mock sigh. "Those noserings were kind of intriguing," he said.

Rael snorted, her gaze riveted to the screen.

"Destruct One," Steen said. Rael envisioned the torp exploding, transforming its cargo into a high-velocity hailstorm of metal and plastic and frozen garbage. "Destruct Two . . . Destruct Three." He paused. "Orbits appear to be within parameters."

And just then Rael saw the fleeing *Solar Queen* arc over the limb of the planet.

Jan was now silent. Rael and the cargo master watched without speaking, every moment stretching the suspense, until suddenly Jellico's voice came:

"Show time." The captain triggered the retros, and they dropped like a stone from heaven toward the planet.

✳ ✳ ✳

"Intruder, dead ahead—"

A double hammer blow hit the *Solar Queen.*

"Ariadne!" exclaimed Lossin; then his neck fur fluffed again. He said something in his own language, and then said, *"North Star."*

By any name, the angular ship now dwindling astern like a reddish comet, its hull glowing at the edges, was a welcome sight—but Rip felt sweat trickle into his eyebrows as he struggled to fathom Jellico's tactics.

Then the *North Star*'s jets winked out, and sudden understanding galvanized him. He shut down the *Queen*'s jets. Moments later the malevolent glare of the colloid blaster detonated astern, wiping out the view of the *North Star* with a wash of flame—

—that followed the ion track of the *North Star,* bending away from the *Solar Queen.*

But the blast still tossed the ship violently upward. The jets stuttered as Rip triggered them again, fighting for control. Gravity slammed him back as the ship jolted violently. He fought the controls, battling against the raging violence of the weapon's wake.

A violent pulse shocked the bridge. Console lights went red. The *Queen* bucked and fought him like a wild animal— without the computer compensating he would have lost the battle. With the autopilot to damp the most violent movements, he brought the ship back on course. But its song was harsh now. There was a burring edge to it that spoke of hull damage, and air friction raking at a wound in the *Queen*'s hull.

Craig Tau's report confirmed the feeling in the controls. "Hull temperature at ninety-five percent and climbing rapidly," Tau reported, his voice carefully passionless. "We lost the port-under coolant tank; discharge in three minutes."

The *Queen*'s cooling capacity had been crippled by the near miss, and her aerodynamics compromised. In less than three minutes, the ship would purge itself of excess heat—that, or risk the certain explosion of a coolant system already overstressed by the loss of a third of its capacity.

And then the jets, their efficiency sacrificed to the gush of superheated gas carrying away the heat from her hull, would no longer sustain her against atmospheric friction, now clawing with increased strength against the sear mark in her flank.

Rip could almost see it, so vivid was the image, just like the wound on the *North Star* when they'd found her.

The *Queen* was dying, and her death would plunge them into the hell that was the rebirth of the Phoenix Trees.

Already the pinwheel of auroral light was all of the planet they could see, so bright it looked as though one of the planet's moons was reenacting its ancient birth from the planet's flank, lifting again from the gouge its genesis had torn in the crust of Hesprid IV.

"Intruder out of range," said Lossin, and in the next breath, "Retrofire ahead, five mark sixty-five, seventy-five hundred kilometers and closing."

It was the first of the pirates, dropping from its slower orbit to intercept the *Queen* in her swifter passage.

Rip tapped frantically at his console.

"One minute to discharge," said Tau. "Hull temperature one hundred ten percent and rising."

Rip felt a sharp increase in the energy of the psi link. The minds of the others were buoying him up, ideas flooding his mind without invasion, sudden shifts of perception that fled even as his rational side tried to grasp at them. He shook his head to break his own focus, and concentrated on his screens.

Vast sheets of lightning tore across the sky below them, and above, yet still below the fleeing ship, the auroral light waxed almost solid. The slow wheel of electrical fire was mesmerizing; from its center reached a whisp of whirling light, a faint tornado of ionized particles questing blindly for the electrical connection that would fulfill the trees' destiny and give rebirth to Hesprid IV.

Were the Floaters now far enough away?

Another sheet of lightning glared up at him from the screen.

Was the *Queen* far enough away?

Not that it mattered.

"Intruder at three mark thirty-nine, thirty-four hundred kilometers and closing."

Intercept course. They were making sure.

Without warning, the perception shift tore at Rip's mind one more time. All four were there, a wheel of energy and awareness and suddenly, without any sense of identity but a compelling clarity, Rip *felt* the pirate captain give the order to fire.

And suddenly, somehow he knew what to do.

Acting instinctively, Rip shut down the jets and triggered the coolant discharge manually, leaving an expanding cloud of vapor behind the fleeing ship that glowed and twisted weirdly as the particle storm from the sun and the EM from the cielanite islands tore at it.

The ship lurched. Again his straps pulled at him. The *Queen*'s nose tipped down, into the maelstrom of light.

Seconds passed in agonizing suspense. Had he imagined it?

A hammer blow worse than the first slammed at the ship, nearly blacking him out. His nose burned; blood. He blinked tears from his eyes, and concentrated fiercely. From the viewscreen, boiling flame flared across the sky above, beaming from a point of light stooping toward them—

—and then bending up, over the ship, into the glowing cloud of gas the coolant discharge had left behind. A sphere of light detonated, expanding in an intricate flower of light.

And then, as if attracted by the beauty of a flower, the tentacle of light reaching from the center of the whirlpool quested outward and gently touched the surface of the sphere.

Almost slowly, light grew beneath the clouds, far below the wheeling auroral light, boiling up brighter and brighter until the clouds went black against the glare and dissipated as a tornado of electrical flame, a narrow tube of hellfire, struck out and upward along the tentacle.

It hit the sphere, which blossomed like an enormous dandelion into a tracery of actinic light that raced around its surface to converge on the spot where the blaster track had created it. From there the world-spanning lightning bolt flashed up and hit the point of light that was the pirate ship. Light flared, a rosette of flame blossomed slowly, then tore to rags and blew away as the energies of the magnetic storm tore at its delicate structure. When the last wisp vanished, there was no trace of the pirate ship.

No one spoke; then Rip heard Tooe's small voice, "We did that?"

Dane's voice came, low and urgent, trying for distraction: "Yes, and no. We created an ionized cloud that turned their blaster beam into a direct tap into the planetary storm. A planet-sized lightning bolt. But nothing would have happened to them if they hadn't fired."

Then the shock wave from the monstrous blast of lightning pummeled the *Queen,* less violent than the uncontrolled ravening of the blaster beam.

Rip fought to damp the ship's shuddering, and at last he felt through the vibration of the controls under his hands that he had succeeded.

"Sections, report," he ordered, his throat dry and raspy.

"Ionospheric oscillation beginning to subside," reported Lossin. "Comsat lag decreasing slightly."

Rip listened intently to the others as he scanned his console, alert to any change. The *Queen* was unstable with the hole in her, and he had to hold her speed down while they were climbing. But climbing they were.

"Manifest shows the coolant tanks blew away about three tons of cielanite," said Dane, reporting last. "I think everything else came through all right, but I'll need a tour of inspection to be sure."

"Do you think the cielanite helped trigger that—" Jasper's voice trailed off.

"Conflagration," said Tau. "Or make up a new word; but I'll bet we never see the likes of that again."

"Not for Tooe! Not for Tooe!" came the fervent assertion, and sudden hilarity swept the ship in the aftermath of tension.

"We still have two pirates to deal with," Rip warned, hating to do it.

In confirmation, Lossin tonelessly read off new coordinates. "Intruder at four mark forty-two, forty-two hundred kilometers and closing . . ." His voice ceased and his eyes widened, the fur of his cheeks puffing out. "Intruder has lost power . . . no . . . jet emissions ragged. They are pulling out of action?"

"Could it have been the shock wave?" Dane asked.

"Acting like something hit them," Stotz said. "Except we know the *Star* has no weapons—"

"We should have a few minutes before the next one's in position," said Rip. "But then what? We can't expect another miracle."

"The gods laugh," said Lossin unexpectedly. "Signal incoming." At Rip's motion, he tapped it into the general com.

". . . hostilities will cease. Weapons fire will be considered an act of war against the Patrol, and will be dealt with accordingly."

"Comsats report five ships vectoring in on Hesprid IV," Lossin said, his voice a plangent bass. "They match Patrol corvette specs. Intruders attempting evasion."

"Ooooh, let's watch the fun," Ali drawled, and again the others laughed, the dizzying hilarity of sudden and intense relief.

Rip breathed slowly in aching lungs as he watched the two pirate ships fall out of sight around the planet. He grinned at the futility of the damaged one fleeing the relentless vectors of the Patrol vessels, which were equally armed, and with much better discipline. The other, with the greater gee endurance of the Shver, might escape. But not for long.

The *Queen* was responding now, albeit sluggishly, and no threat awaited. Rip felt the tension leak out of his shoulders.

The sand shields snapped shut.

"Entering ionosphere," said Lossin. "Ringing continues to damp down."

Rip studied the plot on his screen. If the Tath's projections were right, when the shields next snapped open, they'd truly be out of the ionosphere and into space, which meant they could rendezvous with the *North Star*—and the Patrol.

All they had to do then was convince the Patrol that they had a valid trade with the Floaters.

Rip chuckled to himself. After what they'd just been through, dealing with the Patrol would be a snap.

Murphy willing.

23

★

Tooe woke up and glanced at her chrono, making an automatic calculation. She was glad she no longer had to reckon Hesprid time; it was hard enough translating Terran Standard into Exchange time.

"A week," she said to herself as she bounced out of her bunk and yanked her tunic from the cleaner. The movement sent her backward, which just for a moment took her by surprise. Her body adjusted before her mind did, leaving her with a second of dizziness, and then she laughed and dived at her console, making a note to tell Momo in the long letter she'd been writing about how she—Tooe—had actually gotten so used to gravity she made little mistakes in reaction.

As she tabbed the note in, she noted how long her letter had gotten. So much to report! And different aspects to different people in the klinti. Momo would want to know all about her adjustments to life in grav and then back again, and about the people in the Trader camp, but he would have little interest in the flight from the pirates—other than that they had managed to evade them.

For Kithin, though, Tooe had described how Captain Jellico had played Dead Dog in order to fool the pirates, waiting for the apogee of their complex orbit before firing off a tight-beam to alert the Patrol.

He hadn't known any more than Rip and the others on the Queen whether his message had gotten through, or would be answered, she wrote, then she went on to vividly describe how the captain had guessed when Rip was likely to launch and then made sure the *North Star* was sitting right above his launch position—the last place the pirates would expect— and waiting.

The captain guessed what Rip would do, because it was what he should do—and in his turn, Rip figured out the captain's likely tactics, she wrote. *You have to learn to think like them, Kithin, if you are going to pilot your own ship.*

For Nunku, Tooe saved her report on what had happened to the planet. They were still in Hesprid space, for the Patrol was very thorough on their investigations. All the scientists aboard the Trader ships and the Patrol ships had used this opportunity to focus every available piece of equipment at the planet in order to measure, record, and evaluate the dramatic changes going on there. Nunku the computer expert was fascinated by data gathering.

Also for Nunku, who concerned herself with the futures of the klinti, the news that they were not—alas—to be fabulously wealthy. *We can keep what we mined from the planet, which will see the ships upgraded and refueled, and new cargo, because we made a lawful trade with the Floaters. But even if we could land on that planet again, our Charter is suspended. The Patrol and all the authorities will be wrangling for years, the cargo master says, about the exact status of sentient beings no one can talk to.*

Then for a third friend, whose aspiration was to join the Patrol, she reserved her descriptions of the Terran Federation's peace-keeping arm. By the time the ships had finally rendezvoused, the Patrol had already taken care of the pirates, and they willingly shared their vidrecordings of the encounters.

Tooe had really enjoyed her interview with the austere Patrol captain. An older woman, dark of face and silver of hair, this captain reminded Tooe of Captain Jellico.

It was to Momo that Tooe talked about the Patrol captain.

She asked me a variety of questions about my experiences on Hesprid IV, and when I made jokes, her mouth had quirked in just the same way that the captain's does when he laughs inside.

Tooe paused, considering Captain Jellico. She'd discovered that making him smile just that way was tougher than making some other people guffaw like spacehounds with two much happy-juice inside them, and she was proud of any joke that got such a reaction. *I think now I am beginning to know the captain, a little. You have to know someone to be able to make them laugh. Dane, I can make laugh,* she added.

Dane? How long had she been in her cabin, typing up their experiences?

She glanced guiltily at the chrono, then closed down her computer and zoomed out of her cabin, caroming off the bulkhead and zapping down the corridor to the cargo area.

There she found Dane and Jan Van Ryke at the computer.

"News?" she asked. "My shift yet?"

They both turned around, and Dane said, "Nothing besides our being finished with the recordings. Gleef is programming the comsats to continue data-collection, but Tau thinks we've got enough here to work with; any subsequent changes to the planet will take a long time."

"Work with?" Tooe asked. Then an idea occurred to her, and she exclaimed, "Data Trade?"

"Precisely, my young friend," Jan Van Ryke said, his white brows beetling. He hefted a quantumtape in his big hand, and grinned. "This here is another cargo for us—data. There will be plenty of scientists clamoring for this once we put the word out, and I plan to make some fine trades for contributing to the collective wisdom of the Federation."

Dane nodded at Tooe. "Wilcox says the Patrol is just about finished with us. As soon as they leave, we'll get the cargo distributed."

"Then off to the next port?" Tooe asked. She was so pleased she could not keep still, and both men laughed as she bounded from one wall to another, somersaulting midway between.

"Off to the next port," Van Ryke repeated, and then he said with mock solemnity, "so don't use up all that energy. You'll be working up a fine sweat when we tackle moving cargo over to the *Star*."

"Rigelians don't sweat!" she said, whistling a laugh.

"You'll learn," Dane said, grinning. "Trust me, you'll learn."

Tooe was still laughing over that when she reached the control deck. Not that she had any business there, but she wanted to see everything, to know everything that was going on.

And she noticed when she reached it that the Terrans had gone back to their old gravity habits—their heads were all oriented in one direction, their feet magged to what in grav would be the *Queen*'s deck. She perched overhead, out of the way, and watched Captain Jellico and Tang Ya talking to the Patrol comtech on the big screen. A side screen showed Rip and Lossin on the control deck of the *North Star*.

"So the captain says that that about wraps it up," said the lieutenant on-screen, looking from what had to be one screen to another.

"A week ought to suffice, I think," Jellico said drily.

The lieutenant was young, with some Rigelian in his background. Tooe liked the greenish cast of his scaled skin above the neat black-and-silver Patrol tunic. Now the lieutenant rolled his eyes as he said humorously, "It usually takes longer to file the reports than it did to initiate and carry through the action."

Ya gave a quiet snort. "We have the same thing waiting for us, no doubt, when we reach Trade Admin."

"Not everyone finds a supposedly uninhabited planet full of sentients—and about to blow up—while being shadowed by pirates, requiring a double Nova Class Alert," the lieutenant said, his yellow eyes gleaming. "I've looked up your name in the records. Seems like the lords of space have marked out the *Solar Queen* for more than the usual share of Interesting Times."

Tang Ya grinned, but Captain Jellico gave a slight shrug. "That's life among the Free Traders."

"Well then, that is it—Captain just issued orders for us to close this one down and move on. Shannon?" The lieutenant's head turned slightly as he looked into an ancillary screen, and Tooe glanced into the *Queen*'s side screen and saw Rip's expression alter to query.

The lieutenant nodded behind him, and said, "Piloting team wants you to know they thought that a nice piece of work over the planet, there."

Rip's dark skin took on a deep red hue, but before he could answer, the Patrolman gave a casual salute and closed the connection.

Ya also closed the screen, switching it to an external view. Within moments they saw lights representing the Patrol craft speed away on their run to jump, then disappear.

Jellico hit the comlink. "Thorson. Van Ryke. You can commence the cargo transfer now."

Tooe heard that as a call to duty, and bounced out before the captain and the comtech were even aware that she'd been there.

She dived down through the decks—or started to. When she passed the mess cabin, she heard the rumble of voices, and stopped outside to look in. There she discovered all nine of the former *Ariadne*'s Traders. They either didn't notice her, or it didn't matter to them that she was there.

They were talking in Tathi; after a few seconds she realized they were discussing what to do next.

"I know what I want," Kamsin said, his fur fluffing around his ears. "There is no galley steward on the other ship. *Ariadne, North Star*—names don't matter. It is my home ship. The captain told me himself, just today, that I can sign on as crew if I want. Rip Shannon has spoken for us all. I signed in, and was even spat at by the hoobat. I am now crew."

There was a mild growl of humor from the Tath, overlaid by Siere's hissing laugh.

"They have two medicsss," Siere said. "Regretfully, I mussst now ssseek new berthing. I shall be ssssorry to part from my companionsssss in successs and adversssity."

Several murmured protests, and thanks. Tooe knew that the Torquain medic was popular among the crew.

"I do not know what to do," Gleef said. "I might want to stay, or to go. It is too soon; my spirits are still sore, and I cannot think clearly."

Tazcin spoke then, her voice a mellow boom. "No one has to decide now. We have earned our way, and our place. We can make a decision at the next port—or we can stay longer, and trade work for place if we wish. Captain Jellico has made this clear."

"Dane has called for hands for cargo transfer," Irrba reported suddenly, from his place by the muted comlink.

This reminded Tooe of her duty. As she started away, she saw a stirring among the Traders, and several followed her out.

She bounded ahead, mentally reviewing the cargo, and thinking about the physics of null-grav cargo transfer. This was her field of expertise, and she knew Dane would ask for her help.

She felt a spurt of happiness inside. She would finish her letter in hyper, and send it at the next port, but she no longer felt the pull on her heart to return to the klinti. This was now her job, and her home. She flexed her fingers, happily anticipating the work ahead.

*   *   *

Dane Thorson hooked a toe under the gee-bar near the console and tabbed the control for the last cargo-seal in the *North Star*'s hold. "That's it," he said, looking up at his crew.

They made self-congratulatory noises, and started to disperse, those who were returning to the *Queen* moving out to suit up, and those staying seeking some refreshment after the hours of hard work.

Dane looked down at his manifest symbols, which were blinking peacefully on his com screen. Both ships now had cargo evenly distributed, with an eye to maximum fuel efficiency. It remained only to get the hoobat back to the *Queen*, and to disperse the crewmembers evenly between the two ships. Then they could blast away from Hesprid space, and on to their next port.

He keyed the comlink. "We're done, Rip," he said.

"We'll relay the news to Captain Jellico," Rip replied.

Dane paused, concentrating—but there was no mental echo from Rip.

He let himself float next to his chair and closed his eyes, reaching—

Nothing.

His imagination provided likely locations for the other three. He knew Rip was at the *Star*'s nav controls, and that Jasper and Ali were down in the Engineering areas. But he couldn't "see" them as if from inside their heads. Shield? He wasn't aware of any new ability to shield the others, though it was possible all three had somehow learned it and he had not.

He shrugged it off and finished up his work before going in quest of something to eat.

In the galley welcoming spicy smells greeted his nose. Kamsin was already busy learning about Terran tastes from the stores and recipes that Frank Mura had shared with him.

Dane was halfway through a tasty meal when the comlink lit—transmission from the *Solar Queen*, relayed to both ships. "Ready for acceleration," Captain Jellico said. "Captain Shannon, please begin the countdown, on my mark . . ."

Captain Shannon. Dane grinned as the signal chimed for strap-down, and he got ready for the return of weight. A few seconds later Dane heard the grumble of the jets and felt the ship lurch slightly. They were on their way, blasting out from the ecliptic to their snapout point.

The return of acceleration reoriented his views to up and down, and he paused, letting his brain register the change before he returned to his meal.

Irrba and Parkku appeared a few moments later; both had been down in the engine deck for the transition. They were chattering away in the musical Berran language, Parkku walking about with one of the black-and-white cats perched happily on her shoulder. Dane finished his food, half-listening to the sound of the words. He liked the language, and made a mental note to study it. Especially if the pair decided to stay on as crew.

When he was done he put his dishes in the recycler and started out, his mood good. Rec time now, and he'd earned it! How about a good, old-fashioned blaster-and-zap vid? Or maybe he could hunt up the Berran language tape? Or maybe he could just . . . sleep? Sleep sounded great. He was owed a lot of overdue rack time. He was owed a lot of overdue boring, everyday duty.

As he moved out, he felt a twinge at the back of his head— too brief to identify. A few seconds later he caught sight of Craig Tau, who beckoned.

Dane sighed, and turned to follow.

They went up to the control deck. There Dane saw Jasper and Ali gathered around Rip. All three were silent, Ali lounging with his arms crossed in his familiar pose, Jasper sitting quietly, his hands still, his gaze diffuse.

Tau said, "We managed to finesse the psi link in our report to the Patrol. Rip's sense of that pirate captain firing was easily attributed to the imagination of a good pilot, and as for how we discovered that the Floaters were sentient, as the Patrol captain said, that is the business of scientists; her job was to see that the laws were obeyed. Which we have done."

"Trade Admin," Ali said. "They're not going to stop until they turn our heads inside out."

"I'm afraid that's the truth." Tau nodded, looking around at them. "You are unique, something that will draw the biologists like magnets to iron."

Jasper shook his head slightly. "Except that there won't be much for them to investigate."

Tau looked over. "Explain, Jasper?"

Weeks lifted his hand. "I know I'm not doing anything differently, but in the last week I haven't seen any of the others' dreams, or had them appear in mine. Not in the psi sense. My dreams have just been the usual jumble of images from recent events. Nothing else."

"Same here," Ali said. "I thought I was shielding."

Dane spoke up. "I haven't felt anything—even when I tried."

"Me either," Rip admitted.

"Maybe you are shielding," Craig said, looking around. "Maybe you all are."

"Or maybe it's gone," Jasper said, his expression of hope unmistakable. "We were strongest when the EM on that planet was strongest; it seems to have affected us."

"Except we felt the link before we ever snapped out into Hesprid space," Rip pointed out. "We were feeling it back on Exchange, and didn't even know it."

"Maybe it comes and goes," Ali said, shrugged slightly. "Though I have to admit I wish it would just go. I've been content to have it dormant these past few days."

Jasper nodded slightly. Dane saw no reaction in Rip's face, and realized that the pilot-navigator did not necessarily agree—but as usual he was not going to speak counter to the others.

Tau nodded. "Perhaps the ability has somehow burned out, like bad wiring. Or else it's gone dormant, as Kamil said. Perhaps it can be activated again. I don't know. What I want you to consider is acknowledging its existence, and trying some experiments. The more data we know, the less you'll be regarded as experimental subjects."

"Nobody can force us to agree to any experiments," Ali said, his mouth tight. "We're Free Traders. Not lab specimens. If the Federation has suddenly changed its laws while we've been off the Terran lanes, then I'm for moving out to the rest of the galaxy."

"Right," Tau corroborated in even tones. "Except if you have a widely publicized talent that you know little about, you're more likely to find parties interested in exploiting you waiting at your next port of call. And such parties who don't consider themselves bound by Federation law might be . . . creative . . . in obtaining your cooperation."

Rip laid his hands flat on his knees. "It's a fact, gentlemen. We didn't choose it, but we have it. Ignoring it is stupid. At least we can learn how to control it, if we don't want to use it. I suggest we make some time while we're in hyper to do exactly that. Using it or not can wait for now."

Ali's lips parted, and then he shrugged sharply. "So be it. Captain Shannon has spoken." He straightened up and walked out.

"What you say makes good sense," Jasper said in his quiet voice. "Let me know the schedule, Craig." He went out with his usual soundless tread.

Tau looked from Rip to Dane, smiled a little, then he left.

Rip grimaced. " 'Captain Shannon.' I could bust his vidstar nose for that."

"But it's true. Everyone heard it over the com—I don't think you even noticed. You were probably too busy setting up the run for hyper."

Rip grinned sheepishly. "Oh, I noticed, but I didn't think anyone was listening."

"And I don't think Ali really meant it as a dig. It was an order, but a good one, or he'd have spoken about that."

"I know. He hates this psi thing, and nothing is going to change that, I suspect. I don't think Jasper likes it any better.

Truth to tell, I don't know how *I* feel about it—except it's there. We may as well face it, and learn all we can, or it will end up controlling us, instead of us controlling it."

"I feel the same way," Dane said. "Craig'll give Ali some time to cool off before we experiment. But it really is better to know what we've got."

Rip grinned, then turned back to his work, and Dane left the control deck.

As he started down to his domain, he shook his head. Sounded like even hyper wasn't going to give him a chance to sample that boring duty time. Well, that was fine. He could handle it.

They had two working ships, and excellent cargo. They even had enough crew. Their next port could launch them toward prosperity at last—which they might end up gambling again. Win or lose, this was the life for him. He liked not being able to predict where they would go next, or what would happen. He liked the changes, the widening awareness of all life had to offer.

As for the psi link, he knew he'd made peace with the changes going on inside him. Rip hadn't surprised him with his willingness to accept it; that was what one would expect of a leader. Perhaps the other two would accept, in time, that the farther human beings go from Terra, the less human they become. Or the *more* human they become. It was up to them to define human—and the wider the definition, Dane felt, the better for human potential. Though the four of them were not and never could be entirely what they were, he felt more each passing day like part of the greater universe.

About the Authors

For over fifty years, Andre Norton, "one of the most distinguished living SF and fantasy writers" *(Booklist)*, has been penning bestselling novels that have earned her a unique place in the hearts and minds of millions of readers worldwide. She has been honored with a Life Achievement award by the World Fantasy Convention and with the Grand Master Nebula award by her peers in the Science Fiction Writers of America. Works set in her fabled Witch World, as well as others, such as *The Elvenbane* (with Mercedes Lackey) and *Black Trillium* (with Marion Zimmer Bradley and Julian May), have made her "one of the most popular authors of our time" *(Publishers Weekly)*. She lives in Monterey, Tennessee.

Sherwood Smith is the author of over a dozen novels, including *Wren to the Rescue* and two other Wren adventures. She is also the coauthor, with Dave Trowbridge, of the Exordium series of adventures. Smith lives in California.

Together, Ms. Norton and Ms. Smith wrote a previous

Solar Queen adventure, *Derelict for Trade*. That book and this are new additions to the series created in four previous novels by Ms. Norton, including *Sargasso of Space* and *Galactic Derelict*.